SCHOUSach

PENGUIN BOOKS

THE LUCK OF GINGER COFFEY

Brian Moore was born in Belfast in 1921, emigrated to Canada in 1948, and now lives in the United States with his wife. His first novel, *The Lonely Passion of Judith Hearne*, was published in 1955 and immediately acclaimed. This was followed by *The Feast of Lupercal* (1956), *The Luck of Ginger Coffey* (1960) – which has been filmed – *An Answer from Limbo* (1962), *The Emperor of Ice-Cream* (1965), *I am Mary Dunne* (1968), *Fergus* (1970), *The Revolution Script* (1972), *Catholics* (1972; winner of the W. H. Smith Award, 1973), *The Great Victorian Collection* (1975; winner of the James Tait Black Memorial Prize) and *The Doctor's Wife* (1976). Among the honours Brian Moore has received are a Guggenheim Fellowship, an award from the U.S. National Institute of Arts and Letters, a Canada Council Fellowship, the Authors' Club of Great Britain First Novel Award, and the Governor General of Canada's Award for Fiction.

D1048905

The Luck of Ginger Coffey

BRIAN MOORE

Penguin Books

Penguin Books Ltd, Harmondsworth, Middlesex, England
Penguin Books, 625 Madison Avenue, New York, New York 10022, U.S.A.
Penguin Books Australia Ltd, Ringwood, Victoria, Australia
Penguin Books Canada Ltd, 2801 John Street, Markham, Ontario, Canada L3R 1B4
Penguin Books (N.Z.) Ltd, 182–190 Wairau Road, Auckland 10, New Zealand

—

First published in the U.S.A. by *Atlantic Monthly* 1960
First published in Great Britain by André Deutsch 1960
First published in Canada by McClelland and Stewart Limited 1972

Published in Penguin Books 1965
Reprinted 1977

—

Copyright © Brian Moore, 1960
All rights reserved

—

Made and printed in Great Britain
by Hunt Barnard Printing Ltd
Aylesbury, Bucks
Set in Linotype Times

Except in the United States of America,
this book is sold subject to the condition
that it shall not, by way of trade or otherwise,
be lent, re-sold, hired out or otherwise circulated
without the publisher's prior consent in any form of
binding or cover other than that in which it is
published and without a similar condition
including this condition being imposed
on the subsequent purchaser

To Jacqueline

Chapter One

FIFTEEN dollars and three cents. He counted it and put it in his trouser pocket. Then picked his Tyrolean hat off the dresser, wondering if the two alpine buttons and the little brush dingus in the hatband weren't a shade jaunty for the place he was going. Still, they might be lucky to him. And it was a lovely morning, clear and crisp and clean. Maybe that was a good augury. Maybe today his ship would come in.

James Francis (Ginger) Coffey then risked it into the kitchen. His wife was at the stove. His daughter Paulie sat listless over Corn Flakes. He said good morning but his only answer came from Michel, the landlady's little boy, who was looking out the window.

'What's up, lad?' Coffey asked, joining Michel. Together, man and boy, they watched a Montreal Roads Department tractor clambering on and off the pavement as it shunted last night's snowfall into the street.

'Sit down, Ginger, you're as bad as the child,' his wife said, laying his breakfast on the kitchen table.

He tried her again. 'Good morning, Veronica.'

'*His* mother was just in,' said she, pointing to Michel. 'Wanting to know how long we were going to keep the place on. I told her you'd speak to her. So don't forget to pop upstairs and give our notice the minute you have the tickets.'

'Yes, dear.' Flute! Couldn't a man get a bite of breakfast into him before she started that nattering? He knew about telling Madame Beaulieu. *All right.*

A boiled egg, one slice of toast and his tea. It was not enough. Breakfast was his best meal; she knew that. But in the crying poverty mood that was on her these last weeks, he supposed she'd take his head off altogether if he asked her for a second egg. Still, he tried.

'Would you make us another egg?' he said.

'Make it yourself,' she said.

He turned to Paulie. 'Pet, would you shove an egg on for me?'

'Daddy, I'm late.'

Ah, well. If it was to be a choice between food and begging them to do the least thing, then give him hunger any day. He ate his egg and toast, drank a second cup of tea and went out into the hall to put his coat on. Sheepskin lined it was, his pride and joy; thirty guineas it had cost him at Aquascutum.

But she came after him before he could flee the coop. 'Now, remember to phone me the minute you pick up the tickets,' she said. 'And ask them about the connexion from Southampton with the boat train for Dublin. Because I want to put that into my letter to Mother this afternoon.'

'Right, dear.'

'And, by the way, Gerry Grosvenor's coming in at five. So don't you be stravaging in at six, do you hear?'

What did she have to ask Gerry Grosvenor up here for? They could have said good-bye to Gerry downtown. Didn't she know damn well he didn't want people seeing the inside of this place? Flute! His eyes assessed their present surroundings as Gerry Grosvenor's would. The lower half of a duplex apartment on a shabby Montreal street, dark as limbo, jerry-built fifty years ago and going off keel ever since. The doors did not close, the floors buckled and warped, the walls had been repapered and repainted until they bulged. And would bulge more, for it was a place that people on their way up tried to improve, people on their way down to disguise: all in vain. The hegira of tenants would continue.

Still, what was the use in talking? She had asked Gerry: the harm was done. 'All right,' he said. 'Give us a kiss now, I'm off.'

She kissed him the way she would a child. 'Not that I know what I'm going to give Gerry to drink,' she said. 'With only beer in the house.'

'Sure, never mind,' he said and kissed her quick again to shut her up. 'So long, now. I'll be home before five.'

And got away clean.

Outside in the refrigerated air, snow fine as salt drifted off the tops of sidewalk snowbanks, spiralling up and over to the intersection where a policeman raised his white mittpaw, halting traffic to let Coffey cross. Coffey wagged the policeman the old salute in passing. By J, they were like Russkis in their black fur hats. It amused him now to think that before he came out here, he had expected Montreal would be a sort of Frenchy place. French my foot: it was a cross between America and Russia. The cars, the supermarkets, the hoardings; they were just as you saw them in the Hollywood films. But the people and the snows and the cold – that woman passing, her head tied up in a babushka, feet in big bloothers of boots, and her dragging the child along behind her on a little sled – wasn't that the real Siberian stuff?

'*M'sieur*?'

The other people at the bus stop noticed that the little boy was not wearing his snowsuit. But Coffey did not. 'Well, Michel,' he said. 'Come to see me off?'

'Come for candy.'

'Now, there's a straight answer, at least,' Coffey said, putting his arm around the boy's shoulders and marching him off to the candy store on the corner. 'Which sort takes your fancy, Michel?'

The child picked out a big plastic package of sourballs. 'This one, *M'sieur*?'

'Gob stoppers,' Coffey said. 'The exact same thing I used to pick when I was your age. Fair enough.' He handed the package over and asked the storeman how much.

'Fifty cents.'

By J, it was not cheap. Still, he couldn't disappoint the kid, so he paid, led his friend outside, waited for the policeman to halt traffic, then sent Michel on his way. 'Remember,' he said. 'That's a secret. Don't tell anybody I bought them.'

'Okay. *Merci, M'sieur*.'

Coffey watched him run, then rejoined the bus queue. He hoped Veronica wouldn't find out about those sweets, for it would mean another lecture about wasting his money on outsiders. But ah! Coffey remembered his boyhood, the joys of a penny paper twist of bullseyes. He smiled at the memory and discovered that the girl next to him in the queue thought he was smiling at her. She smiled back and he gave her the eye.

For there was life in the old carcass yet. Yes, when the good Lord was handing out looks, Coffey considered he had not been last in line. Now, in his prime, he considered himself: a fine big fellow with a soldierly straightness to him, his red hair thick as ever and a fine moustache to boot. And another thing. He believed that clothes made the man and the man he had made of himself was a Dublin squire. Sports clothes took years off him, he thought, and he always bought the very best of stuff. As he rode downtown on the bus that morning there wasn't a soul in Montreal who would say there goes a man who's out of work. Not on your earthly. Not even when he went through the doorway of the Unemployment Insurance Commission and marched right up to *Executive & Professional*, which seemed the right place for him.

'Fill it out at the table over there, Mr Coffey,' said the counter clerk. Nice young fellow, no hint of condescension in his tone, very helpful and natural as though this sort of thing happened to everyone. Still, pen in hand, *write in block letters or type,* Coffey was faced once again with the misleading facts of a life. In block letters, he began:

Born 14 May 1917, Dublin, Ireland.

Education Plunkett School, Dublin. National University of Ireland, University College, Dublin.

Specify degrees, honours, other accomplishments (He had not finished his B.A., but never mind.) Bachelor of Arts. (Pass.) 1940.

List former positions, giving dates, names of employers, etc. (Flute! Here we go.) Irish Army 1940–45. Commissioned 2nd Lieut, 1940. 1st Lieut, 1942. Assistant to Press Officer, General Headquarters. Kylemore Distilleries, Dublin, 1946–48, Special Assistant to Managing Director. 1949–53, Assistant in Advertising Department. Coomb-Na-Baun Knitwear, Cork, 1953–1955, Special Assistant.

Cootehill Distilleries, Dublin.
Coomb-Na-Baun Knitwear, Dublin.
Dromore Tweeds, Carrick-on-Shannon.
} August 1955–December 1955, Special Representative for Canada.

List Present Position His position as of this morning, 2 January

10

1956, was null and bloody void, wasn't it? So he put a line through that one. Then read it all over, absent-mindedly brushing the ends of his moustache with the pen. He signed with a large, much-practised signature.

The wooden plaque in front of the young man who looked over his application bore the name *J. Donnelly*. And naturally J. Donnelly, like all Irish Canadians, noticed Coffey's brogue and came out with a couple of introductory jokes about the Ould Sod. But the jokes weren't half as painful as what came after them.

'I see you have your B.A., Mr Coffey. Have you ever considered teaching as a profession? We're very short of teachers here in Canada.'

'Holy smoke,' said Coffey, giving J. Donnelly an honest grin. 'That was years ago. Sure, I've forgotten every stitch.'

'I see,' J. Donnelly said. 'But I'm not quite clear why you've put down for a public relations job? Apart from your – ah – army experience, that is?'

'Well now,' Coffey explained. 'My work over here as Canadian representative for those three firms you see there, why that was all promotion. Public relations, you might call it.'

'I see .... But, frankly, Mr Coffey, I'm afraid that experience would hardly qualify you for a public relations position. I mean, a senior one.'

There was a silence. Coffey fiddled with the little brush dingus in his hat. 'Well now, look here,' he began. 'I'll put my cards on the table, Mr Donnelly. These firms that sent me out here wanted me to come back to Ireland when they gave up the North American market. But I said no. And the reason I said no is because I thought Canada was the land of opportunity. Now, because of that, because I want to stay, no matter what, well, perhaps I'll have to accept a more junior position here than what I was used to at home. Now, supposing you make me an offer, as the girl said to the sailor?'

But J. Donnelly offered only a polite smile.

'Or – or perhaps if there's nothing in public relations, you might have some clerical job going?'

'Clerical, Mr Coffey?'

11

'Right.'

'Clerical isn't handled in this department, sir. This is for executives. Clerical is one floor down.'

'Oh.'

'And at the moment, sir, ordinary clerical help is hard to place. However, if you want me to transfer you?'

'No, don't bother,' Coffey said. 'There's nothing in public relations, is there?'

J. Donnelly stood up. 'Well, if you'll just wait, I'll check our files. Excuse me.'

He went out. After a few minutes a typewriter began to clacket in the outer office. Coffey shuffled his little green hat and deerskin gauntlets until J. Donnelly returned. 'You might be in luck, Mr Coffey,' he said. 'There's a job just come in this morning for assistant editor on the house organ of a large nickel company. Not your line exactly, but you might try it?'

What could Coffey say? He was no hand at writing. Still, needs must and he had written a few army releases in his day. He accepted the slip of paper and thanked the man.

'I'll phone them and tell them you'll be on deck at eleven,' J. Donnelly said. 'Strike while the iron's hot, eh? And here's another possibility, if the editor job doesn't work out.' He handed over a second slip of paper. 'Now, if nothing comes of either of those,' he said, 'come back here and I'll transfer you to clerical, okay?'

Coffey put the second slip in his doeskin weskit and thanked the man again.

'Good luck,' J. Donnelly said. 'The luck of the Irish, eh, Mr Coffey?'

'Ha, ha,' Coffey said, putting on his little hat. Luck of the Canadians would suit him better, he thought. Still, it was a start. Chin up! Off he sloped into the cold morning and pulled out the first slip to check on the address. On Beaver Hall Hill, it was. Up went his hand to signal a taxi but down it came when he remembered the fourteen dollars left in his pocket. If he hurried, he could walk it.

Or Shanks mare it, as his mother used to say. Ah, what's the sense giving Ginger any money for his tram, she'd say; he'll never use it. Doesn't he spend every penny on some foolishness the minute you put it in his pocket? And it was true, then as now. He was no great hand with money. He thought of himself in those far off days, hurrying to school, the twopence already spent in some shop, whirling the satchel of schoolbooks around his head, stopping at Stephen's Green to take out his ruler and let it go tickety, tak, tak among the railings of the park. Dreaming then of being grown up; free of school and catechism; free from exams and orders; free to go out into a great world and find adventures. Shanks mare-ing it now along Notre Dame Street, remembering: the snow beginning to fall, a melting frost changing grey fieldstone office fronts to the colour of a dead man's skin, hurrying as once he had hurried to school. But this was not school. School was thirty years ago and three thousand miles away, across half a frozen continent and the whole Atlantic ocean. Why even the time of day was different from at home. Here it was not yet mid-morning and there, in Dublin, the pubs would be closing after lunch. It made him homesick to think of those pubs so he must not think. No, for wasn't this the chance he had always wanted? Wasn't he at long last an adventurer, a man who had gambled all on one horse, a horse coloured Canada, which now by hook or crook would carry him to fame and fortune? Right, then!

So Shanks mare he went across Place d'Armes under the statue of Maisonneuve, an adventurer and a gambler too, who had sailed out in 1641 to discover this promised land, and Shanks mare past the Grecian columns of a bank and do not think what's left in there, but Shanks mare alone up Craig Street, remembering that he was too far away now from that wireless network of friends and relations who, never mind, they would not let you starve so long as you were one of them but who, if you left home, struck out on your own, crossed the seas, well, that was the end of you as far as they were concerned.

And Shanks mare up Beaver Hall Hill, last lap, all on his onlie-oh, remembering that any man who ever amounted to anything was the man who took a chance, struck out, et cetera. But oh! he was close to the line today. Only he knew how close.

And at last, Shanks mare-ing it into a big office building, riding up in an express elevator to the fifteenth floor, he was

13

let out into a very grand reception hall. Up he went to a modern desk that was all glass and wooden legs which let you see the legs of the smashing blonde receptionist behind it. She smiled at him but lost her smile when he said his name and in aid of what Ginger Coffey had blown in. She was sorry but Mr Beauchemin was presently in conference and would you just sit over there for a moment, sir? And would he just fill in this form while he was waiting? In block letters, please. In block letters he pondered once again the misleading facts of a life.

When he had set them down, he handed back the form and the girl read it over in front of him. Which mortified him. There were so few things you could write down when faced with the facts of a life. 'Fine, sir,' she said in a school-mistressy voice. 'Now, perhaps while you're waiting, you'd like to familiarize yourself with our house organ. Here's our latest issue.'

That was very kind of her, he said. He took the glossy little magazine and went back to the *banquette* to study it. *The Nickelodeon* was the name of the house organ. He wondered if that was funny on purpose but decided not. Canadians saw nothing comical in the words *house organ*. He flipped through the glossy pages. Pictures of old codgers getting gold watches for twenty-five years of well-done-thou-good-and-faithful. Wasn't it to avoid the like of that that he had emigrated? He skipped through the column of employee gossip called 'Nickel Nuggets' but looked long at the photos on the 'Distaff Doings' page. Some of the distaffers were very passable pieces indeed. Well now, enough of that. He turned to the main article which was entitled 'J. C. Furniss, Vice-Pres. (Traffic) A PROFILE'. It seemed that even J.C. himself had started in humble circs as a chainman (whatever that was). Which was the rags-to-riches rise the New World was famous for. Which cheered a fellow up because at home it was not like that. At home it was Chinese boxes, one inside the other, and whatever you started off as, you would probably end up as. Which was why he had come here. Which was why, this morning, he had been stumped when faced with the facts of a life.

For the true facts you could not put on an application form, now could you? For instance, when Ginger got out of the

14

army Veronica's relatives had influence at Kylemore Distilleries and the job they offered him was a real plum, they said. Special Assistant to the Managing Director. Plum! Two years as a glorified office boy. Get me two tickets for the jumping at the Horse Show, Ginger. Book me a seat on the six o'clock plane to London. Go down to customs and see if you can square that stuff away, Ginger. Orders, orders. And, after two years, when Ginger asked for a raise and more responsibility, the managing director gave him a sour look and kicked him downstairs into the advertising department. Where, when he tried some new ideas, the advertising manager, a Neanderthal bloody man, name of Cleery, called him in and said: 'Where do you think you are, Coffey? New York? Remember, the thing that sells whisky in this country is being on good terms with the publicans. Now, get back to your desk at once.'

Orders. Taking guff from powers that be. So, the minute Ginger heard of an opening in a place called Coomb-Na-Baun Knitwear in Cork, he resigned and over Veronica's protests moved his family down there. But Cork was not New York either. Ah, no. Orders, orders. Fifty years behind the times. Taking guff. Never free.

In fact he might never have got free if his father (R.I.P.) hadn't died, leaving two thousand quid to Ginger, enough to pay their debts and start them off again. Again, he did it over Veronica's protests, but this time, by J, he decided to get right out of the country. Far too late now to do the things he once had dreamed of: paddling down the Amazon with four Indian companions, climbing a peak in Tibet or sailing a raft from Galway to the West Indies. But not too late to head off for the New World in search of fame and fortune. So he went up to Dublin and took his old boss out to lunch. Filled the managing director of Kylemore Distilleries with Jammets best duck à l'orange and asked him point blank if Kylemore would be interested in opening up a North American market. They would not, said the managing director. 'All right then,' Coffey said. 'You'll be the sorry ones, not me.' And went straight across the street to Cootehill Distilleries, Kylemore's chief competitor. But flute! At Cootehill they told him they already had a man in New York. 'Well,' said Coffey. . . . 'Well – what about

Canada, then?' And yes, they were willing to let him have a crack at selling their whisky in Canada. Seeing he was paying his own way out there, why not? A small retainer? Yes, they might manage that.

Right then! Before he sailed he lined up two sidelines. A North American agency for Coomb-Na-Baun Knitwear which the Dublin office gave him over the Cork office's objections. And a little sideline as American representative for Dromore Tweeds of Carrick-on-Shannon which was part-owned by an old school pal of his. And so, six months ago, after a round of good-byes for ever, he, Veronica and Paulie sailed out to Montreal, taking the great gamble. His own boss at last.

Except that now, six months later, he was his own boss no longer. And so, at a quarter to twelve, *The Nickelodeon* read from cover to cover, he smiled at the receptionist, still hoping. She came over. 'I'm afraid Mr Beauchemin will be tied up until after lunch. Do you think you could come back at two-thirty?'

Coffey thought of Mr Beauchemin trussed up on his office carpet. He said yes, he thought he could.

Down he went in the express elevator, across the lobby and out into the street. The noon crowd scurried along icy pavements from central heat to central heat. Six office girls, arms linked, high voices half lost in the wind, edged past him in a tottering chorus line. Bundled against the wind, no telling what they looked like. He followed them for a while, playing an old game of his. That very instant a genie had told him they were all houris awaiting his pleasure, but only one must he choose and he must not look on any of their faces. He must choose from the rear view. All right, then, he decided on the tall one in the middle. His choice made, he followed them to the intersection of Peel and Ste Catherine streets and as they paused for the traffic light he came level and inspected their faces. She had a long neb. He should have picked the little one on the outside right. Anyway, none of them was half as pretty as his own wife. He turned away.

Businessmen clutching hatbrims butted impatiently past his aimless strolling figure. A taxi, its tyre chains rattling in the brown sugar slush, pulled up beside him to disgorge six rotarians who ran up the steps of an hotel, their snow-filthy rubbers tracking the wine-coloured carpet. A bundle of newspapers, hurled from the tailgate of a truck by a leather-jacketed leprechaun, fell by his feet. He paused, read the headline on top, as a newsvendor rushed from a kiosk to retrieve.

WIFE, LOVER SLAY CRIPPLE MATE

Which reminded him. He had not phoned Veronica.

Slow stroll across Dominion Square, everyone hurrying save he, every face fixed in a grimace by the painful wind, eyes narrowed, mouths pursed, driven by this cruel climate to an abnormal, head-bent, helter-skelter. He passed a statue of Robert Burns, reflecting that this snow-drifted square was an odd place for that kiltie to wind up. And that reminded him of failures: Burns' brew was called for a lot more often on this continent than usquebaugh. 'Usquebaugh is the name of it, Mr Montrose, yes, we Irish invented it, quite different from Rye or Scotch. I have a booklet here, Irish coffee recipe ...' Promotion, they called it. You had to promote before you could sell. But, to those thicks back in Ireland, promotion was not work.

Dear Coffey,
Yours of the 6th to hand. Before we approve these expenses which seem very high to us, our directors would like to know how many suppliers you can guarantee. So far, in our opinion, you have not ...

That was in the beginning of October. He should have seen the writing on the wall. But instead, he started to use his own savings to keep the ship afloat. He had to. Those thicks refused to pay the half of his expenses. And then, a month later, three letters with Irish postmarks arrived in the same week, as though, behind his back, the whole of Ireland had ganged up on him.

Dear Coffey,
I regret to inform you that at the last meeting of our board of directors it was decided that in view of current dollar restrictions and the heavy 'promotion' expenses you have incurred, we feel unable at this time to continue our arrangement with you. Therefore, we are no longer prepared to pay your office rent or to continue your retainer after this month. ...

Dear Coffey,

Four orders from department stores and single orders from six other shops which have not been repeated do not justify the money you are charging us. And advertising at the rates you quote is quite out of the question. Coomb-Na-Baun Knitwear has always enjoyed a modest sale on your side of the water without any special promotion and so we feel at this time that it is wiser all around for us to cancel our arrangement with you. ...

Dear Ginger,

Hartigan says we would be better off sending an out-and-out traveller to cities like Boston, New York and Toronto to show samples and take orders as the British tailoring firms do. High power American methods do not go over in Carrick-on-Shannon, so if you will kindly let us have back the swatches ...

He burned those letters. He economized by giving up their flat and moving to this cheap dump of a duplex. But he did not tell Veronica. For two weeks he sat in his rented office, searching the want ads in the newspapers, dodging out from time to time for half-hearted inquiries about jobs. But the trouble was, what his trouble always was. He had not finished his B.A., the army years were wasted years, the jobs at Kylemore and Coomb-Na-Baun had not qualified him for any others. In six months he would be forty. He thought of Father Cogley's warning.

The pulpit was on the right of the school chapel. Ginger Coffey, aged fifteen, sat under it while Father Cogley, a Redemptorist Missioner, preached the retreat. There's always one boy — Father Cogley said — always one boy who doesn't want to settle down like the rest of us. He's different, he thinks. He wants to go out into the great wide world and find adventures. He's different, you see. Aye, well Lucifer thought he was different. He did. Now, this boy who thinks he's different, he's the lad who never wants to finish his studies. Ireland isn't good enough for him, it's got to be England or America or Rio-dee-Janeero or some place like that. So, what does he do? He burns his books and off he runs. And what happens? Well, I'll tell you. Nine times out of ten that fellow winds up as a pick-and-shovel labourer or at best a twopenny

18

penpusher in some hell on earth, some place of sun and rot or snow and ice that no sensible man would be seen dead in. And why? Because that class of boy is unable to accept his God-given limitations, because that class of boy has no love of God in him, because that class of boy is an ordinary lazy lump and his talk of finding adventures is only wanting an excuse to get away and commit mortal sins – Father Cogley looked down: he looked into the eyes of Ginger Coffey who had been to confess to him only half an hour ago – And let me tell that boy one thing – Father Cogley said – If you burn your books you burn your boats. And if you burn your boats, you'll sink. You'll sink in this world and you'll sink in the next –

And woe betide you then –

It was all missionary malarkey, of course. But although he had forgotten all else that was ever preached to him, Coffey had not forgotten that sermon. He had thought of it often ; had thought of it that third week of December when Veronica found out. She wept. She said she had seen this coming for a long time. (It was the sort of thing she *would* say.) She said if he did not land a job by Christmas, they must go home the first ship in the New Year. She said they had six hundred dollars put aside for their passages home and he had promised her they would go back if it did not work. It had not worked. And so – Look at us – she said – We know no one here. No one would lift a finger if we froze to solid ice in the streets. You promised me. Let's get out before we have to sing for our passage. At home, there's people know you. You can always find something. Now, there's a ship leaving Halifax on the tenth of January. I'm reserving our tickets –

– But, it's not even Christmas yet – he said – What's the hurry? I'll find something. Chin up! –

Christmas came and went, but the snow was their only present. They saw the New Year in, with Veronica starting to pack as soon as the radio played Auld Lang Syne, while he, alone in the dun-coloured duplex living-room, decided that on January second, as soon as the offices were open again, he would humble himself and go down to the unemployment commission. Because he would have to find *some* job. Because, you see, there was one thing he still hadn't told her. He no longer had the money for the tickets. In fact, all that was left was – never mind – it was a frightener to think how little.

And today was D-Day. The wind was stronger now. The snow had stopped and his ears began to hurt as if someone had boxed them. He looked into a restaurant, saw people lined three deep beside the hostess rope, the waitresses stacking dishes, placing paper place mats and fresh glasses of water before anyone who dared to dawdle: no, there was no shelter in Childs. But he must phone Veronica – start preparing her. So in he went.

'That you, Kitten?'

'Did you get the tickets, Ginger?'

'Well, no, not yet, dear. That's what I'm phoning you about. You see, dear, right out of a clear blue sky I met a man on my way downtown who told me about a job. So I'm going for an interview.'

'What man?'

'You wouldn't know him, dear. The point is, I have an interview arranged for half-past two this afternoon.'

'Today's the last day to pick up those tickets,' she said. 'If you don't get them they'll sell them to someone else.'

'I know, dear. The point is, I'm going to wait until after I've had this interview. I should be finished by three. That leaves lashings of time to pick up the tickets, if nothing comes of it.'

'But what job *is* this?'

Flute! He reached in his weskit and pulled out a slip of paper. It was the second slip which Donnelly had given him but he had started reading it out before he realized his mistake. 'Wanted,' he read. 'Aggressive publicity man for professional fund-raising group, province-wide cancer research campaign. Apply H. E. Kahn, Room 200, Doxley Building, Sherbrooke Street.'

'But that doesn't sound permanent at all!' she said.

'Well, never mind, dear. It would tide us over.'

'If we're going to stay,' she said. 'You've got to get something permanent, Ginger. At your age, you can't afford to be chopping and changing any more. You know that.'

'Yes, dear. We – we'll talk about it later. Good-b . . .'

'Wait! Ginger, listen to me. If this job is only a few weeks' stopgap, don't you take it. Get those tickets.'

'Yes, dear. Bye, bye, now.'

He replaced the receiver and stepped out of the booth. There must be a law of averages in life as well as in cards. And surely if anyone's luck was due for a change, his was?

A Childs' hostess beckoned with her sheaf of menus but he thought of the fourteen lonely dollars left in his pocket. He went outside but it was too cold to hang about the square. Then where? He looked across the snowy park; three old dears were going up the steps of the basilica. Warm it was in God's house. How long was it since he'd been in a church? Not since he'd left home, not that he'd missed it, either. Maybe . . . ? Well, it wouldn't hurt him, now would it?

The interior darkness was familiar. He listened to the murmur of water pipes, located a bench near a radiator and moved in. Catholic churches were all the same. The pulpit on the right (shades of Father Cogley!) and on the left the Altar to Our Lady (Distaff Doings) with a bank of votive candles underneath. He remembered how, as a boy during the boredom of mass, he used to count the candles, sixpence a big one, threepence a little one and try to estimate the profit to the priests.

Coffey's father, a solicitor, had been buried in the brown habit of a Dominican Tertiary. Enough said. His elder brother Tom was a missionary priest in Africa. And yet neither Coffey nor Veronica were what Dublin people called pi-odious. Far from it. In fact one of his secret reasons for wanting to get away to the New World was that in Ireland, church attendance was not a matter of choice. Bloody well go, or else, tinker, tailor, soldier, sailor, rich man, poor man, you were made to suffer in a wordly sense. Here, he was free. . . .

And yet . . . Staring now at the altar, he remembered the missioner's warning. Supposing it were not all nonsense? Suppose his brother Tom, worrying about the Moslems stealing his African converts, was right after all? Just suppose. Suppose all the prayers, the penances, the promises were true? Suppose the poor in spirit would inherit the kingdom of heaven? And not he.

For he was not poor in spirit. He was just poor. Well, what about him? If he did not believe all this stuff about an afterlife then what did he believe? What was his aim in life? Well ... well, he supposed it was to be his own master, to provide for Vera and Paulie, to ... to what? Damned if he could put it into words. To make something of himself, he supposed. Well, was that enough? And would he? Maybe he was one of those people who get the best of neither world, one of those people the Lord had no time for, neither fish nor fowl, great sinner nor saint? And maybe because he had never been poor in spirit, had never been one for pleading and penances, maybe God had lain in wait for him all these years, doling him out a little bad luck here, a little hope there, dampening his dreams, letting him drift further from the time and tide that led on to fortune until now, at the half-way mark in his life he was stranded in this land of ice and snow? If there was a God above, was that what God wanted? To make him poor in spirit? To make him call pax, to make him give up, to herd him back with the other sheep in the fold?

He looked at the tabernacle. His large ruddy face set in a scowl as though someone had struck it. His lips shut tight under his ginger moustache. I never could abide a bully, he said to the tabernacle. Listen to me, now. I came in here to maybe say a prayer and I'll be the first to admit I had a hell of a nerve on me, seeing the way I've ignored you these long years. But now I cannot pray, because to pray to you, if you're punishing me, would be downright cowardly. If it's cowards you want in heaven, then good luck to you. You're welcome.

He picked up his little green hat and left the church.

At two-thirty Mona Prentiss, receptionist, went into the office of Georges Paul-Emile Beauchemin, public relations director of Canada Nickel, and handed him Coffey's application form. Yes, the man was outside and had been waiting since this morning. Would Mr Beauchemin care to see him?

Mr Beauchemin had time to kill. He had just finished buying someone a very good lunch in exchange for two hockey tickets. In half an hour, at the mid-week meeting, he planned to hand the tickets over to Mr Mansard. Mr Mansard was a vice-president and a hockey fan. So Mr Beauchemin was in a good mood. He said to show the guy in.

Miss Prentiss came back up the corridor. 'Will you follow me please, sir?' And Coffey followed, suddenly wishing he'd worn his blue suit although it was shiny in the seat, watching her seat – melon buttocks rubbing under grey flannel skirt, court heels tic-tac, cashmere sweater, blonde curls. A pleasant rear view, yes, but he did not enjoy it. Sick apprehension filled him because, well, what were his qualifications for *this* job? What indeed?

'This is Mr Coffey, sir,' she said, shutting the door on them. And hooray! The face that fits. Because, by some miracle, Coffey had met Mr Beauchemin, had met him last November at a party in the Press Club where the Coffeys had been Gerry Grosvenor's guests.

'Hello there,' Coffey said, jovially advancing with his large hand outstretched, the ends of his moustache lifting in a smile. And Beauchemin took the proferred hand, his mind running back, trying to place this guy. He could not recall him at all. A limey type and, like most limey types, sort of queer. Look at this one with his tiny green hat, short bulky car coat and suède boots. A man that age should know better than to dress like a college boy, Beauchemin thought. He looked at Coffey's red face and large military moustache. Georges Paul-Emile Beauchemin had not served. That moustache did not win him. Oh no.

'I don't suppose you remember me?' Coffey said. 'Ginger Coffey. Was with Cootehill Distilleries here. Met you at a Press Club do once with Gerry Grosvenor, the cartoonist.'

'Oh yes, eh?' Beauchemin said vaguely. 'Old Gerry, eh? You're – ah – you're Irish, eh?'

'Yes,' Coffey said.

'Good old Paddy's day, eh?'

'Yes.'

'Lots of Irish out here, you know. Last year I took my little girl out to see the Paddy's day parade on Sherbrooke Street. Lot of fun, eh?'

'Yes, isn't it?' Coffey said.

23

'So you're not with – ah – ' Beauchemin glanced at the application form – 'not with Distillery any more?'

'Well no. We had a change of top brass at home and they wanted me to come back. But I like it here, we were more or less settled, kiddy in school and so on. Hard changing schools in mid-term, so I decided to chance my luck and stay on.'

'Sure,' Beauchemin said. 'Cigarette?' Perhaps this guy had been sent by someone from upstairs. It was wise to check. 'How did you know we were looking for an editorial assistant, eh?'

Coffey looked at his little green hat. 'Well, it was the – ah – the unemployment commission people. They mentioned it.'

Reassured (for if it had been a brass recommendation he would have had to send a memo) Beauchemin leaned back, openly picked up the application form. A nobody. Seventeen from fifty-six is thirty-nine. Let him out on age.

'Well, that's too bad,' he said. 'Because – what did you say your first name was again?'

'Ginger. Had it since I was a boy. Red hair, you see.'

'Well, Gin-ger, I'm afraid this job's not for you. We want a junior.'

'Oh?'

'Yes, some kid who's maybe worked a couple of years on a suburban weekly, someone we can train, bring along, promote him if he works out.'

'I see,' Coffey said. He sat for a moment, eyeing his hat. Fool! Stupid blundering fool! Why didn't you wait to see if he remembered you? He doesn't know you from a hole in the wall, coming in with your hand out! Oh God! Get up, say thank you and go away.

But he could not. In his mind, a ship's siren blew, all visitors ashore. He and Veronica and Paulie, tears in their eyes, stood on the steerage deck waving good-bye to this promised land. This was no time for pride. Try? Ask?

'Well,' Coffey said. 'As a matter of fact, my experience has all been on the other side of the water. I imagine it's quite different here. Maybe – maybe I'd need to start lower on the scale? Learn the ropes as I go along?'

Beauchemin looked at the man's ruddy face, the embarrassed

eyes. Worked for a distillery, did he? Maybe they let him go because he was too sold on the product? 'Frankly Gin-ger,' he said. 'You wouldn't fit into the pension plan. You know it's a union-management deal. The older a man comes in, the more expensive for the others in the plan. You know how these things work.'

'But I wouldn't mind if you left me out of the pension plan.'

'Sorry.'

'But – but we New Canadians,' Coffey began. 'I mean, we can't all be boys of twenty, can we? We have to start some-where? – I mean,' he said, dropping his eyes to his hat once more. 'I'll put it to you straight. I'd appreciate it if you'd make an exception?'

'Sorry,' Beauchemin said. He stood up. 'I tell you what, Ginger. You leave your name and address with Mona outside. If we think of anything we'll get in touch with you, okay? But don't pass up any other offers, meantime. All right? Glad to have met you again. Give my regards to Gerry, will you? And good luck.'

Beauchemin shook hands and watched Coffey put on his silly little hat. Saw him walk to the door, then turn, and raise his right hand in a quick jerky movement of farewell, a kind of joke salute. A vet, Beauchemin thought. I was right. They do okay, free hospitals, pensions, mortgages, education; the hell with those guys. 'Be seeing you,' he said. 'And shut the door, will you?'

In Room 200 of the Doxley Building, Sherbrooke Street, an aggressive publicity man for a professional fund-raising group, province-wide cancer research campaign, put his little green hat between his feet and stared at H. E. Kahn to whom application must be made.

H. E. Khan wore a blue suit with narrow lapels which curved up to the points of his tight, white, tab-collared shirt. His black tie knot was the size of a grape and the tie itself was narrow as a ruler. The mouth above it was also narrow, narrow the needle nose, the eyes which now inspected the form on which, for the third time that day, the applicant had set down the misleading facts of a life. H. E. Kahn was a swift reader. He turned the form over, read the other side, his young, convict-shaven head bent, showing a small monkish tonsure at the crown. Yet for all that hint of baldness, Coffey estimated that H. E. Kahn could not be more than thirty years old. Which was older than the three other young men he had noticed at work in the outer office, older than the two pretty stenographers who sat facing each other, transcribing from dictating belts behind Coffey's back, and older certainly than the other applicant who had filled up a form as Coffey did and now waited his turn outside.

H. E. Kahn finished his reading and leaned back in his swivel chair until the tonsure on his head touched the wall. 'You speak French?'

'No, I'm afraid not.'

'French might have helped.'

'I suppose so.'

'Not essential, mind you, but I see you're not a local man. Not a Canadian, are you?'

'No, I'm Irish.'

'Irish, eh? That so? I've been in Ireland. Shannon airport. Got a wonderful camera deal there coming back from Paris last summer.'

H. E. Kahn's chair jack-knifed to desk level, his hand crumpling the application form. Balled, the form accurately described a parabola over Coffey's shoulder, holed into the secretary's wastepaper basket. 'Sorry, Mr Cee. You wouldn't suit us.'

Coffey stood up. 'Well, thanks for seeing me, anyway.'

'My pleasure. Hey, Marge, hey send that other guy in, will you? And Jack? JACK? Shoot me over that special names list. Nice meeting you, Mr Coffey. See you.'

'See you,' Coffey repeated mechanically. In hell he hoped.

But afterwards, out in the street, he wondered if that had been fair. After all, Kahn had been polite enough. Was it because Kahn seemed to be a Jew? No, he hoped that wasn't it. Coffey did not agree with many of his countrymen in their attitude to Jews. None of his best friends were Jews, but that was no reason to dislike Jews, was it? Besides, he had not particularly liked Beauchemin either and that wasn't because Beauchemin was French-Canadian. Of course not. So, what

26

was it, apart from the fact that neither man had wanted to employ him? *They were younger than he.* That was the first thing he had thought about both of them. And Donnelly too, the man in the unemployment commission. Younger. All day he had been going hat in hand to younger men. And yet – Suffering J. I'm not told, Coffey thought. Thirty-nine isn't old!

Walking, he turned the corner of Ste Catherine Street and saw again this morning's tabloid headline: WIFE, LOVER SLAY CRIPPLE MATE. He remembered the unbought steamship tickets. Flute! Better stay downtown a while.

At a quarter to five he arrived in the street where he lived. Dawdling still, walking a little off the track of other pedestrians, watching his abominable snowfeet mark the white, new-fallen snow, waiting until five when Gerry Grosvenor would come because with Gerry on hand, the dreaded scene about the tickets would be staved off for another hour or so. And, as he reached the lane running alongside his place, he saw, with relief, that Gerry's sporty little car was here and had been here for some time because there were no tracks on the snow where it had driven in. Which was peculiar.

Gerry Grosvenor, a political cartoonist on a big magazine called *Canada's Own*, was, Coffey supposed, their only real pal in Canada. Someone in Dublin who had known Gerry during the war had given Ginger a letter of introduction to Gerry and from the first go-off Gerry had taken to them like first cousins and favourites. Which was all well and good, but awkward because when Coffey moved from his other flat and the cash started running out, he had to duck Gerry Grosvenor. For dammit, Gerry was a social sort and popular, and the last thing in the world Coffey wanted was for Gerry to start looking down on him. So, as he unlocked the door of the duplex, he was shocked to hear Gerry's voice say: 'There now, there now. Cheer up. It won't be so bad as you think.'

What was that? Vera was sniffling, that was what. What was she sniffling about? Had she found out about the tickets? How? Lord bless us and save us. Bloody females! Sobbing out her private affairs to some outsider, had she no dignity, the woman? He hesitated, dreading his entrance, wanting to hide.

27

There was one safe place. Paulie was not at home, and Veronica would never expect to find him there. He slipped into Paulie's tiny nest, cluttered as all her other rooms had been, and sat on the bed for a breather.

Three-quarter profiled in their tin-finish frames, Paulie's favourite singers, film heroes and guitar players smiled on Daddy in autographed contempt. He avoided their glossy stares and picked up Bunkie, his daughter's oldest plaything, a wooden-headed pyjama case doll. Other talismen, less favoured, lined her dressing-table: a copy of *Little Women*, a worn beaded purse which had once been used by Coffey's mother at a Viceregal ball, a glass snowflake paperweight, a pencil case Coffey had made for her in a woodworking shop. The pencil case, now chipped and broken, was filled with bobby pins and head combs. Paulie was growing up.

He looked again at the doll's wooden head, its painted features half-obliterated by childish kisses, childish tears. Ah, Paulie ... what happened to us? Once, I wasn't able to stir without you running after me, oops-a-daisy, come to Daddy, whirling you up in the air, my Goldilocks and me the Big Bear. The games we played, the childish shrieks of fun. But now you never look at me. What happened? If only you were a boy?

But they had never had a boy. And whose fault was that? Not his, although she sometimes tried to make it seem so. You see, she got pregnant the month he married her. At the time, he had just been commissioned and everyone expected Ireland to go into the war. So they waited and waited. About the time Paulie was born, the thicks in the government announced that Ireland would stay neutral. And Veronica blew up when Coffey wanted to desert and move to the British side. He wanted to see some action but she said his duty was with his family. Family! He wanted adventure, not diapers. So he sulked for a month or so and she got the priest after him for practising birth control. He said he was damned if any priest would dictate whether or not he'd have another child. The priest then threatened to refuse Veronica the sacraments and if there was one thing Coffey would not stand for, it was being threatened. They would not have another child, he said. Not yet. Not until he was good and ready. When would that be, she asked. Soon? Yes, soon. He promised her. Soon.

But they never had one. The years had passed: he no longer knew if she even wanted one. Ah, children ... children ... his large hand caressed Bunkie's head. He put the doll on the coverlet and awkwardly tidied the bed. He was acting like a child himself, come to think of it. Hiding like this. He went out, listened in the corridor, but heard no further weeps. So he risked it into the living-room.

'Hello there, Ginger,' Gerry Grosvenor said, getting up. He was tall, and so neat he reminded Coffey of a dummy in a men's furnishing window. Yet for all his height and neatness, for all his thirty years, his Gillette-blue chin and black-haired hands, adolescence, like an incurable disease, had never quite left him.

'Hello, Gerry, lad,' Coffey said jovially. 'Hello there, Kitten.'

Yes, she had been sniffling.

'So you never picked up the tickets?' she said.

'What was that, Kitten?'

'I phoned at quarter to five,' she said. 'You hadn't picked them up then and they were closing in a few minutes. Does that mean you got a job?'

Coffey did not answer her at once. Instead, he winked at Gerry. Sure, women are always starting a barney over nothing, eh, Gerry lad? But Grosvenor did not return the wink; left Coffey in the field, alone. 'No,' Coffey said, turning back to her. 'I did not get a job.'

'Then why didn't you buy those tickets?'

'Look, we'll talk about that later, Kitten. Now, what about a beer? Are there any beers in this place, by any chance.'

'In the kitchen,' she said.

'Gerry, will you have another?' Coffey asked.

But Grosvenor shook his head. His round brown stare which reminded Coffey of a heifer watching you cross a field, was now fixed and glassy. He was ploothered, Coffey decided.

'No, I have to run,' Grosvenor said. 'I have another appointment. Now, don't worry, Vera and Ginger. I'm going to see what I can do, okay?'

'Listen. Have a short one for the road, won't you?' Coffey

said, knowing that the minute Gerry left, the roof would fall in.

'No, I'm late now,' Gerry said. 'Bye, Ginger. Bye, Veronica.'

Veronica did not move out of her seat, did not even say good-bye. Which mortified Coffey for, no matter, she might at least be polite to visitors. Angry, Coffey followed Gerry out into the hall. 'I'm sorry I was late home, old man,' he said. 'I hope Veronica hasn't been bothering you with our troubles.'

Grosvenor bent his head to drape a long woollen scarf about his neck, then looked at Coffey with round brown cow eyes. 'But I'm your friend,' he said. 'I mean to say, I didn't know you were having trouble. I mean, your troubles are my troubles, right? That's the essence of any relationship, isn't it?'

'I suppose it is,' Coffey agreed. Canadians were terribly slabberry, he'd noticed. Even the men were always telling you how much they liked you. Shocking way to carry on, especially when you'd be daft to heed one word of it. Still, there was an excuse for old Gerry. He was drunk. 'There we are,' Coffey said, helping Gerry on with his overcoat. 'Steady as she goes.'

'I mean, I thought you *wanted* to go home,' Grosvenor said. 'But now that you don't – well, I'll see what I can dig up. Right?'

'Right,' Coffey said, guiding him to the front door. 'And thanks very much, Gerry.'

'Listen,' Grosvenor said, stopping, fixing Coffey once more in his drunken stare. 'Going to look into a possibility right now. Call you tonight, okay?'

'Fair enough. I'll be at home.'

''Kay,' Grosvenor said. He stumbled on the step, went down the path to the street in a shambling, head-heavy walk. It occurred to Coffey that Gerry was not fit to drive.

'Gerry?' he called – because if he drove Gerry home it would put off Judgement Day a while longer. . . .

'Bye,' Grosvenor shouted back. 'See you, Ginger.'

Ah well. Slowly, Coffey shut the front door. Slowly he made his way back into the living-room. She had not moved from her chair. She sat, her dark hair framing her pallor, her long fingers laced over one knee, the leg drawn up, her large dark eyes looking up at him, implacable and waiting.

'Well,' he said, sitting on the arm of the sofa. 'Pal Gerry

certainly has a skinful in him this afternoon, wouldn't you say?'

She did not answer. He smiled at her, still trying to jolly her. 'Do you know, I could have sworn for a moment he was going to kiss me, out there in the hall,' he said.

'Kiss who?'

'Me,' he said, trying to smile at her.

'Why didn't you get those tickets, Ginger?'

'Now . . .' he said. 'Look dear,' he said, 'listen, do you know where I went today?'

No answer.

'First thing this morning,' he said. 'I went down to the unemployment commission. You know, the labour exchange? And do you know, right off they gave me two jobs to look into. They were very decent. So, I spent the whole day at interviews and – and listen, Vera, I admit I didn't get anything. But it was just a start and tomorrow they're going to have another try at placing me – '

'Tomorrow you're going to get those tickets,' she said.

'Ah now, look here, Kitten. Sure you don't want to go home to Ireland any more than I do. Now, why not wait a while – '

'No. We've waited too long already.'

'But just another week wouldn't kill us?'

'Ginger,' she said. 'I'm doing this for your sake, if you only knew it. We're getting those tickets tomorrow and that's all about it.'

'For *my* sake?' he said. 'Am I the one who wants to go home?'

'We're buying those tickets,' she said. 'That's final!'

'It is not final,' he said, suddenly losing his temper. 'We can't buy the tickets, so shut up about it, will you?'

'What?'

'How the hell do you think I've carried on this last while?' he said. 'It costs a fortune, this country.'

'You spent the money? *You-spent-the-money?*'

'I couldn't help it, Kitten. There were expenses – at the office – things you never knew – '

'One,' she said. 'Two – '

'All kinds of bills – '

31

'Three – Four –'

'Ah, now, cut it out, Kitten. I'm sorry. I'm not a good manager, I never was. I'm sorry.'

'Five – Six – Seven –'

'I said I was sorry, Kitten. God knows it's not just my fault. Those thicks at home, not paying my expenses. I skimped on lunches, even.'

'Eight – Nine – Ten!' she took a long breath. 'I am not going to lose my temper,' she recited. 'I-am-not-going-to-lose-my-temper.'

'Good, that's the girl. Now, cheer up, sure, listen, I'll get a job soon and it'll be all for the best. You'll see.'

'Go away,' she said. 'What on earth good does saying you're sorry do?'

'Vera?'

'If you just knew what you've done,' she said, beginning to cry. 'If you had just the *faintest* idea. You've torn it, this time. You really have.'

'Ah, now, Kitten –'

'Go away. Eat your supper.'

'Aren't you eating, dear?'

'*Get out!*'

Ah, well. Women were peculiar cuss. They had nervous troubles men knew nothing about. Ah, she had been acting very peculiar this last while, cold and fed up and so on. That was nervous troubles, he was sure. If you read medical books, it was all explained in there. So, leave her be. She'd come around.

He went into the kitchen and found sausages and potatoes warm in the oven. A little mental arithmetic indicated three for him, three for her, and two for Paulie. He took his portion and settled down at the kitchen table. The sink tap dripped on to stacked pots and pans. Upstairs, someone knocked on a radiator and a moment later the basement furnace whirred and coughed into life. Lord save us, what a dump this was, was it any wonder Vera hated it? Coffey was hungry. He ate his sausages and helped himself to more gravy and potatoes. Fork half-way to his mouth, he noticed her standing in the door, her face pale, her eyes bright. Still in a rage. He put the forkful in his mouth and winked at her.

'How much *do* we have left?' she said.

He smiled, gesturing that his mouth was full.

'Answer me. The truth, mind!'

Eight and fourteen – well, make it an even – 'About a hundred dollars,' he said.

'Oh my God!' She went away.

He finished the spuds and wiped his plate with a bit of bread. What did Vera know about money anyway? An only child, brought up by a doting mother, pretty, with plenty of beaux, until she met and married him. And, even so, in all those years of marriage, the army years, the years at Kylemore and in Cork, had she ever bloody starved? Had she? Give him credit for something. And remember, Vera, you married me for better or for worse. This is the worse. Ah, but supposing she won't put up with the worse?

Now that was nonsense. She loved him in her way and despite her temper. And she had Paulie. He could hear the two of them talking now in the living-room. Paulie, home from her dance practice, had gone straight in to see Vera. And, as usual, not even hello for Daddy. They were like sisters, those two, always gossiping away about womany wee things he knew nothing about.

There was the phone. He got up to answer because Vera hated the phone.

'Ginger?' It was Gerry Grosvenor. 'Listen, how would you react to a hundred and ten a week?'

'Get away with you!'

'No, seriously, there's a job going as a deskman on the *Tribune*. And the managing editor happens to be a friend of mine.'

'Deskman?' Coffey said. 'But Gerry lad, what's that? What does a deskman do? Make desks?'

'Copy editor,' Grosvenor said. 'Easy. This is on the international desk, all wire copy, very clean. It's just writing heads and putting in punctuation. Nothing to it.'

'But I have no experience on a newspaper. I never wrote a headline in my life.'

'Never mind that. Would you take the job?'

'Would a duck swim!'

'Okay. Wait. I'll call you back.'

Coffey replaced the receiver and looked down the long railroad corridor hallway. Total silence from the living-room which meant she and Paulie had been listening. So he went in. 'Hello, Apple,' he said to Paulie. 'Had a good day in school?'

'Was that Gerry?' Veronica asked in an angry voice.

'Yes, dear. He says he can get me a job. Hundred and ten dollars a week to start.'

'What job?'

'On the *Tribune*. It's an editing job. I pointed out that I'd no experience, but he said not to worry.'

'I'd worry,' Veronica said. 'If I were you. This isn't acting the glorified office boy, or playing poker and drinking pints in barracks.'

He gave her a look intended to turn her into Lot's wife there on the sofa. Imagine saying that in front of Paulie!

'Go and have your supper, Apple,' he told Paulie. He waited as, unwillingly, Paulie trailed out of the room. 'Now, why did you say that in front of the child, Vera?'

'She might as well know.'

'Know what?'

'What sort of a selfish brute she has for a father.'

Suffering J! No sense talking, was there? He went out and while he was in the bathroom, the phone rang again. He hurried up the corridor.

'Yes,' she said to to the phone. 'Yes – wait, I want to explain something. I mean apropos of this afternoon. Ginger doesn't *have* our passage money home. He spent it ... Yes ... So that leaves me no choice, does it? ... Yes ... yes, here's Ginger. I'll let you tell him yourself.'

'Ginger,' Gerry's voice said. 'It's all set. I've given you a good build-up and old MacGregor wants to see you in his office at three tomorrow afternoon.'

'Thanks a million, Gerry. But what did you tell him?'

'I told him you'd worked on a Dublin newspaper for two years and said after that you'd been a Press officer in the Army and that you were a public relations man for Irish whisky out here. It sounded good, believe me.'

'But, Holy God!' Coffey said. 'It's not true. I never worked on a newspaper.'

At the other end of the line there was a Remembrance Day hush. Then Grosvenor said: 'Ginger. The point is, do you want this job or don't you?'

'Of course I do, but –'

'But nothing. Everybody bullshines out here. Every employer expects it. The point is to get in. After that, doing the job is up to you.'

'But maybe I can't do it,' Coffey said.

'Beggars can't be choosers,' said Vera's voice. She reached out, took the receiver from him and said: 'Thanks, Gerry, you're an angel. Thanks very much . . . Yes . . . Yes, I know . . . good night.' She replaced the receiver, turned away, walked down the hall and went into their bedroom. He followed her but she shut the door. When he tried the door, it was locked.

'Vera, I want to talk to you.'

'Go away,' she said. She sounded as if she were crying again.

'Listen,' he said. 'Don't you want any supper?'

'No. And go away, will you? Please! Sleep on the living-room sofa. I want to be alone.'

Ah, well. What was the use? He went back to the kitchen where Paulie was at table, reading some trashy magazine. He got out Vera's sausages and offered Paulie one but she shook her head and, still reading, carried her dishes to the sink.

'Stay and have a chat with me, Apple?'

'I have to study, Daddy.'

'Just a minute, miss,' he said, surprised at the anger in his voice. He saw she was surprised too. It wasn't like him to be cross. 'Sit down,' he said. 'I want to ask you something.'

'Yes, Daddy?'

'Apple, do you want to go back to Ireland?'

'Jeepers, no. I like it here.'

'Why?'

'Well, the kids are more grown up here. And school's more – oh, it's just nicer, that's all. Besides, I said good-bye to everybody at home. I'm going to look silly going back now. I wish we weren't going back, Daddy.'

'Well, we're not,' he said. 'It's much better here. You're right. I wish your mother could see that, though.'

'But Mummy's never wanted to go home.'

'Is that so?' he said. 'That's not the way I hear it.'

'She likes it here, Daddy. Honestly she does. She's just afraid you won't find a job, that's all.'

'I'll get a job,' he said. 'No need to panic.'

'Sure. Of course,' Paulie said. 'Can I go now, Daddy?'

'All right, Pet.' You'd think he was a leper or something, she was that anxious to run away from him. Children ... children. . . .

He ate the remaining three sausages and lit a smoke. If Veronica really wanted to stay over here, why the blazes couldn't she say so? No bloody faith in him, that was it. Suffering J!

He went into the living-room with the *Montreal Star* but he was too upset to have a read of it. He went back into the kitchen and brought out two quarts of beer. Last of the last. He poured himself a glass, lay down on the sofa and switched the radio on, trying to salvage something out of this miserable bloody evening. He searched for music for music hath charms and had better have because, looking back on the day, he had a savage bloody breast on him, all right. Hat in hand to younger men, wife snivelling to strangers, asked to lie his way into some job he'd be caught out in, and what else? Oh, a savage bloody breast!

And all there was to drink was this gassy Canuck beer that gave him heartburn. And to sleep on, this bloody sofa that was too short. No faith. If your nearest and dearest had no faith in you, then how could a man give his all? Where would he be unless he still could hope? Without hope, he'd be done for. Aye, a savage bloody breast.

'Daddy? Dad-dee?'

'Yes, Apple,' he said, sitting up in hope.

'Daddy, I can't hear to study with all that noise. Could you turn the radio off?'

'Right, Pet.'

Not even able to enjoy a bit of music. Bloody females! He lay back, entering a world where no earthly women were. In that world soft houris moved, small women of a Japanese submissiveness, administering large doubles and sweet embraces in rooms filled with comfortable club sofas and beds. In that world, men of thirty-nine were Elder Brothers, prized over any

36

Greek stripling. In that world, a man no longer spent his life running uphill, his hope in his mouth, his shins kicked by people with no faith in him. In that world, all men had reached the top of the hill; there were no dull jobs, no humiliating interviews, no turndowns; no man was saddled with grinning wives and ungrateful daughters, there were unlimited funds to spend, the food was plentiful and non-fattening, there were no Father Cogleys handing out warnings, no newspapers worrying you with atom bombs, no sneerers and mockers waiting to see you fail, no rents to pay, no clothes to buy, no bank managers. In that world you could travel into beautiful jungles with four Indian companions, climb a dozen distant mountain peaks, sail rafts in endless tropic seas. You were free. By flicking your fingers in a secret sign, you could move backwards or forwards in time and space, spending a day in any age that took your fancy, but as a leader of that age, the happiest man of that day. In that free world. . . .

In that world, both quarts finished, Ginger Coffey fell asleep

Chapter Two

HE came to consciousness, aware of a telephone ringing. Sunlight struck down on him from the window in a white column filled with tiny floating feathers of dust. He turned his eyes from that light and, as in a frame from a film, saw his wife pass by in the corridor. The ringing stopped.

He had lain all night in his clothes. Mother of God, she would think he'd been drunk. Up with him now! He undressed, dropping clothes in a heap, found blankets and a sheet in the cupboard, made up the sofa as a bed and hopped back in his underpants, closing his eyes as she passed back to the bedroom. Yes, that was a little victory.

Relaxed, he lay for a while, listening to the voice of a French-Canadian radio announcer upstairs, listening to the thump and shuffle of Madame Beaulieu's feet on the ceiling, remembering that last night he had been supposed to tell Madame whether or not they would keep this apartment for another month. Oh, well. Tell her tonight, when he knew about the new job. The job. That started him thinking of the day ahead, remembering that Veronica now knew the worst about the tickets, remembering that she would want to know how he had spent the money and what they were going to do. Ah, dear God!

He exhaled noisily, feathering up the ends of his moustache. As usual, you must balance the good with the bad. And if there was no good at the moment, then think of the important things. Health and strength and a wife and daughter. And here you are in a foreign land listening to French on the radio and you a man who has cut loose from all the old codology and cant at home, a man who struck out alone in search of fame and fortune. So, you're not dead yet. Now, raise your big carcass out of this excuse for a bed. Lift it. One, Two, Three, and Up! And up he got, feeling a touch of heartburn after last night's beer, a twinge in his knee as he went heavily down the dark corridor to knock on her door. 'Veronica?'

He went in. Nobody there. She had already made up the bed.

He put on his dressing-gown and slippers and wandered back up the corridor to the bathroom. When he came out, he saw the pair of them in the kitchen. Paulie, her head in pincurls, eternal book propped up against the milk jug as she finished her corn flakes. That child didn't eat enough and Veronica didn't seem to care. But when he looked at Veronica, he forgot to be angry. She was in her dressing-gown, her dark hair down about her shoulders. She smiled at him. 'Did you sleep all right?' she asked.

'Like a top,' he said, kissing the end of her nose.

'I'm sorry about last night,' she said. 'I had a terrible headache. It made me grumpy.'

He looked to see that Paulie was not watching, then ran his hand down his wife's back, giving her buttocks a little slap. 'Sure, that's all right,' he said. 'Was that the phone I heard earlier?'

'Yes, Gerry rang. He wants us to have lunch with him today before you go for your interview. His treat, he said.'

'Isn't he the decent skin, though?' Coffey said. 'You told him yes, I hope.'

'Of course. Now, eat your breakfast.'

There must have been at least two eggs in the helping of scrambled eggs she ladled out to him. He peppered and salted it, warmed by the sunlight, by this matutinal kindness, sure that it was a good omen somehow. He thought of J. F. Coffey, journalist. He liked the sound of that. Or better, Coffey the editor, Coffey of the *Tribune*. Yes, it was a grand morning, right enough. Maybe today his ship would come in.

'Was Madame Beaulieu around yet?' he asked.

'Not yet.'

'Well, we'll tell her about the place tomorrow,' he said. 'Although, if I get this job, I don't fancy staying on in this hole.'

'I've been thinking,' Veronica said. 'If we're really going to stay I'm going to get a job as well. Paulie's out until after three, five days a week. There's no need for me to sit at home, is there?'

No need for her to get a job either, was there? He could take care of his own. Ah, this was old stuff, her wanting a job, wanting to slave away in some shop. Ah, for God's sake! But he held his whist: let her dream, the woman. He finished his eggs, ate four pieces of toast and sat idle over his third cup of tea while Paulie rushed off to school and Veronica washed the breakfast dishes. And after, following Veronica down the corridor in the morning sunlight, everything quiet, everyone else off to work, he stood in the bedroom door watching her as she took off her dressing-gown and stood in her pink slip. His Dark Rosaleen.

'Lay out my old blue suit, will you?' he said. 'I'd better wear it today. They're shocking conservative in their clothes over here.'

Obediently she leaned into the closet to get the suit and at that moment the sight of a fold of her slip caught between the cleft of her buttocks aroused him to a sluggish, familiar desire. Married as long as they were, desire was not something a man could waste. He dropped his own dressing-gown and pulled her down on the bed. He kissed her, fumbled her slip off her, then remembered. He looked at her, and obedient, she went to the bathroom. He shut his eyes, carefully nursing his desire until she came back. Then, forgetting her years of complaints about his roughness, his selfishness, he took her, tumbling her naked beneath him. Animal, his breathing harsh in the morning silence, he laboured towards that moment of release and fulfilment. And afterwards, fell down beside her, pulling her on top of him, crushing her face against the reddish, greying hair on his chest. He exhaled in contentment; dozed off to sleep.

Then minutes later, he awoke to find her sitting up in bed beside him, smoking a cigarette, her cheek reddened by contact with his unshaven chin. He was in good form, this morning: her body, familiar as his own, still could rouse him to another round. He reached up, taking hold of her breasts, smiling at her, his moustache ends curling upwards in anticipation.

'No, Ginger.' She drew back, put her cigarette in his mouth, slipped off the bed and went into the bathroom. That was women for you, they never enjoyed anything. He heard her begin to run a bath.

'Ginger?'

40

'Yes?'

'Ginger, promise you'll tell me the truth?'

'Promise.'

'Who do you love more? Paulie or me?'

'Love both of you, Kitten.'

'But if anything happened to Paulie that would be worse for you than if anything happened to me, wouldn't it?'

'Nothing's going to happen to anyone,' he said. 'Oh, Kitten, I feel it in my bones. Today is going to be the day that counts. There's a law of averages in life. You just have to wait for your chance to come up.'

'But, supposing you had to decide in a matter of life or death? I mean between Paulie and me. You know, one of those things about save the mother or save the child. Which would you save?'

'Will you, for the love of Mike, shut up and get on with your bath?' he said contentedly.

'No, answer me. Which one would you save?'

'Well, I suppose if a ship was sinking, I'd save Paulie. I mean, she'd have all her life before her. Kids of her own and so forth.'

'And what makes you think I can't have any more kids?' she said. 'Good grief, it's not my fault we hadn't any more kids. And I still can have them, otherwise why did you send me off to the bathroom this morning? What do you think I am – a grandmother? Most men – let me tell you – most men still find me *very* attractive, do you hear?'

'Listen, Kitten,' he said. 'I didn't mean that. I was only saying that Paulie has her whole life before her. We haven't.'

'Maybe *you* haven't,' she said. The bath water began to run again. 'But *I* have,' she said. 'God, you're selfish!'

After her bath, she cheered up. She put on her best black suit for lunch because they both knew Gerry would take them to some posh place. Yes, he was the soul of generosity, Gerry, always lending them his car for a run up north, inviting them out to parties and for lunch. Not that Ginger hadn't held their end up, when he could. Matter of fact – although Vera didn't know it – that was where some of the return passage money went. Although, even in these last days when Coffey had to cut his entertaining to a duck egg for lack of spondulicks, Gerry never let that make one bit of difference. None of your eyes right and cross the street for him when a pal was down on his luck. Ah, no. Dead on, Gerry was. A heart of oak.

Still, for all his decency, Gerry could be a strain at times. Talk? A gramophone. And, being a political cartoonist, he fancied himself as in the know. He was always up in Ottawa and to hear him talk about the place it was the hub of the bloody universe. He referred to the head men in the Canadian Government as Lester and Louie. He had once had tea with Madame Pandit and when he talked politics he let slip names like Joe Enlee or J. F. Dee or Rab or Mac or Masy Dong or Mick O'Yan as if he was related to all of them.

But today, for a change, Gerry talked about Ireland. He said he was glad they were not going back there. He said until he had met the Coffeys he had considered Irish people bigoted, untrustworthy and conventional. Although he had some very good Irish friends, he said. But he had been relieved to find that the Coffeys were not nationalists or religious. Although he admired people who believed in something, didn't they? Of course, none of *his* Catholic friends ever went to church, he said. Which was a relief to him. Yes, the Irish were wonderful people, imaginative, romantic and creative. Wonderful people.

Coffey winked at Veronica.

Then Gerry talked about the interview that was coming up: 'Confidence,' Gerry said. 'That's the important thing in an interview. Now, in Canada, we don't go in for the hard sell. On the contrary –' and his face loosened in that self-satisfied smile peculiar to him when discussing his country – 'I like to think that Canadians combine the best facets of British reticence with a touch of good old American down-to-earthness. And that's the tone I took when I sold you to MacGregor. I made him feel I was doing him a favour.'

This time, it was Veronica who winked. Ah, God knows, Coffey thought, when you come right down to it, she's a darling. Not that Gerry would notice that, he was so wrapped up in himself. But she was a darling.

After the lunch with Gerry, the Coffeys walked over to the

Tribune building and just the fact of having her with him made Coffey less nervous about the interview to come. Into the lobby they went and she stopped to straighten his tie. 'I'll wait for you here,' she said.

'But there's no need, Kitten. I mean, even when you have an appointment in this country, they often keep you hanging around for hours on end.'

'Doesn't matter,' she said. 'I'll be nervous no matter where I wait. Oh Ginger. What if they find out you've no experience?'

'Steady the Buffs,' he said, smiling at her. But the sickness came suddenly upon him. No faith, she had. No faith. 'Don't worry,' he said. 'Why I'll bet you a –'

'I know,' she said. 'A brand new frock. I could run a dress shop if I collected on half your bets. Now go on, and good luck.'

So, into the elevator he went, sick with nerves, praying that –

'Fourth floor. Editorial,' the elevator man said. Funny, whenever you were in no hurry to get some place, elevators, buses, taxis, all went like the wind. Coffey stepped out, hearing the elevator door shut behind him, feeling shabby and ill at ease in his old blue suit, pausing to stare at his image in the brass plaque in the corridor. The plaque said CITY ROOM and in it he seemed all squeegeed up, head tiny, eyes aslant like a Chinaman. Exactly how he felt. But you'll do, he told himself. Keep your chin up and some day you can buy yourself a brass plaque like this to remind yourself of the day your luck changed and you started in a whole new career. Right, then! He went in.

On the fourth floor of the *Tribune*, the night's business was just beginning. Under fluorescent lights, lit all year around, a few reporters studied the afternoon papers. A police radio blared routine calls in a corner and in the near-by teletype room a jammed machine tintinnabulated incessantly, calling for attention. In the centre slot of a large horseshoe desk a fat man in a woollen cardigan sliced open the afternoon's crop of wire service photographs. He looked up as Coffey approached. 'Yes?'

'May I speak to Mr MacGregor, please?'

'Boy! Take this man to Mr Mac.'

An indolent adolescent shoved a rubber cylinder down a communications tube, then hooked a beckoning finger. Across the City Room he led and down a corridor to a partitioned-off office on the opened door of which a small brass plaque announced: MANAGING EDITOR. The boy pointed to the plaque, then went away, wordless. Inside, Coffey saw three young men in shirtsleeves looking over the shoulders of an old man who was seated at a large, scarred desk. He was a thin old man with a pale, bony face, a pumping blue vein in his forehead and eyebrows thick and crumbling as cigar ash. His voice, a Low Church Scottish rumble, could be heard clearly in the corridor. For once, Coffey was not comforted by the fact that he faced an older man.

'Dorrothy Dix? Where's Dorrothy Dix?'

'Here, Mr Mac.'

'Okay. Now, where's the funnies?'

'Here, Mr Mac.'

'Make sure that Blondie is up top and then Dick Tracy and *then* Li'l Abner. *Not* Rex Morrgan, M.D. Some bleddy rascal in the composing room changed the order in the Early last night.'

'Right, Mr Mac.'

'Okay. Now, away with ye.'

The three young men clutched up page proofs and galleys and rushed out, jostling Coffey in the doorway. For the love of J, how was he going to tell this sulphur-breathing Scottish Beelzebub that he was an experienced sub-editor? Grosvenor must be daft.

The old man spiked a scrap of paper like Calvin drowning sin. His eye picked out Coffey in the doorway.

'Come in. State your business.'

'My – name is Coffey. I believe Gerry Grosvenor spoke to you about me?'

'Grrosvenor? Och, aye, the cartoonist. Come in, come in, sit you down. Where's my notes. Aye, here we are, Desk-man aren't you?'

'Yes, sir.'

'What paper did you wurrk for in the old country?'

44

Confidence, Grosvenor had said. The time and tide that leads on to fortune. One good lie and – But as Coffey opened his mouth he was taken with a sort of aphasia. The old man waited, becoming suspicious. 'I – ah – I worked on the *Irish Times*, sir.'

'*Times*, eh? Good paper.'

'Yes. Yes, isn't it?'

'Grrosvenor said you were in the Army?'

'Yes, sir.'

'Officer weren't you? Serve overseas?'

'I – was in the Irish Army, sir. We were neutral during the war.'

'Indeed?'

' – I was a Press officer,' Coffey added, trying to correct the hostility in that 'Indeed?'

'Press officer?' the old man said. 'Trying to keep the facts from the public, that is the services' job. However, I need a man who has some knowledge of wurrld events. Most Canadians have none. What about you?'

'I – ah – I try to keep up, sir.'

'Grrosvenor tells me you were a publicity man for a whussky company?'

'Yes, sir.'

'Scotch whussky?'

'No sir. Irish.'

'No wonder you were out of a job then. Did you wurrk on the foreign desk at the *Times*?'

'Yes, sir. Ah – part time.'

'What do you mean, part time?'

'Well, ah – summer holidays and so on. Filling in.'

The old man nodded and consulted his notes again. Coffey fingered his moustache. A good touch that, summer holidays. He was pleased with himself for thinking of it.

'When was it you wurrked for the *Times*?'

'Oh – after I got out of the army. About – ah – six years ago.'

'How long did you wurrk there?'

'About – (what had Grosvenor said?) – about eighteen months.'

'I see.' The old man picked up one of the phones on his desk. 'Give me Fanshaw,' he said. 'Ted? When you were in Dublin, did you ever hear tell of a subbie on the *Times* by the name of Coffey? . . . Aye, about five years ago . . . Hold on.' He covered the mouthpiece and turned to Coffey. 'What was the name of the foreign editor?'

Coffey sat, his eyes on his little green hat.

'Well?'

He raised his eyes and read a title on the bookshelf behind MacGregor. *Holy Bible.*

'Right, Ted,' the old man told the telephone. 'Disna matter.' He put the phone down and glowered at Coffey under the crumbling ash of his eyebrows. 'If you'd been a Scot,' he said, 'you'd have come in here wi' references in your hand. But you carry nothing besides your hat and a lot of cheek. Och, aye. You may fool the likes of Gerry Grrosvenor, but there isn't an Irishman born that I'd trust to pull the wuul o'er my eyes!'

Coffey, his face hot, stood up and put his hat on.

'Where are you going?' MacGregor said.

'I'm sorry I took up your ti . . .'

'Sit down! Are you hard up for a job? Tell me the truth.'

'Yes, sir.'

'Okay. Can you spell? Spell me phosphorous.'

Coffey spelled.

'Correct. Are you married?'

'Yes, sir.'

'Children?'

'One daughter, sir.'

'Hmm . . . Have you a vice?'

'Advice sir?'

'Are you deaf ? I mean, have you a weakness? Booze or horses or wimmin? Own up, now, for I'll find out, anyway.'

'No, sir.'

'Okay. You say ye've been a P.R. That may be. But what a P.R. knows about the wurrking of a newspaper could be written twice over on the back of a tomtit's arse and still leave room for the Lorrd's Prayer. So you'd best start at the bottom. Do you agree?'

Coffey took a deep breath. He was too old to start at the bottom, suffering J.

'Well? Don't stand there gawking.'

'Well, sir, it depends. I'm not a boy of twenty.'

'I'm proposing to start you off in the proofroom,' the old man said. 'So that you can acquaint yourself with the rudiments of our style. That's the best training there is.'

'A – a p-p-proofreader, did you say, sir?'

'I did. My readers are not unionized, thank the Lord. And I happen to be shorthanded there at the moment. If you wurrk well I might try you out on the floor as a reporter. You might even wind up as a deskman if you play your cards right. What do you say?'

'Well I – I'd have to think about that, sir. How much – how much would that pay?'

'Forrty dollars a week, which is more than you're wurrth. Start at six tonight. Go and think it over now, but let me know no later than half past four, if you want the job.'

'Thank you –'

'Clarence?' Mr MacGregor shouted. 'Where's Clarence?'

A fat man rushed in, notebook at the ready.

'What's the last two paras of Norrman Vincent Peale doing in the overset, Clarence?'

'Don't know, Mr Mac.'

'Bleddy well find out, then.'

The fat man rushed out. Mr MacGregor spiked another galley. 'All right, Coffey. Good day to you.'

Coffey went away. Forty dollars a week, reading galleys. A galley slave. He passed along a corridor lined with rolls of newsprint, wandered across the wide desert of the City Room and out past the brass plaque to the elevator. The red light flashed above the elevator door. Going down. Down, down, all his high hopes failed; with Veronica waiting below, Veronica who wanted to know that the bad days were over, that they could move to a better place –

'Ground floor,' the elevator man said. 'Ground floor. Out.'

There she was under the big clock, the nervous beginnings of a smile on her face. Poor Kitten, it was not fair to her, not fair at all, she'd be in such a state –

Maybe, through Gerry Grosvenor, maybe he might just manage? Maybe. And so, he went towards her, his mind made up. Don't tell her now. Smile instead, be the jolly Ginger she used to love. He kissed her, squeezed her and said: 'Steady as she goes.'

'Did you get it, Ginger?'

'I did, indeed.'

'Oh thank God.'

'Now, now,' he said. 'What's that? Sniffles? Come on, come on, it's laughing you should be. Listen – let's – let's go and have a cup of tea. How would you like to sail into the Ritz, just like the old days?'

'Oh, Ginger, I'm so glad for you.'

'Glad for *me*? And aren't you glad for yourself, Kitten? Ah, it's going to be super. Just super. Come on now. We'll take a taxi.'

'But we can't afford it, Ginger.'

'Come on, come on,' he said, out in the street now, signalling a cab. 'Let me be the judge of that. In with you. Driver, The Ritz-Carlton Hotel, on the double!'

He leaned back in the taxi, put his arm around her shoulders and hugged her, watching the city rush past: pretending. Making her feel as she did in the first weeks they landed, two people in a new and exciting country, him with three good agencies to make his fortune and all the old fogies at home confounded. Sweeping her off to the Ritz for tea, happy as sandboys, the pair of them.

'But, how did the interview go?' she said. 'What did he ask you?'

'Why, first rate, first rate,' said he. 'The old fellow took to me like a long lost relative. He's going to show me over the different stages of the job, let me work a while in each department until I get my hand in.'

'Isn't that marvellous,' she said. 'We must phone Gerry and thank him.'

'Plenty of time. Tea first.'

'Ginger, how much are they going to pay you?'

'Hundred and ten, but that's only a start. There's no telling how far I can go in a job like this. You may be looking at an important citizen, Kitten. J. F. Coffey, the editor.'

'But Ginger, do you think you can do it?'

'Didn't Gerry say I could?'

'Yes, but. . . .'

'Gerry has perfect faith in me,' Coffey said. 'And you have none. Isn't that a nice thing?'

'No, I didn't mean that,' she said, contrite. 'It's just that I hope nothing goes wrong this time.'

'What would go wrong, would you tell me? Now, come on. Here we are.'

He helped her out of the taxi under the brass carriage lanterns of the hotel, already lit in the grey winter afternoon. Up the steps they went, past the black wood panels of the entrance hall, and into the heat of the lobby. He took her coat and removed his own, dodging off into the cloakroom. He had to get hold of Gerry. For one thing Gerry might be able to tell him how long he'd have to wait before they made him a reporter. And, for another, Gerry would have to help him because this was Gerry's fault after all. They would just have to keep mum, Gerry and he, and try to get through the weeks until he was made a reporter. Wasn't that the best plan? Well, if it wasn't, it was the only plan he could think of at the moment.

So when he checked the coats, he hurried down the back stairs to the row of public telephones in the basement. He called *Canada's Own.*

'How did it go, Ginger?'

'Disaster. Listen, Gerry, he caught me red-handed. Now listen – I haven't had the heart to tell Veronica the truth. And listen – he's offered me a job and I have until half past four to make up my mind. It's in the proofroom, but that's only temporary. He's promised to promote me to reporter. Now, if I take it, maybe I can last out a few weeks without Vera being any the wiser. Until they make me a reporter, you see?'

'But did MacGregor give you a definite date for this promotion?' Gerry asked.

'No, he didn't. I think it won't be long, though.'

'How do you know? I wouldn't put it past that old bastard

to con you into this, just so's he can get himself a non-union proofreader on the cheap.'

'But dammit, what's the use in talking, I'll have to take it,' Coffey said. 'I've told Vera I have a job.'

'It's up to you,' Gerry said. 'But if you start small, you'll wind up small.'

'Yes, but beggars can't be choosers –' Coffey began. Then he stopped. In the little mirror in front of the telephone, he saw Veronica's face. He turned around.

'Let me speak to Gerry,' she said.

At once, Coffey hung up.

'Why did you do that? You're too late, anyway. I heard you.'

He took her arm. 'Now, listen – listen, Kitten, it's not as bad as you think. Let's – let's go up and have a cup of tea. I want to talk to you.'

Carefully he led her up the stairs. They went into the Palm Court, a room that reminded Coffey more of a drawing-room in some big house than a place where you could buy a cup of tea. He guided her to a sofa in a corner and at once called a waiter, taking as long as he could to order tea and crumpets, postponing the inevitable. But, at last, the waiter went away. 'Now listen, Kitten,' Coffey said. 'It's a sort of apprenticeship, that's all –'

She was sniffling. He passed her his handkerchief, then looked anxiously around at the other people in the room. 'Vera, please!' he said. 'People are watching.'

'Go and sit by yourself, then.'

'Vera, I didn't mean that. Now, cheer up.'

'Why?'

'Well, this thing is only temporary, just for a week or so.'

'Does Gerry think it's temporary?'

'Of course he does.'

'Word of honour, Ginger?'

'Word of honour. It's just a training period –'

'Proofreading, isn't that what it is?' she said. 'How much are they going to pay you during this "training" period?'

'Ah – seventy dollars a week. We can manage on that.'

'How much? Do you want me to phone Mr MacGregor and check?'

Nervously, Coffey touched the parting in his moustache. 'All right,' he said. 'Forty is what it is. But that's only for a week or so.'

'Oh? How many weeks? Ginger, for once in your life, why can't you tell me the truth?'

'Well . . .' he said. 'Well, anyway, this is Grosvenor's fault, not mine. Bloody daft caper, asking me to tell this old codger I had experience. Sure he trapped me in no time, made me look like a bloody idjit. God, wait till I see Mr Gerry Grosvenor. Him and his bloody schemes.'

'It's Gerry's fault,' she said. 'Not your fault, of course. Oh, it's never your fault, is it, Ginger?'

'Well, it wasn't my idea to pretend I was something I'm not.'

'A proofreader,' she said. 'That's what you are. That's all you are. How are the three of us going to live on forty dollars a week?'

'But he promised to make me a reporter. And then an editor, he said. Now, that's true, Kitten. Here – have a crumpet.'

'You *can't* afford a crumpet,' she said, weeping.

'Ah now, for the love of Mike, will you ever give over that boohooing, Vera. What sort of way is that to carry on?'

'Listen to me,' she said. 'Li – listen to me. I'm not going to put up with this any more, do you hear? God knows,' she said, her tears now coming uncontrollably. 'I've tried. You'll never know how hard I've tried. I was even ready to go home even though I hated to go home. But I thought it was the only way to save us. That wasn't easy. No, it wasn't easy, believe you me.'

'I know, Kitten. I know.'

'And then – then last night you walked in and admitted that you'd been lying to me for weeks. Letting me pack and write Mother and make plans and everything. After you'd promised on your word of honour you'd never touch a penny of that passage money.'

'I know,' he said. 'I should have told you. I'm sorry, Kitten.'

'You're sorry. That makes it all right, I suppose? What good does saying you're "sorry" do? Is that supposed to make me stay with you?'

'What do you mean, *stay* with me?'

'You heard me,' she said. 'I'm going to get away before it's too late.'

'Is that so?' he said, with all the sarcasm he could manage in his sudden fright. 'And what about Paulie? Did you ever think of Paulie?'

'Oh, who's talking! Don't you know the only thing that's kept us together, this past while, is Paulie?'

She doesn't mean that, he thought. Ah no, she doesn't mean that. He looked at her.

'Not that you care about Paulie,' she said. 'Not that you care about any of us except yourself. If you did care, we'd never be in this mess.'

'Now, is that fair, Vera? Just because I happen to be between jobs –'

'Ginger, Ginger,' she said, shaking her head. 'Aren't you always between jobs?'

'What do you mean?'

'Isn't the job you're in always a burden to you, isn't it always no good, according to you? And isn't there always a crock of gold waiting for you in the next job you're going to get? Ginger, will you never learn anything? Will you never face the facts?'

'*What* facts?'

'That they let you go in nearly every job you've had. Why do you think Mr Pierce sent you down to the advertising department? Why do you think Mr Cleery in the advertising let you go? I'll tell you why. Because you're a glorified secretary, that's all you are, that's all you can ever hope to be. But you can't see that, you had to tell them how to run their business, you that knew nothing about it.'

'Glorified secretary, my foot,' he said. 'Those old codgers were living in the dark ages,' he said. 'Fifty years behind the times.'

'Yes,' she said. 'Everybody's out of step except our Ginger. Same thing when we were in Cork, wasn't it? And then you were coming over here to Canada, setting yourself up to do a job you never did in your life, a job you had no experience in. How could you sell whisky or tweeds or anything, you that had no experience?'

'If it wasn't for those thicks at home –'

'Oh yes. Blame them. Blame anybody except yourself. And today – walking in, bold as you please, asking to be made an editor. You that knows nothing about it.'

'That was Gerry's idea.'

'But you went along with it, didn't you?' she said. 'Oh yes, it's Gerry's fault. Do you know the thing I can't stick about you? It's never your fault. *Never.* You've never had the guts to admit you were wrong.'

'That's nonsense,' he said.

'Is it? Then is it my fault you spent the ticket money home? Is it, Ginger?'

'Ah, what's the sense in raking all that up again, Vera? Former history.'

'Former history! It happened yesterday!'

'Shh,' he said, looking around the room.

'Yes, shush,' she said. 'People are watching. And you care more about people than you do about me. Playing the big fellow, spending our passage money.'

He looked at his hands. He joined his fingers in the childhood game. A game between him and all harm. *Here's the church –*

'Well, from now on, don't bother to tell me anything,' she said. 'Not even lies. Because I don't want to hear. I'm sick of lies and dreams and schemes that founder as soon as *you* put your hand to them. I'm sick of your selfishness and your alibis. You can go to hell for all I care.'

– and here's the steeple. Open the gates –

'Tomorrow morning,' she said, 'I'm going to look for a job of my own. And when I get it, I'm moving out.'

'What about Paulie?'

'I'll take Paulie,' she said. 'Then you won't have to worry about anybody except yourself. Which will suit you down to the ground.'

– and let in the people. And here is the minister coming upstairs –

'In the meantime,' she said, 'I'd advise you to take this proof-reading job. Come down off your high horse, Ginger. It's just about what you're fit for. A proofreader.'

– and here is the minister saying his prayers – He separated his hands, looked at her, at last. 'For better or worse,' he said. 'For richer or for poorer. Ah,' he said bitterly, 'you could sing that, if you had an air to it.'

'You'd better go,' she said. 'You have to let Mr MacGregor know at half past four, don't you?'

'There's plenty of time. It's not even four. Besides –'

'Oh God's teeth, Jim, why are you so dense? Don't you understand *anything*?'

She never called him Jim, except when things were desperate. She wanted rid of him, this minute, that was what she wanted. All right. *All right*. He stood up and took the bill. 'I'll have to wait for change,' he told her.

She took a ten-dollar bill out of her bag. Where did she get that, he wondered. 'Go on,' she said. 'I'll pay the bill.'

But he could not move. Suffering J, they weren't going to leave things like this, were they? Ah, Vera –

'Are you leaving, or must I?' she said.

He tried to grin. 'Just looking for the cloakroom tickets, dear. I have yours in my pocket somewhere.'

He fumbled for a while.

'Breast pocket,' she said.

'Oh, yes. Silly. I always put it there and then forget. Vera – listen to me –'

'No,' she said. 'And stop standing there like a dog waiting for a pat on the head. You're not getting any pat. Not any more. Now, go away.'

He saw her hands tremble on the catch of her purse. Listen, listen, listen, he cried silently, for God's sake don't let this happen. But he had said listen so many times, in so many rows, for so many years. And she had said listen, as often. Listen to me, they cried to each other. Listen! Because neither listened any longer. She stared at him. Her face was pale, her eyes were fixed and bright and, now that it had been said, he saw that all her irritations, all the fits of temper he had discounted, all that was hate. She hated him.

Still, as he went away across the room, he turned back to her once more. Tried to smile, hoping that somehow she, sure that she, wouldn't she signal, call him back?

But she did not. She sat watching him, willing him to go. Go away, doggy.

So he went.

Chapter Three

It was twenty past four. For several minutes he had been standing in the lobby of the *Tribune* building wondering whether he should go upstairs. After all, MacGregor had said it would only be a short while until he was made a reporter. And you wouldn't heed Gerry, would you? Why should Gerry know whether MacGregor was tricking him or not?

But he had heeded her. That was why he was here. Ah, sure that was a lot of malarkey, that stuff about them letting him go in those other jobs he had. A lot of malarkey too about him being selfish and putting the blame on other people – all nonsense – sure, what did she know, the woman? But it was not nonsense that she said she wanted to leave him. Not nonsense that he had seen a hatred in her look. She would get over it. Sure, she would. She had just been letting off, as women do, with the first hurtful thing that came into her head, hadn't she? She didn't hate him; not Vera. Not his Dark Rosaleen?

He was troubled as he had rarely been. It was hard to find something to be cheerful about in what she had said and the way she had looked at him. And so, he had to think of something else. He thought of J. F. Coffey, journalist. There was some good in that thought. Say what you like, he had a foot in the door there. Maybe MacGregor would promote him in a week or so? Probably would. All right, then. Take the job. Show her she's wrong.

At twenty-five past four he went in, took the elevator up and once again presented himself at the open doorway of the managing editor's office. 'Excuse me, sir?'

'Aye?'

'I – ah – I would like to take the job, sir.'

Mr MacGregor pulled out a sheet of paper. 'Right,' he said. 'Full name?'

'James Francis Coffey.'

MacGregor wrote it down. 'Hours, six to one, five nights a week. Except when you take the late trick until two. Saturdays off, and one rotating day per week. If sick, report to me pair-sonally by phone before three in the afternoon. Okay?'

'Yes, sir.'

'One more thing, Coffey. I have fifty gurrls wurrking in the mail room, one floor down. Dinna interfere with them, d'you hear?'

'Yes, sir.'

'Now go to the composing room and ask for a man called Hickey. He'll give you a style book. Study it before you start wurrk tonight.'

Galley slave. Suffering J, that was apt. Coffey went back down the corridor and asked directions of a man in shirt-sleeves. He followed the directions and after several turnings entered a large room, loud with noise. In even rows, like children in some strange classroom, the linotypers threaded their little lines of words. Men with wooden mallets hammered leads into place; others, wearing long blue aprons and green eyeshades, plucked strips of lead from a table, fitting them in, tossing the rejects backwards to crash into large tin hellboxes. A foreman in stiff white collar and black knitted tie moved with ecclesiastic tread up the aisle. As he drew level with Coffey, he leaned over, hand to his ear, in smiling dumbshow inquiry as to the visitor's business.

'Mr Hickey?' Coffey shouted, over the machine roar.

The foreman showed comprehension by a nod and led Coffey across the room to a small, cleared area, surrounded by rows of Linotype machines. There, in Dickensian concentration, sat three old men, each facing a pigeonhole desk, each scanning a galley proof. At once their strange apartheid, combined with the extreme shabbiness of their clothing, reminded Coffey of MacGregor's remark. These were outcasts in a union sea. As he drew near he saw that each desk was double, with seats for two men.

'Hickey?' he shouted.

Without looking up from his work one old man elbowed the next, who rapped on his neighbour's desk with a pencil, who, hearing the rapping, turned slowly in his stool. His eyes, huge and shifting under lenses thick as an aquarium window, float-ed up to find the interrupter. Then he stood, buttoning about him a darned, many-stained cardigan of navy blue wool.

'Mr Hickey?'

The red face nodded, the shifting eyes indicated that he must follow. The old man's large, gently sliding posteriors moved between rows of Linotypes, leading Coffey into the comparative quiet of the locker room. There, Mr Hickey paused, his distorted eyes searching for enemies, his raw, red hands knitting together a home-made cigarette.

'Yes?' he said. 'New man?'

'How did you know?' Coffey said, surprised.

'Gets so you can tell,' Mr Hickey said. 'Hitler send you?'

'Who?'

'Hitler. The boss.'

'Oh! You mean Mr MacGregor. Yes, he told me to ask you for a style book.'

Mr Hickey wheezed like an ancient organ. 'MacGregor,' he said. 'Never call him by that name, son. Hitler's the name. Because he's –'

And then came a slow, enjoyed recital, noun, adjective, verb, of fourteen well-rehearsed obscenities. When he had finished, Mr Hickey reached into his darned cardigan to produce a small red booklet. 'Style book,' he said. 'Now, go on down the street, one block to the left of here. In the tavern on the corner you'll find the night men. Look for a fellow with a crutch. That's Fox, head of the shift. It's pay-night, so they all like to come in together. Better come in with them, okay?'

'Okay,' Coffey said. 'And thanks very much.'

'Thanks?' Mr Hickey seemed surprised. 'For what, fella? This job, you don't have much to be thankful for. God bless, fella. Be seeing you.'

The tavern described by Mr Hickey was unnamed. Above its door was an electric sign: *Verres Sterilisés – Sterilized Glasses,* a sign which no one read but which conveyed to the passing eye that here was a place to drink, a place which shut late or never, a place unlikely to be well-frequented. This last was its deception, Coffey found. Forgotten, faded, off the main streets, in a downtown limbo where property owners allowed buildings to live out a feeble charade of occupation until the glorious day when all would be expropriated in a city slum clearance drive, the tavern, instead of dying, had burgeoned in a new and steady prosperity. As Coffey pushed open its doors he was met by a beer stench and a blast of shouted talk. Two waiters in long white aprons, each balancing a tray containing a dozen full glasses of draught beer, whirled in and out among the scarred wooden tables, answering thirsty signals. Slowly Coffey moved up the room, searching for the man with a crutch. The customers put him in mind of old Wild West films: they wore fur caps, peaked caps, toques. They wore logging boots, cattle boots, flying boots. They talked in roars, but they numbered also their solitaries. These sat alone at smaller tables, staring at the full and empty bottles in front of them as though studying the moves in some intricate game.

No one heeded Coffey as he moved on. At the far end of the room a huge jukebox, filled with moving colours and shifting lights, brooded in silence amid the roar of voices. Near it, disfigured with initials, an empty phone booth; symbol of the wives and worries the tavern's customers bought beer to forget. Coffey paused by the phone. What if she were sitting in the duplex this minute, already sorry for what she'd said? She could be. Yes, she might be.

He went into the booth and shut the door on the noise. He dialled and Paulie answered. 'Is that you Bruno?' she said.

'Who's Bruno, Pet?'

'Oh, it's you, Daddy.'

'Is your mother home yet?'

'She was in but she went out again.'

'Where?'

'She didn't say, Daddy.'

'And she left you all alone, Pet?'

'Oh, that's all right, Daddy. I'm going to supper at a girl friend's house and her mother's giving me a lift home in their car.'

'Oh.'

'I must go now, Daddy. I'm late already.'

'Wait a minute, Pet. Did Mummy tell you I've got a job?'

'No.'

'Well, I have. A – an editing job on a newspaper. Isn't that good?'

'Yes, Daddy.'

'Well – well, tell your mother I phoned her, will you, Apple?'

'Okay, Daddy.'

'And listen, Apple – don't be too late getting home, will you?'

But Paulie had already hung up. Who the blazes was selfish – he or a woman who would go out of the house and leave her little girl all alone? Suffering J! Ah well – let's have a beer. Where's this man I'm supposed to meet? Fox with a crutch.

He came out of the phone booth and stood solitary among the shouting drinkers searching for the cripple's sign. On the top of a radiator by the far wall, he saw an aluminium cane with a rubber-covered elbow grip. Near-by, sticking out into the aisle, a built-up boot. Its owner was a tall, vaguely professorial man with fairish hair and a grey stubbled chin. Coffey went over.

'Mr Fox?'

The cripple ignored him. 'First million,' he said to his companions. 'That's the caste mark. As long as they made it long enough ago for people to forget what it was made in, they become one of Canada's first families.'

One of the men at the table, a bald, sweating person in a navy blue shirt and a vermilion tie, looked up, saw Coffey. 'Fu-Fox,' he said. 'Wu-wanted.'

'Oh,' The cripple sprawled backwards in his chair, letting his gaze travel slowly from Coffey's brown suède boots to the tiny Tyrolean hat. 'New man, eh?'

'Yes. How did you know?'

'How did I know? Hear that, Harry?'

Both Fox and the stammerer were seized with a laughing fit. Fox cleared glasses and bottles from in front of him in a rash sweep of his arm, laying his laughing face on the beer-wet table top. He was, Coffey realized, half seas over.

'Sit down,' said a third reader, pulling out a chair for Coffey. He was very old, strangely dressed in a duck-billed fawn cap, fawn windbreaker and high, elastic-sided boots. A feathery white goatee grew precariously on his caved-in jaws and as he reached forward to shake hands, Coffey was put in mind of the recruiting poster's Uncle Sam. 'My name's Billy Davis,' he said. 'And this here is Kenny.'

Kenny was little more than a boy. His face, tortured by eczema, looked up at Coffey in a lost, posed smile. His right hand clutched the neck of a beer bottle. He sat primly on the edge of his chair.

'Drink up, Paddy,' Fox said, signalling a waiter. 'You're behind.'

A waiter came and Fox paid for four glasses of draught beer which he at once lined up in front of Coffey. His companion, Harry, seemed to consider this a further occasion for laughter. 'Now, Paddy,' Fox said. 'Let's see you sink these. Go ahead.'

'Thanks very much,' Coffey said. 'That's very decent of you. My next treat, I hope?'

'Drink!' Fox shouted. 'One, two three, four. Go ahead.'

Lord knows, Coffey liked a wet as well as the next man. But there was something lunatic about this. He began on the first beer. Bald Harry's upper lip dripped sweat. The boy widened his fixed smile a fraction, in encouragement. The old man nodded his goatlike chin. Glass empty, Coffey put it down and reached for a second.

'Good man,' Fox said. 'Away you go. One swallow.'

It took two swallows.

'Number three, now,' Fox said.

But as he raised the third glass to his lips, Coffey paused. Wasn't this daft? What was he doing, drinking himself stocious for a clatter of strangers?

'What's up?' Fox said.

'Nothing. Only that it's against nature, guzzling like this. What's the rush?'

Fox and Harry exchanged glances. 'A good question, Paddy,' Fox said. 'And it answers mine. Booze is not your problem, right.'

They must be joking. It must be some sort of joke, this chat?

'Never mind him,' the girlish boy said. 'Say, that's a dandy overcoat you have. Sharp.' He touched Coffey's sleeve.

'Wu-women?' Harry said. 'Du-do you think that's his pu-problem, Foxey?'

'Why must I have a problem?' Coffey said. 'What are you talking about?'

'Every proofreader has,' Fox said. 'All ye who enter here. Look at Kenny.' He leaned over as he spoke and put his arm around the boy's shoulders. 'You know what Kenny's problem is, I suppose?'

'Shut up,' the boy said. 'Lousy gimp.'

'Hostility to the father figure,' Fox shouted. 'Classic!'

Feathery fingers plucked at Coffey's wrist. The old man thrust his Uncle Sam visage close. His mouth opened, showing gaps of gums policed by ancient dental survivors. 'Could be money,' he said. 'That's everybody's problem, am I right, fellow?'

'That's right,' Coffey said, uneasily jovial. 'It's the root of all evil, they tell me.'

'Wrong!' Fox shouted. 'Why, money is not evil, Paddy my boy. Money is the Canadian way to immortality.'

'Cu-Christ, here he gu-goes again,' Harry said.

'Quiet now,' Fox shouted. 'I have to explain the facts of life to our immigrant brother. Do you want to be remembered, Paddy? Of course you do. Then you must bear in mind that in this great country of ours the surest way to immortality is to have a hospital wing called after you. Or better still, a bridge. We're just a clutch of little Ozymandiases in this great land. Nobody here but us builders. This is Canada's century, they tell us. Not America's, mind you. Not even Russia's. The twentieth century belongs to Canada. And if it does, then you had better know our values. Remember that in this fair city of Montreal the owner of a department store is a more important citizen than any judge of the Superior Court. Never forget that, Paddy boy. Money is the root of all good here. One nation, indivisible, under Mammon, that's our heritage. Now drink up.'

Coffey reached for his fourth glass of beer. Might as well. She didn't bloody well love him any more so what did it matter if he got drunk. Today was enough to drive any man to drink.

'Tonight, Coffey, you will become a proofreader. You will

62

read all the news. War in China, peace in our time. Mere finger exercises. Later, Coffey, if you show promise, we may let you read something more important. The Quebec Social Notes, for instance. Or the Governor-General's speech to the Crippled Deaf Mute Division of the United Sons of Scotland. And if you continue to show promise – if you make no mistake, allow no errors typographic or orthographic to slip into print, then we may even let you read an advertisement. And some day, you may become a senior man, a man who reads *only* advertisements. Because, Coffey, news is cheap. Here today and gone tomorrow. But advertisements cost money. They count. So you must get them right, do you hear? Compree?'

'Compree,' Coffey said, raising his hand to signal the waiter.

The old man nodded and smiled. 'It's money that counts, all right,' he said. 'Ten men run this country, did you know that? Ten big finenceers. And did you know there's a book tells you who they are and how they made it. You'll want to read that book, being a New Canadian. Yes, you will. You can borrow my copy, if you like.'

Yes, Coffey said, he must dip into that some time. He paid for another round of beers.

'Are you just pu-passing through?' Harry asked him. 'Or du-do you pu-plan to stay for a while?'

Coffey took a long pull of his beer. 'Passing through,' he said. 'Matter of fact, I'm just in the proofroom so's I can pick up the *Tribune* style. MacGregor's going to make me a reporter.'

As he said this, he saw Fox screw up his left eye in a large drunken wink. Harry collapsed in a fresh rush of laughter. The old man shook his head. 'Big finenceers,' he mumbled. 'Scab labour, that's what we are.'

'But – but what's the matter?' Coffey asked. 'I mean, what's funny about it?'

Again Fox winked at the others. 'Nothing funny,' he said. 'I just hope you succeed, that's all.'

Coffey stared at their knowing faces. What did they mean? Had he been tricked? 'Look fellows,' he said. 'Tell me. I want to know. Do you think he *will* make me a reporter?'

'Stranger things have happened,' Fox said. 'Drink up.'

'Big finenceers,' the old man mumbled. 'I remember one time –'

But Coffey no longer listened. He sat dumb, drowsy with beer, the glasses multiplying in front of him, the style book forgotten in his pocket. Were they making a joke of him? Was MacGregor tricking him, what was going on? Was it for this he had travelled across half a frozen continent and the whole Atlantic ocean? To finish up as a galley slave among the lame, the odd, the halt, the old?

'Money,' Fox was saying. 'Oh, let me tell you, you can be a four-letter bastard all your life but never mind. If you die with enough in the bank, the *Tribune* will write you a fine editorial eulogy –'

Had he been wrong to bet his all on Canada? Would he have been better to stick in those dead end jobs at home, plodding along, day in and day out, until he dropped? – listen to these fellows – they seem to think Canada is the back of beyond –

'Nu-nother depression,' Harry said. 'You just wu-watch it. They sneeze in the States and we get pneumonia here.'

Was that true? Was it a backwater, like the land he had fled? Had he made the mistake of his life, landing himself up here among these people, either mugs like old Gerry, or full of gloomy prophecies like these fellows? Bloody Canada! Bloody Canadians!

'Just a poor clutch of Arctic-bound sods –' Fox was saying.

For if Veronica was going to leave him, then hadn't this been the greatest mistake ever?

'Greatest mistake this country ever made was not joining the United States – ' Fox said.

There was always Paulie. I've got a job, Pet, he'd told her. Yes, Daddy. Daddies are supposed to get jobs. Not very great to have a job, is it? Not this job. Yes, if he lost Veronica, he would lose Paulie too. And would have no one.

'Drink up,' Fox said. 'Last call, boys.'

'Must phone,' he said, standing up. 'Just a moment.'

Because, ah, Vera didn't mean it, did she? She was just upset, she would say she was sorry now. Never mind, dear, he'd

say. My fault. I love you, Kitten. I love you too, Ginger. Yes
. . . she'd be over it now –

He dialled. 'Vera?'

'It's me. Paulie.'

'Oh, Paulie,' Coffey said, closing his eyes, leaning his forehead against the cool glass of the booth. 'Is your mother there,
Pet?'

'I told you she went out.'

'Out?'

'Daddy, are you drinking?'

'No, no, that's a way to speak to your Daddy! Listen,
Apple. Give her a message. Tell her to phone me. All right?'

'Where?'

'The *Tribune*. It's a newspaper. All right?'

'Okay. I'll leave a note for her,' Paulie said.

'Listen – Paulie?'

'What is it?' Paulie asked crossly.

'Paulie . . . You don't think I'm selfish, do you? I mean –
listen, Apple. You're still my own little Apple, hmm?'

'Oh, stop it, Daddy!'

'Not cross at me . . . I mean . . . listen, Pet. I mean Paulie . . .
Daddy's not bad, is he? Mmm? . . . Paulie?'

– Dizzy, all that beer in a hurry, but that pane of glass was
so cool against his forehead –

'Listen, Pet . . . won't be home. Want to speak to Mummy . . .
tell her . . . Apple . . . Tell her, Daddy's sorry –'

Fox banged on the door of the booth. 'Saddle up,' he
shouted. 'Come on galley slave. Hitler's Legion rides again.'

'Paulie – Paulie?'

Brr-brr-brr-brr, the phone went. He shovelled the receiver
back on to its cradle, and looked at it dully. No, Paulie didn't
care . . .

He stepped out of the booth and stumbled. 'I'm drunk,' he
said. 'I'm plootered.'

'Never mind,' Fox said. 'So are we all, all honourable men.
Take his arm there. Hurry! Hurry!'

Into the men's wash-room behind the composing-room, Old
Billy Davis led Coffey, fumbling drunk. Stood him beside the
basins, took hold of Coffey's jaws, forcing them open as though

5   65

he would administer a pill, but instead darted his finger into Coffey's mouth, pulled it out again and forced Coffey's head down towards the washbasin. Then waited, placid and fragile in his fawn windbreaker, as his victim, hands gripping the basin, retched wildly, flooding the bowl.

'Once more?'

'No ... no.' Coffey moaned, coughing until the tears came.

'Better now? All right. Follow me.'

Out of the men's locker-room in a trembling run, past the compositors' lockers, through the lanes of Linotype machines to the row of steel desks. Hands reached past, claiming galleys, shuffling copy, spiking galleys, busy, everyone busy, no voices heard above the chattering mumble of machines. Drained, but still ill, Coffey made a cradle of his arms and rested his head on the dirty steel desk top. J. F. Coffey, Editor, J. F. Coffey, Journalist. In a weak moment he felt the tears come: she did not love him; she hated him and why shouldn't she, rotten with drink, he was, great drunken lump, J. F. Coffey, journalist, plootered his first night on the job. Ah God! He hated this great lump, blowing into his thick red moustache, self-pitying fool. ...

'Hey, hey,' Fox said, shaking him. 'Wake up, Paddy. Hitler's coming. Here you are.' A half-finished galley appeared in front of Coffey's face. And just in time.

Mr MacGregor was coming through. Bony old arms hanging naked from shirt sleeves, blue vein pumping in his pale forehead, fanatic eye, starved for trouble. As he swept out on his nightly visitation, office boys, delinquent deskmen, guilty reporters, all avoided his eye, practised the immobility of small animals as a hawk moves over a forest. But on the instant MacGregor entered the composing-room, some of the ferocity drained from his walk. Here, old battles had been fought, old forts abandoned. Here, the enemy was in full command, camped permanently within MacGregor's walls. Strikes, scabs, shutouts; all had failed. Hedged around by clause and contract, the managing editor was forbidden to lay a finger on one stick of type, denied the right to speak one word of direct command. The composing-room foreman waited his nightly sortie with the amused contempt of a Roman general dealing with the chieftain of a small hill tribe. Here, each night, MacGregor relived his defeat.

And so, as was his custom, his impotence sought its revenge. Alone in that union camp, the proofreaders were still his servants. 'Who let this pass?' he shouted, shaking a galley high above the dirty steel desks. 'Who let this pass?'

Fox raised his grey stubbled chin, took the galley, consulted the pencilled initials. 'Day man,' he said.

'Jesus Christ! Got this name wrong, see? Friend of the publisher. Jesus Christ!'

Fox looked at the ceiling as though engaged in mental arithmetic. His fellow workers read proofs with awful intensity. 'Not our shift, sir,' Fox said. 'And we're late, sir. Still short of men.'

'I gave you a new man tonight. Where is he? New man – aye – let's see – '

As he spoke, Macgregor ran around the desks and snatched up the half-finished galley. 'Well, Coffey, let's see your wurrk?' He spread the galley on the desk top, scanning it, block-reading not for sense but for typographical errors. Years of practice gave him an unerring eye for flaw, but tonight, he saw no flaw. Four errors on the galley, four caught, so far. A new man? He did not believe it. He turned on Fox. 'These aren't his marks. They're yours.'

It was a guess, but once he had made it, MacGregor snatched some of Fox's galleys off the spike and compared. 'Aye, these are your marks,' he said in triumph. 'Coffey?'

'Yes, sir.'

'Show me your other galleys.'

Behind his high desk, the composing-room foreman had been watching. He saw the new man's face, red, confused, turn upwards towards his tormentor. Poor sod. The foreman stepped down from his desk, approached, stopping MacGregor in midshriek. 'Your men are behind here, Mr Mac,' he said. 'All this talk is holding up the work. You're short-staffed here, as usual. And we're late.'

'We're doing our best, damn ye!'

But MacGregor turned away, spiked the galleys and made off without another word, fearful of a new defeat, a new infestation of mediators, arbitrators, international representatives and similar union incubi and succubi. The foreman winked at Coffey's bewildered face and returned to his desk. The linotypers, prim and efficient on their little stools, smiled as at an old and favourite joke and – monks performing a rite of exorcism – the proofreaders downed galleys and intoned a short chant of MacGregorian abuse. Then, the obscenities observed, Fox leaned across the desk and fed Coffey his first galley of the night. 'All right,' he said. 'Coast's clear. Do your best.'

At ten the bell rang for supper break. At ten-fifteen it rang again and they went on to work until one. Sober now, Coffey found that he could do the job. Soon he was reading galleys only seconds slower than old Billy and half as quick as Fox. He was surprised, and pleased, because, all his life, do you see, he had been in jobs whose only purpose seemed to convince some higher-up that you were worth the money he was paying you. But in this job, you read your galley and made your corrections and if you looked across the room, you could see the make-up men going on with the next step in the process. Within an hour or two, a newspaper would come off the press and tomorrow morning, people would buy it, would read it over breakfast. You made something. There was no coming the old soldier, either. You signed your initials at the foot of each galley and if you let something slip, it could be traced back to you.

It was a new and satisfying feeling.

And so, at one in the morning, when Coffey rode home on the bus, a newly-printed newspaper on his lap, he had, by his habitual processes of ratiocination, convinced himself that the day was not a defeat but a victory. A little victory. He had a job: he was working alongside a bunch of Canadians in a far-off country, pulling his weight with the best of them. As for Vera, she would be over her bad temper by now. He would make a cup of cocoa for her, bring her into the kitchen and tell her all about this evening. He would kiss her and they would say they were sorry, both of them. Hard-working Ginger. Not selfish, no. Doing the best he could.

There were no lights on in the duplex when he let himself in. In the outer hall, he listened for signs of life as he emptied snow out of the turnups of his trousers. Quietly, he passed by Paulie's room and went into the darkened master bedroom, fumbling for the curtain drawstrings. The curtains screeched on their runners, opening with a quick flounce. Moonlight fell on his wife's slender body, wrapped like a furled sail in all the bed-sheets.

'Veronica?' he whispered.

But she slept. Ah well, let her sleep: he would make up with her tomorrow. He undressed in the moonlight, looking out of the window. Snow, dead and thick and white, shaded the arms of the tree opposite; wedged itself in clefts of branches; cake-iced the roofs of houses across the street. The city was quiet, its traffic noises muted by the snowfall. He yawned and reached for the curtain drawstrings, sending the rings screeching on their runners, closing the room to blackness again. He slipped into bed and lay, listening to her breathe. How strange life was! Only this morning he had lain here beside her, happy after joy, not knowing what the day would bring. Only this afternoon he had walked away across the Palm Court, in dread of her leaving him. Only a few hours ago he had sat in a room full of machines, doing something he had never done before. How could people say life was dull? Ah, look at her now, asleep and at peace. If only there had been no bitterness, if only those things had not been said. If only he could take part of the day away, erase it with a kiss.

And why not? He snuggled against her. She was tall but his chin touched the top of her head, his feet slipped under her soles, a pedestal for her feet. Oh, how warm and soft she was, her nightgown rucked about her waist. Warm she was. And warm he loved her.

'Don't,' she mumbled. 'No.'

He smiled in the darkness and moved his hand up to cup her breast.

'Stop it. Please, Gerry. Stop.'

He lay very quiet. He could hear his own heart. She must hear it too, it was thumping like an engine. Slowly, he reached out and fondled her breasts, his loins cold, his heart hammering.

'No, Gerry. Please. Not now.'

He took his hand away. Slowly, careful not to wake her, he turned his back to her and lay, eyes open in the dark, his large body still as a statue on the lid of a tomb. He listened to her breathe. The intake was regular, yet irregular in the way of sleep. She was asleep. Yes, she was dreaming a dream.

Do you remember that summer you were stationed at the Curragh and you got a great crush on an eighteen-year-old girl who never even knew you fancied her? Didn't you dream about her many's a night that summer, and did that mean that you slept with her? Or even kissed her? Haven't you been unfaithful to Veronica a thousand times in dreams?

Still, she only knows one Gerry. That long drink of water? Besides, she's thirty-five, five years older than he is. But he's a bachelor, he has a sports car and he's free with his money. And she wept her troubles to him the other day. *He*'s why she wants to leave you. It's plain as the nose on your face.

But was it? It could be a dream. One sentence in her sleep after fifteen years of marriage didn't make a whore of her, did it?

He lay, his eyes open in the darkness. He blinked his eyes and felt something wet touch the corner of his mouth, seeping through the edges of his moustache. He was not going to boohoo like a baby, was he? Was he? No.

But Suffering J! It was hard to hold on to his hopes.

Chapter Four

NEXT morning, after she had fed him breakfast, she said she was going downtown to see about a job.

'What job?'

'It's a millinery place that's run by a friend of Gerry Grosvenor's. They need a saleslady.'

'Oh.'

'I won't be back for lunch,' she said. 'And if you go out, you'd better buy something to put in your sandwiches tonight.'

'All right.' He looked down at his plate. He had noticed she was wearing her good black suit.

'Paulie?' she called. 'Get a move on, you'll be late for school. Good-bye, Ginger. Are you going to be at home all day?'

'I suppose so.'

'I'll phone you later on, then.'

He heard the front door close. No kiss good-bye. He sat, his tea growing cold, hardly noticing Paulie who rushed in, ate, and fled late to school. Let her go. Let them all go.

A ruler went tickety-tak-tak down the staircase which connected his apartment with the landlady's upstairs.

'*M'sieur?* Want to play with me?'

He looked up, met eyes lonelier than his. 'Come on in, Michel,' he said. 'Let's have a game, the pair of us.'

The little boy had brought his building blocks. Coffey cleared a space at the kitchen table and gravely, thirty-nine and five years old, they built a house with a long sugar lump chimney. They played at building for more than an hour until Michel's grandmother called from upstairs. Alone again, Coffey sucked a sugar lump. . . . Maybe if he went down to Grosvenor's office, ostensibly to discuss the proofreading job, and somehow brought the conversation around to Veronica? If he had any gumption at all, wouldn't he see in Grosvenor's eyes, the guilt or innocence of last night's phrase?

All right. He shaved, dressed himself in his suit of Dromore

71

Tweed, and took a bus to the financial district. It was a quarter to twelve when he got off the bus. He went into a drug store, already crowded with typists on their lunch hour, and in a phone booth at the rear, surrounded by display cards showing smiling girls half naked under sun lamps, he phoned Gerry Grosvenor.

No, Mr Grosvenor had just stepped out for a moment. Would he mind calling back, please? And what was his name, again? Coffey. Yes, he would call back. He hung up; stared at the display cards of pretty, half-naked girls. There were so many pretty girls in the world. Why couldn't that long drink of water find one, instead of coming after a friend's wife, a woman of thirty-five who was not *that* pretty? Suffering J!

At five minutes to twelve he phoned again; this time from the lobby of Grosvenor's building. Oh, she was very sorry but the other girl had just told her that Mr Grosvenor had stepped out to lunch. Would he care to phone after lunch? He would? Fine, then.

Flute! He stepped out of the phone booth and was immediately jostled and pushed into a corner by the flow of people hurrying from the elevators. Everybody was in such a hurry here! Everybody shoving and pushing you aside! Canadians had no manners! Raw, cold country with its greedy, pushy people, grabbing what didn't belong to them, shoving you aside! Land of opportunity, my eye!

Now, stop that, he told himself. Don't blame the whole country for one twister of a cartoonist. Stop it. So, he stopped it. He went over to the news stand in the lobby and bought a package of cigarettes. No sense behaving like a lunatic because of one little word in a woman's dream. Ah, why didn't he go back to the house and forget all this nonsense of waiting for Grosvenor. For it *was* all nonsense. In the noon rush of people, it seemed incredible. He had imagined the whole thing.

Someone caught at his sleeve. 'Ginger. Hello there.'

'Oh, hello, Gerry,' he said guiltily.

'What are you doing in this part of the forest?'

'Well – ah – I just dropped by to have a word with you. I mean about that proofreading job. I took it, you know.'

People were passing, bumping against them as they stood,

stuck driftwood, in the current towards the revolving doors. 'Look, we can't talk here,' Grosvenor said. 'Let me give you a lift uptown.'

He followed Grosvenor's tall thin back into the merry-go-round of the doors. A cold wind met them as they stepped out into the cavern of the street and as Coffey paused to put up his overcoat collar, Grosvenor jumped boyishly out into the traffic, snapping his fingers for a cab. A cab careened out of the traffic lane and drew up, inches away from Grosvenor's body. But flute! He was unharmed.

'Come on, Ginger, hop in. Okay driver, go on up Beaver Hall Hill. I'll let you know where, later.'

They settled in the back seat, side by side. 'Well, Ginger,' Grosvenor said. 'Lucky day, eh?'

'What?'

'Veronica's new job, of course. Didn't she tell you?'

Coffey's ruddy face stared straight ahead. 'No,' he said.

'Well, she was hired this morning at Modelli. It's a chi-chi sort of hat shop. The pay is forty a week and a sales bonus which should bring it up to fifty-five most weeks. Not bad for a start, eh?'

'Not bad,' Coffey said. Fifteen dollars a week more than me, that's not bad.

'Well, now, and what about you?' Grosvenor said. 'So you took the proofreading job, did you?'

In the side panel of the cab, enshrined under a tiny light, was a police permit photograph of the driver. *Marcel Parent. 58452.* Coffey looked at this photograph, then at the back of the driver's head. God, it was mortifying trying to talk in private while *Marcel Parent. 58452*, listened in on every syllable.

'I gather Vera knows the truth about the job,' Grosvenor said. 'Too bad. I wonder is there anything I could do, I mean about getting you promoted?'

Coffey shook his head. What did he care about jobs now? What did it matter?

'I might phone old Mac and try to find out how long he intends to keep you in that sweatshop?'

'No,' Coffey said. 'Don't bother.'

'Look, there's no sense in your staying on there if it's a dead

73

end,' Grosvenor said. 'After all, don't forget, that's the lowest job in the newspaper business. You can do better than that.'

Thank you, Marcel Parent, for looking into your driving mirror to see what sort of specimen would accept the lowest job in the newspaper business.

'So what else is new?' Grosvenor asked.

You tell me, Coffey thought. But he said: 'Nothing. Are you having lunch with anyone?'

For the first time, he saw a flicker of uneasiness in Grosvenor's eyes. 'Well, yes, as a matter of fact I am,' Grosvenor said. 'It's a business lunch. I'd like to have you join us, but it would bore you stiff.'

'No, I didn't mean that,' Coffey said. 'I was just wondering where – where you could drop me off.'

'Anywhere you say, Ginger.'

'Well, just drop me anywhere that suits you. Where are you going?'

'The Pavilion,' Grosvenor said. 'So I'll drop you on the corner of Ste Catherine and Drummond, okay?'

'Fair enough.'

When the taxi stopped at the corner of Drummond Street, Grosvenor refused Coffey's share of the fare. 'I'm loaded,' he said. 'Lots of expense account money these days. Be seeing you.'

'Be seeing you,' Coffey echoed. He watched the cab move away. Seeing you, yes, and seeing you, aren't you one of the drippiest drinks of water I've ever laid eyes on? Expense account or not, artist or not, what could she see in you, you self-satisfied sausage?

Still, Veronica had phoned Grosvenor this morning. Not him. And wasn't Grosvenor just the boy who would invite a person to lunch to celebrate anything under the sun? He was indeed.

Ah, nonsense.

But he turned around, hurried down Drummond Street and went into the Pavilion. At the entrance to the dining-room, he hesitated, wanting to turn back. A head waiter came from behind a stand-up desk, tapping a sheaf of menus against his stiff shirt front. 'Have you a reservation, sir?'

'No. I'm just looking for a friend of mine.'

'What name, sir?'

'A Mr Grosvenor.'

'Oh yes, sir. This way please.'

The head waiter sailed out among the tables like a ship's figurehead, turning to make sure that Coffey followed. Halfway across the room, he stopped and pointed. 'Over here, sir. This way.'

'Never mind. I – I see he's busy.'

Busy he was. In a corner, at a tiny table behind a pillar, the pair of them deep in chat over martinis. Out of the dining-room Coffey fled, running down the steps into the street, a boy escaping a pair of bullies. But wasn't it them who should have run from him? He stopped on the street corner, out of breath. Why had he ever gone in there? And why had he bolted? He should have faced them but how could he start a row in front of a roomful of people? To fight or not to fight. To run or stand. What did it matter? He crossed the street and stood in line for a bus. Every hour of last night had moved as slowly as a sun crossing the midsummer sky. And yet he had managed to get up this morning with a reasonable amount of doubt. But now . . .

Now, it made sense. Even her anger when he told her he had spent the ticket money. She had been prepared to go home to Ireland with him, that was the worst of all. She had been willing to stick with him.

He stopped off on the way back and bought some polony for sandwiches. He bought two pears for Paulie. Poor Paulie. No wonder Veronica didn't care if the child ate properly. No wonder she let Paulie run around with ink spots on her school tunic. Why shouldn't she, when her mind wasn't on her family at all? Ah, a lot of things made sense now.

When he entered the outer hall of their apartment, little Michel was sitting on the staircase, waiting for him. 'Hey, *M'sieur*. See what I got?'

'Yes, just a minute, Michel.' He unlocked the door of his apartment and put the grocery bag inside. A toy made a noise behind him. It was a small robot, battery-operated: its cubed legs moved with a slow grinding of cogs, its eyes lit red and

75

there were little antennae coming out of its head. As Coffey watched, the toy fell. The legs had not gained purchase on the slippery linoleum.

'It's too slidey here,' the child complained.

'Oh. Well – bring him in, why don't you? There's a carpet in the hall.'

They went into Coffey's place. The boy placed the toy on the worn carpet runner. 'Watch now, *M'sieur,* I press this button.'

Coffey squatted to watch. Robot cogs ground, robot eyes glowed. The mannikin, stiff-legged, rocked slowly forward. 'By the holy,' Coffey said. 'That's a grand toy. Where'd you get it?'

'My Mamma give it to me.'

'See this little door in his back?' Coffey said. 'That's where the battery is.'

'Don't touch him. He's *my* toy!'

'Sorry,' Coffey said. 'Here you are.'

But the child handed the toy back at once. *'Montrez – montrez?'*

'Now hold on, old son,' Coffey said. 'You know I don't parleyvoo. Wish I did, though. . . . There you are. See that little thing in there? That's what makes him work.'

'Why?'

'Well, it keeps him alive. It's his juice.'

'Why does juice make him walk?'

'Well, if you have no juice – Look here, Michel, why don't you go on upstairs now? I feel tired.'

'But there's nobody upstairs,' Michel said.

'Where's your Mamma?'

'Mamma's out. *Gran'mère* is sleeping. Please, *M'sieur*. Play with me?'

Coffey sighed. 'All right,' he said. 'Let's take it in the kitchen.'

They went into the kitchen. Coffey unloosened his tie and sat down. For fifteen minutes Michel played with the robot while he, with a pretended show of interest, answered the childish questions. He looked at Michel's ragged little head bent over the toy. Was it because he had never given her a son that she had done this to him? Was that far-fetched? But oh! What reason could be stranger than the strangeness of the fact?

76

'He's broke, *M'sieur*. He's broke, he don't work.'

'Wait a sec. Let's see.' Coffey took the robot, opened the back and fiddled with the wires. Probably a bad connexion. He straightened the contacts.

'Will he work now?'

'Let's see. Put him on the floor, Michel.'

'For the love of Mike, why didn't you close the front door?' Veronica's voice shouted down the corridor. 'You'll freeze the place.'

Man and child exchanged glances, strangely united in apprehension. Coffey stood up as she came into the kitchen. 'Did you have lunch?' he said.

'You know damn well I had lunch. Why did you run off like that?'

'*M'sieur,* he still won't work.'

'Go home, Michel,' Veronica said.

'Now, just a moment, dear,' Coffey said. 'Michel's been keeping me company, haven't you, Michel?'

'I want to talk to you, Ginger. Gerry's outside.'

'Look, Michel, push the button like this. See? Now, I'll bet you he'll even walk upstairs with you. Try? All right? Off you go, lad.'

Michel rubbed the tears from his fat little cheeks. He took the robot which was now moving and grinding perfectly. 'Oh, thanks, *M'sieur*,' he said. 'Thanks, thanks.'

And ran off down the hall, the robot in his hand. Slowly, Coffey stood up. Oh, to be a boy ... tears one moment, all wiped away the next. A world of toys. Nothing so terrible a kindness would not change it. Oh, to be a boy. . . .

Too old for toys, he turned to face her; waited for what new bead she would string on her rosary of lies.

'Gerry's here,' she repeated. 'I didn't want him to come, but he insisted. He wants to talk to you alone. And, Ginger ...'

'What?'

'Ginger, I don't want you to fight with Gerry. It won't do any good, do you hear?'

He turned away without answering and went down the hall. He opened the front door and there was Grosvenor.

'May I come in a moment?' Grosvenor asked and came in,

walking as though he entered a house where someone was ill. Together, with Coffey leading the way, they went back along the railroad corridor passageway to the living-room. Coffey opened the door and, out of habit, stood back to let his visitor pass. As he did, he saw Veronica sitting in the kitchen, shoulders bent as though anticipating a blow. Irrationally, he wanted to go to her and tell her everything would be all right. But how could he tell her, he who did not know how wrong things were? And why should he, he thought, in sudden anger. This was not *his* fault.

He went in after Grosvenor and carefully shut the door. He looked at Grosvenor as though seeing him for the first time. Grosvenor was nine years younger than he; taller too. Yet Coffey knew he could win. One good clout and Grosvenor would burst like a paper bag. He waited as Grosvenor took off his overcoat and laid it on a chair. Then Grosvenor produced cigarettes and a lighter initialled G.G. He offered both. Coffey shook his head. They stood back, fighters after the traditional handshake.

'I saw you go out of the restaurant,' Grosvenor said. 'I called after you, but you didn't hear me. So I thought, under the circumstances, I'd better come up and explain. I'm not the sort of man who hides behind a woman's skirts, Ginger.'

Only go up them, Coffey thought.

'I'm not going to lie to you, Ginger. I've been in love with Veronica ever since I met her. At first, I thought there was no hope for me. Now, I realize there is. I'm going to fight for her, Ginger.'

Grosvenor waited but Coffey did not speak. 'I'm sorry this has happened, Ginger. Believe me, no matter what, I think of you as a friend.'

'Do you, now?' Coffey said. 'Trying to stuff another man's wife, is that your idea of being a friend?'

'Now wait, Ginger. I know you're angry and you have every right to make ugly remarks about me. But not about Veronica. Veronica's a wonderful girl and she's been terribly loyal to you.'

'She's my wife,' Coffey said. 'I don't need you to tell me what she's like.'

78

'You don't?' Grosvenor said. 'I'm not sure about that. If you knew her, you wouldn't have spent your ticket money home. And I'd have lost her.'

'You haven't got her yet. Nor will you.'

'Maybe not, Ginger. But she wants to leave you. You know that.'

'Will you shut your gob!' Coffey shouted. 'This is a private matter between me and Veronica – '

'Now wait, I'm nearly finished, Ginger. I've told Veronica that any time she's ready, I'll take care of her. I've promised to give her all the things she needs: love and consideration. And security.'

'You louser,' Coffey said. 'What the hell do you know about love? All you want is to get up some woman's skirts, you skinny bastard you.'

'I knew you'd say that,' Grosvenor said. 'But let me set you straight on one thing. This is love, not lust. What Veronica and I feel for each other is precious. I know that sounds corny, Ginger, but it happens to be the truth. We're in love, and we intend to stay in love until we die.'

'Get out,' Coffey said. 'Get out before I flatten you.'

'Wait a minute, Ginger, I'm not finished yet. I came here to settle this – '

'Right, then. Put up your dukes!'

'I don't mean fighting, Ginger. Fighting isn't going to settle anything. Now – wait a minute – '

But Coffey hit him, his fist thudding against Grosvenor's cheek. Grosvenor's head cracked back; his knees joined ludicrously like an opened scissors. He stood, holding his face with both hands as Coffey hit him again, first on the side of the head, then, with all his strength, in the body. Grosvenor stumbled. His hands went to protect his stomach. Immediately, Coffey finished him with a blow in the mouth, then stood back, his knuckles skinned on Grosvenor's teeth. Grosvenor fell against a sofa and sat down on the floor, his mouth widening in a trickle of blood like a sad clown's grin.

'Get up,' Coffey said, waiting.

'Go on,' Grosvenor said, thickly. 'Hit me. Hit me if it does you any good.'

'Get up.'

'No,' Grosvenor said.

Coffey stood sucking his knuckles, staring at Grosvenor. He had never met one like this before.

'Hit me if you want,' Grosvenor said, still sitting on the floor. 'But the fact is, I didn't come to fight, I came to talk. Veronica tells me she doesn't think you'd have any religious objections to getting a divorce. Is that true?'

Coffey ignored him. He opened the living-room door and called: 'Veronica?'

She came, from the kitchen.

'Is it true you want a divorce, Vera?'

But she had seen Grosvenor sitting on the floor. She went to him, bent over him. 'Oh, Gerry,' she said. 'What happened? What did he do to you?' She turned to Coffey. 'How could you?' she said. 'He was only trying to help.'

How could he? He looked at her, looking at her face which he knew so well and did not know at all; saw the thing he had seen yesterday. Hate. He could not bear that hate. He lowered his gaze to the worn pattern of the carpet, the fleur-de-lis, blue and gold. 'Paulie's coming with me,' he said.

'You have no money, Ginger. You can't look after her.'

'I have some,' he said.

'No, Ginger. I went to the bank yesterday. I took all that was left.'

He remembered the ten-dollar bill she had paid the tea with. So that was it. 'Paulie's coming with me,' he repeated.

'Look, Ginger,' Grosvenor said. 'In case you're worrying about the effect this might have on Paulie, I give you my word to keep out of things until this is settled between you – '

'*Your* word of honour?' Coffey said. 'You specimen!'

'You're a nice one to talk,' Veronica began. 'You that – '

But he could not bear to hear her. He left the room, went into the bedroom and shut the door. Confused, he began to open closets and drawers, throwing shirts, socks and underwear in a heap on the bed. No, she wasn't going to get Paulie. She wasn't going to leave him all alone now, with nobody, with nothing. He and Paulie, just the two of them –

But where? And on what?

80

He sat down on the bed, in large, trembling dignity. His image in the dresser mirror looked at him: large, trembling. Look at him, would you, sitting there with his great big ginger moustache, in the hacking jacket he spent hours picking out in Grafton Street, with the tie to match. When, what matter, ties will not make the man, no, nor throwing her across this bed yesterday morning, pleased with yourself for being the great stud, when all the time she was dreaming of Grosvenor. Look at yourself, would you. Take a good look.

He looked at him. A stupid man, dressed up like a Dublin squire. Looked at the frightened, childish face frozen now in a military man's disguise. He hated that man in the mirror, hated him. Oh, God, there was a useless bloody man, coming up to forty and still full of a boy's dreams of ships coming in; of adventures and escapes and glories still to be. When, what were the true facts of that big idjit's life? Facts: James Francis Coffey, failed B.A.; former glorified secretary to the managing director of a distillery; former joeboy in the advertising department after he was kicked downstairs; former glorified secretary to the manager of a knitwear factory; failed sales representative of three concerns in this new and promised land. Facts: husband of a woman who wanted out before it was too late; father of a fourteen-year-old girl who ignored him. Fathead! Great Lump! With nine solitary dollars between him and all harm.

The mirror man looked sad. Yes, he hated that man, that man he had made in the mirror, that mirror man who had unmade him. No one honoured that foolish sad impostor, no one loved him. Except he: for only he knew that the big idjit had meant no harm, had suffered many's a hurt. Ah, poor fraud, he thought. You're all I have. Yet, even I don't like you.

Quiet footsteps passed in the corridor. Whispers. The front door shut. That was Grosvenor leaving, he supposed. He looked at his face and his face looked at him. Well now, you, what are you going to do?

Speak to Paulie when she comes in? Ask her –

What good will that do? She's her mother's girl.

No, no, I'll explain. I'll show her how we can manage, just the two of us.

Yes, the mirror man said. You've managed rightly, until now, haven't you? Judging by today.

Now, wait – I'll get a job, I'll get two jobs, I'll work day and night if need be –

But the front door had opened. Paulie's voice called: 'Mummy? Are you there, Mummy?'

He stood up, pulled down the peaks of his doeskin weskit and went into the hall. 'Paulie?' he said. 'Would you come into the kitchen for a second?' He waited as she removed her duffel coat and overshoes and followed him down the corridor. As they passed the living-room, he saw the door was shut. They went into the kitchen. 'Sit down, Pet,' he said. 'I want to have a word with you.'

'What about?'

She was tall for her age, Paulie. Her hair was reddish, like his own. She had his large hands and something of him in her pale, placid face. As he drew out a chair for her, he noticed again the patch of ink on the shoulder strap of her tunic.

'I was wondering,' he said. 'How would you like to move to a new flat, Pet?'

'Anything would be better than this dump. Are we going to move, Daddy?'

'Well, I mean just you and me,' he said.

'What about Mummy?' Paulie asked, her pale blue eyes worrying at him. 'What happened? Did you have a row?'

'No – it's just that – well, Mummy's got a job. It would suit her better if she stayed on here for a while. I mean alone.'

'I can't see any sense in that, Daddy. You *did* have a row, isn't that it?'

'Look, Pet,' he said. 'It's just that – well, I need you more than Mummy does.'

'I'd have to do the cooking, you mean. And make the beds and stuff?'

'Oh, I'd help you, Apple. It's not for that. It's for company I'm asking you.'

Paulie picked at her fingernail. The sink tap dripped on a plate. 'I want to stay here,' she said. 'Let's both stay here, Daddy. All right?'

He nodded, uncomfortably. To get her to come he would

have to tell the truth and how could he? No matter what, as his mother used to say, a child has only one mother. And Paulie, tall and fourteen, was still her mother's child.

'All right,' he said. 'We'll talk about it later. Listen, Pet. I have some polony in the fridge. Would you make me three sandwiches for my supper tonight? And I left two pears there for you, as a present.'

'Oh, thanks,' she said, off-hand. 'Do you want mustard in your sandwiches?'

'Yes, please.' Mustard, no I don't want mustard, I want you. He watched her at the refrigerator and after a moment's hesitation, turned and left the kitchen. He went to the living-room and knocked on the door. Veronica was sitting on the sofa.

'Did you tell her?' Veronica asked.

'What do you mean, tell her? It's pretty hard to tell a child that her mother is some class of whore.'

'What are you talking about?' she said. 'How dare you?'

Hope, sudden and joyful, made him raise his eyes from the carpet, blue fleurs-de-lis on gold – 'What? You mean there's been nothing between you and Pal Gerry?'

'Of course not. Who do you think I am?'

'What did you expect me to think, Vera?'

'I wouldn't know. Did you try to get Paulie to go with you?'

He nodded, eyes on the carpet once more.

'Well?'

He shook his head.

'Good for her,' Veronica said. 'She has some sense.'

'Has she? I wonder.'

'She knows if she stays with me, I'll look after her,' Veronica said.

'So would I. Don't sneer. So would I!'

'I'm not sneering, Ginger. I'm sorry for you.'

'Sorry?' He looked at her. He'd sorry her. 'I'm going to work now,' he said. He left the room, calling to Paulie. 'Apple? Are those sandwiches ready yet?'

'Hold your horses, Daddy. I'm making them.'

He went to the hall, put on his coat and hat. Paulie came out with the sandwiches in a brown paper bag. She gave them to him and he took her by the shoulders, kissing her pale cheek.

'Daddy,' she said. 'Could I have a dollar? I want to go to a movie with some girls tonight.'

He took out his wallet. He had nine dollars left. Nine between him and all harm. He gave one to his Paulie. Now there were eight.

He went out, closing the apartment door behind him, and in the common hallway put on his overshoes. Money, oh those proofreaders were right. Money made this world go round. If he had enough money Veronica wouldn't be leaving him. If he had enough money he could have wooed Paulie to come with him, promised a housekeeper, promised her treats. Money, that was Our Saviour. Not love, mind you, not good intentions, not honesty nor truth. Because if you couldn't make money, they would leave you, wife, child, friends, everyone. It looked that way, didn't it? It did. It did indeed.

'*M'sieur?*'

Jesus, there he was again, sitting on the stairs, the robot on the step beside him.

'*M'sieur*, you want to play a game?'

'No, Michel. I have to go to work now. Play with your toy. Your little man there. Tell him a story, maybe?'

'What will I tell him, *M'sieur?*'

'Tell him your name and all about you. All about where he's going to live and who he's going to meet. Tell him some of the stories I told you.'

'*Bien,*' the child said. He picked up the robot and put it on his knee. Coffey bent over, rumpled the boy's ragged crop of hair. 'Good man yourself,' he said. 'So long, now.'

'Wait. Let's play the wish.'

'All right,' Coffey said. 'But hurry up.'

As he had done many times before, he leaned over and put his ear close to Michel's mouth. The little boy put his arm around Coffey's neck. 'What do you wish for?' he whispered.

The wish game. Wish, if he could wish, what would he wish for? Not for adventures now, not for travels, not for fame. For love? Was it any use to wish for love?

'You wish first,' he said to the boy. 'You first.'

'I wish,' the childish voice breathed in his ear. 'I wish we

84

had a whole lot of toys and you and me could play with them all the time. Because I love you, *M'sieur*.'

Awkwardly, Coffey disengaged himself and stood up. He looked down at Michel's head, big and vulnerable on the slender, childish neck. Oh, to be a boy. . . .

But children must grow up. 'Good-bye, Michel,' he said.

He went to work. There was no time for the facts of his situation, the disasters of his day. All the world's news waited: it must be read, corrected, initialled, sent back to Linotype, rechecked, cleared. The presses waited. The edition was running late. And yet, at eight o'clock, in the midst of it all, a copy boy came through the aisles of Linotype machines towards the dirty steel desks where proofreaders helter-skeltered among galleys, late, all late. Linotype gremlins, double line, transpose, insert, delete, new lead, add front, all had to go, no time for talk now, hurry, hurry. Late.

'Phone for Coffey?' the copy boy shouted. 'Got a Coffey here?' Coffey looked up, waiting Fox's permission to go; but Fox was too busy, they were all too busy, and so, a man leaving the sinking ship, Coffey stood, ran guiltily to the corridor where the phone was, passing the service elevator which waited to rush plates down to the presses. Late, late.

'Ginger?' It was Veronica on the line.

Above the phone stand was a printed card:

NO PERSONAL CALLS DURING WORKING HOURS
G. E. MACGREGOR
MAN. ED.

'Yes, what is it?' Coffey said.

'Madame Beaulieu's just been in here raising the roof. You were supposed to tell her whether we were keeping the place on or not.'

'Look,' he said. 'I've no time to talk now, I'm in a hurry – '

'Well, hold on. Because I told her we weren't going to stay and she says in that case we have to move out by tomorrow morning at the latest. She has another tenant – '

'But that's impossible, Vera. Why – '

'No, it's not. I've already made arrangements about Paulie

85

and me. We're moving to a ladies' boarding-house tonight.'

'But that's not fair –'

'Paulie wants to go with me,' she interrupted. 'And I have to move tonight because I'm starting work tomorrow morning. Gerry's coming to take our stuff in an hour or so. That's why I called you. We won't be here when you get back.'

'Ah now, wait a minute – where are you going?'

'I'm not telling you the address,' she said. 'I'll be in touch with you. And listen, I've left ten dollars for you on the dresser under the mirror –'

'You skunk!' he shouted. 'Waiting until I was out of the house –'

'Ten dollars is all I can afford, Ginger. I'll need the rest to get Paulie settled.'

'I'm not talking about money – Vera? Listen, Vera, wait until tomorrow, at least –'

But as he spoke, he saw young Kenny running towards him along the corridor, gesticulating. 'Hitler,' Kenny whispered. 'Hurry.'

MacGregor. Involuntarily, and at once, Coffey hung up. In a winding rush, he followed young Kenny back to the proof-room. Late, late. *No personal calls*. He rushed back to reading and read in a daze, not even thinking of what had happened, mesmerized by MacGregor's imminent arrival, afraid to do anything which would incur that ancient's wrath. It was only later, during supper break, that he realized the enormous consequences of her telephone call and the strangeness of his own behaviour. Even then, he could not believe it had happened. She and Paulie would be there when he got home. They *must* be there.

But that night, when he arrived back at the duplex, they were gone. Even their clothes were gone. He went to the dresser mirror, found the ten dollars and looked for a note. But there was no note.

At eight o'clock the following morning, Madame Athanase Hector Beaulieu knocked on the door. When he opened, she bent down, picked up a pailful of soaps and rags and marched in.

'The rent was only paid until yesterday,' she said. 'Today, you should not be here. I have to clean this place, my husband's bringing a tenant to see it in his lunch hour.'

'Fair enough,' Coffey said. 'Carry on.'

Madame Beaulieu opened the hall closet. Coffey's raincoat and little hat hung forlorn on the long rack. 'All this stuff,' she said. 'I want it out.' She shut the closet and marched down the corridor into the kitchen, sniffing and peering like a social worker in a tenement. 'My husband warned me,' she said. 'He told me, Bernadette, he said, these people come from the other side, they have no references, you don't know who they are. And I told my husband, don't worry, I said, they're nice people, you don't have to worry. But, look what happened. You never told me you weren't keeping the place on. You should have told me.'

'I'm sorry, yes, I know I should,' Coffey said. 'Very sorry indeed. Look – perhaps I can give you a hand to clear up in here?'

'No.'

He went back into the bedroom and dressed himself. He must pack. He was not used to packing for himself. It seemed impossible that at any moment Veronica and Paulie wouldn't come in and help him. It seemed impossible that he did not know where they were. Or what to do now. Or where to go.

An hour later, he carried two clumsily-stuffed suitcases into the outer hallway which connected his apartment with the one upstairs. Beside the suitcases he placed the overflow: three paper bags full of socks and handkerchiefs and a lamp which, for some reason, Veronica had not bothered to take. Then, carrying his raincoat, a cloth cap and a package of books tied with string, he went down the railroad corridor of that dismal place for the last time. He put his key on the kitchen table. 'I just came to give you this and say all the best, Madame. And to thank you for everything.'

Madame Beaulieu was scouring the kitchen floor. She did not answer; did not look up. Ah well ... there was a lady he never cared to see again.

He went outside and sat islanded by his possessions in the common hallway, waiting for the taxi he had ordered. He thought of Michel. Quietly, so that Madame would not hear him, he ascended the flight of stairs to his landlady's place. Quietly, he knocked on the door. 'Michel?' he whispered.

The little boy opened, all joy. Coffey squatted on his heels, grinned at Michel and in a sudden sadness pulled the child towards him, planting a bristly moustache kiss on the soft childish cheek. Michel, tickled, snatched off Coffey's hat and placed it on his own head, laughing.

'Looks grand on you,' Coffey said. 'Now, wait a sec.' He took the hat from Michel's head, removed the two Alpine buttons and the little brush dingus and handed them to the boy. 'And here,' he said, closing Michel's plump little paw around a dollar bill. 'That's to buy the car I promised for your birthday. Now, be a good boy, won't you, son? I have to go.'

'Please. Stay and play?'

'Must go. Bye bye.' Gently, he pushed Michel back into the apartment, closed the door, and ran downstairs, his chest tight and hurting. What's the world coming to, he wondered, when at my age, I've just said good-bye for ever to the only person in the world who seems to love me? Michel: what will become of him? What will become of me?

'Where to?' the taxi driver asked.

He tried to grin. 'By the holy, I have no notion. I'm looking for a cheap room downtown. Some place clean.'

'What about the Y?' the driver said.

'Fair enough. The Y it is, then.'

Chapter Five

AT the Y.M.C.A., they rented him a basement locker for his possessions and asked for a week's room rent in advance. That was nine fifty in all, which left him exactly seven dollars and forty-five cents until his first pay day. And while he put that worry out of his mind as not his greatest, still it occurred to him that his new life would not be easy.

The room was furnished with a bed, a Bible, a chair and a dresser. When he sat in the chair, his knees touched the bed. When he lay on the bed he could reach out and open the door, pull down the window-blind, open the dresser drawers and get at the Bible, without ever putting his feet on the ground. So, bed it was then. He removed his shoes and jacket and lay down. Opposite his window a forty-foot neon sign flashed on and off every eight seconds.

BUBBL BATH CAR WASH
DAY & NIGHT

Did it flash on and off all night? He pulled the window-blind down and the sign light beat like a hot red wave against the dun darkness which resulted. He shut his eyes.

He was alone: for the first time in fifteen years no one in the world knew where Ginger Coffey was. For the first time in fifteen years, he had stopped running. He exhaled, feathering up the ends of his large moustache. Yes, it was good to rest.

Of course, there were things he should do. He should find his wife's hidey-hole, for one. He could hang around outside Paulie's school and shadow her home to wherever they were staying. But why should he? Hadn't he been far too soft with the pair of them? Wouldn't it serve them right if he never tried to find them, if he just disappeared altogether and settled in here like a mole gone to ground. Not a bad life either: sleeping late every morning, eating his breakfast in some cafeteria, going for walks, seeing the odd film, having a daily swim in the pool downstairs and then each night, to work at six. No ties, no responsibilities, no ambitions. By the holy, that would be a grand gesture. To retire from the struggle, live like a hermit, unknown and unloved in this faraway land.

Hermit, eh? No sex?

No sex. Wasn't that the height of freedom to be able to tell any woman to go to hell? Any woman, no matter how beautiful, no matter how much she begs. Sending them all away, spurning all ambitions, content to be a proofreader to the end of his days.

But wouldn't that be ruining his whole life, out of pure revenge?

Well, and supposing it was, wasn't it a grand revenge? Because, God! he knew her; she'd be expecting him to run after her, to plead and beg and argue and shout. Well, to hell with her. Let her try to be the breadwinner, she'd find it wasn't so easy. No, the good doggy wouldn't beg any more. As of this morning, Good Doggy was a Lone Wolf.

Yes, but wasn't it a crime to abandon your wife and child?

Who abandoned who, anyway? Didn't they throw me over?

But you'd be lonely, you'd have no friends?

Well – well, he wouldn't talk to the fellows at work. And now and then pass the time of day with a waitress or a fellow lodger here. He would be a mystery man, the hermit of the Y.M.C.A. After thirty years or so, he would die in his sleep and people would say – Didn't notice Mr Coffey around lately. Wonder what happened to him? Never knew much about him, dignified man, lived all alone, kept to himself, probably had some shocking tragedy in his life. A quiet mysterious man – Wouldn't that be a grand way to go? Nobody with a word against you, nobody judging whether you were good, or bad. Your secrets interred with your bones.

In the day-darkness, he began to daydream of that future life. A hermit in the city, his tongue cracked from unuse, he lay on his narrow pallet in that tiny cell listening to a radio down the hall. A woman's voice sang:

> – Don't you be mean to Baby
> 'Cause Baby needs lovin' too!
> Embrace me –

From now on, all the world would be like that faraway woman, singing without him, not knowing if he lived or died. He thought of all the rich and beautiful women in the world; of how many thousands of rich and beautiful women must be in this city, this minute. To hell with them. He had turned his back on them. They could be as rich and lovely as they liked. What were they to him, or he to them? Why, if he dropped dead here this instant, that woman would go on singing. Which was shocking, the bloody inhumanity of it. Singing over a dead man.

Of course, to be fair, the only reason that woman would go on singing was because she did not know him. After all, he could make himself known; could ring her up on the telephone if he wanted to. But if he did, would she even speak to him? Supposing he waited for her as she came out of the radio station and stepped up to her, his tongue cracked with unuse: 'Madam, for years now, yours has been the only woman's voice heard in my hermit's cell.' Would she pause, the tears coming to her eyes, would she put out her gloved hand, leading him towards her limousine, saying take me to your room and tell me all about yourself? What is your name? Why is a handsome, intelligent man like yourself living this hermit's life? Why? Ah, it was criminal of that wife and daughter to abandon you. You gave them up? Why? Because you had your pride, you refused to stay where you were no longer wanted. Ah, you are a saint, James Francis Coffey. A saint to have put up with them so long.

But he would never meet her, that unknown singer. And if he never met her, if he never met anyone from now on, nobody would know about his renunciation of all ties, all ambitions. What good was it doing something, if nobody in the whole world knew you were doing it? What was more terrible than being alone all your life, nobody caring if you lived or died? Why, if he went on being a proofreader for the rest of his days, living in a place like this, he might never have another intimate conversation with a living soul. What sort of man was he that he could even consider such a thing? Look at yourself, would you? Lying in this dump, all alone. And that damned singing woman. Ah, shut your gob, woman!

'Turn that bloody thing off,' he shouted.

But the singing continued. Nobody heard. Holy God, nobody heard him, shut up in this cell. He could die this instant, call for help – suffocate – and nobody would hear!

He got off the bed, put on his shoes and went out into the corridor. The doors to the other rooms were open. Nobody there. He was alone here, he could die here, that was what Vera and Paulie had done to him. He went down the corridor. One door was shut. One door behind which that bloody woman caterwauled her song. In a sudden mindless rage, he ran towards that door, thumped on it, shouting. 'Turn that off. Turn it down, do you hear?'

Nobody answered. The horrible endearments went on. *"Cause Baby needs lovin' too!"* He grabbed the door handle and the door opened inwards, spilling him into pitch blackness. A light snapped on. One of the thinnest men Coffey had ever seen stood on the bed in his undershorts, his long hair rumpled like a cockscomb. The horrible woman sang from a miniature radio dangling like a camera around the thin man's neck. The tiny room, twin to Coffey's, was jammed with developing trays, film packs, muscle-building equipment, a stripped-down radio transmitter, a judo mat, a tape-recorder and a huge pile of men's magazines.

'You bastard,' the man said. 'Look what you done. You just ruined five bucks' worth of colour film.'

'I'm sorry.'

'Sorry isn't enough. Come on in. Let's get a little natural light on the subject.'

The stranger ripped a blanket from his window, switched off the overhead light, shut off the radio, and sank down on the bed, crosslegged, like an Indian holy man, sweeping the pile of men's magazines to the floor. 'Sit down,' he said. 'Know what you done? You ruined my entry for the Popular Photography contest, that's what. Two hours I spent in the cab of a crane to get this shot and now it's ruined. The least you can do is pay for the film. Five bucks.'

'But I – well, I'm very short of money,' Coffey said. 'I can't afford to pay you. I'm sorry –'

'Now, wait a minute, let's discuss it,' the thin man said.

'This is a problem in human relations. My name is Warren K. Wilson, by the way. What's your name?'

'Ginger Coffey.'

'Okay, Ginger. Now, you've got a job, right?'

'Yes. But I'm just a proofreader. I don't earn much –'

'Well, get another job, why don't you?'

'It's not so easy,' Coffey said. 'I've been trying.'

'What do you mean, it's not easy? There's plenty of work in this country if you know how to go after it. You live here in the Y?'

'Yes.'

'Single?'

'No – ah – my wife's not with me just now.'

'Oh – Oh,' Wilson said. 'You got a wife, have you? Not so good. I happen to know about a couple of jobs that's going up north this week. I'm heading up to Blind River myself Monday morning. Of course, you married guys are screwed. Now, let's see. What are your hours on this proofreading job?'

'Six at night until one in the morning.'

'Perfect. Can you drive a truck?'

'As a matter of fact, I can. At least, I drove one in the army. I have a driver's licence.'

'Right. How'd you like a job making deliveries, here in Montreal? Eight to four, six days a week and it pays sixty bucks.'

Coffey stared at the judo mat on the floor. Driving a truck? Was that what he had come to Canada for?

'See, I just quit this job yesterday,' Wilson said. '*Tiny Ones*, it's a diaper service outfit. Suppose I get you taken on there? That worth five bucks to you? You owe me the dough anyways.'

'Diapers?' Coffey said. 'Isn't that sort of a – sort of a dirty job?'

Wilson bent forward, his body half-disappearing under the bed, his knobbly backbone curved like Charlie Chaplin's walking stick. Up he came with a package of cigarettes. He lit one and blew a smoke ring. 'I done the job for two months,' he said, staring at Coffey through the ring. 'Do I stink?'

'Sorry. No, of course not, I just meant –'

'Disinfectant,' Wilson said. 'Every sack of returns smells

93

like perfume. And anyways, if you want to get somewhere in this world, you've got to push. Now, look at me. I'll go anywhere and work at any job that pays. And you know why? Because I'm studying. Look at this.' He pointed to the radio transmitter. 'Now, this is on loan to me from the American Home Radio and Television Engineers College. That's a low-power broadcasting transmitter. I bet you didn't know that radio and TV repairs is one of the fastest growing industries on this whole continent?'

'No, I didn't.'

'Well, it's a fact. Now, once I get my diploma as a graduate of the A.H.R. and T., I can pick up fifty a week in my spare time. At least, that's what the ad says.'

'It sounds very good.'

Wilson put his finger into a second smoke ring. 'Right. But when I make that extra jack, know what I'm going to do? Invest in German cameras. And then I start studying another course. How to be a magazine photographer. Now there's life! Movie stars posing for you, flying in planes all around the world, meeting all kinds of personalities. How do you like that?'

'Yes,' Coffey said. 'That sounds interesting, I suppose.'

'You *suppose*? I'm telling you. Now, you take me, that's why I can move anywheres I want. I'm mobile, see. And I don't miss my fun. Any time I feel like it I just check into a hotel, buy a quart of liquor and ask the bellboy to send a pig up.'

'A pig?'

'Right. Why jump in the ocean, eh? I mean, look at you, you're tied down, you can't go no place unless you bring the wife along. And because you're tied down you got no ambitions, right?'

'My wife just left me.'

'Well then, what are you worrying about? Big guy like you, whyn't you come up north with me, you'll get hired right away. Look –' Wilson bounded up from his crouch on the bed and struck a strong man pose. Large knobbly muscles lumped out all over his back. 'I had to work to get like you are,' he said. 'I done it on a home gym set in Toronto. Built myself up from a runt to a Mr Junior Honourable Mention. That's what I mean about getting ahead. You see, I was doing this home study course. There's a place in Chicago gives you a diploma that guarantees you a job as a private investigator any place in the States. Well, I done fine in the test but I failed the physical. So I took this body-building course and, like I say, I built myself up to a Mr Junior Honourable Mention. That's something, eh?'

'But why didn't you become a private detective?'

'Bad timing,' Wilson said. 'When I wrote back to the college in Chicago they said I was too late. All the private eye licences was given out for that year and they want me to do the course over again. Well, eff that, I said. So I started this TV course, instead. I mean –' and he leaned over and gripped Coffey's arm – 'I mean – say, your deltoids are like dead mice, you want to build them up – anyways, as I was saying, you got to keep moving, do whatever comes along. Now, how about coming up north with me next week?'

'Well, I – I – what was this truck driving job you mentioned earlier?'

'Oh, *that* job. You want to take that instead? You could make more money up north, you know.'

'Yes ... but my wife ... I have a little girl here. Perhaps I'd better stay here.'

'Okay, suit yourself. Now, let's see ...' Wilson scrambled around under the bed once more and came up with a writing pad and a ball-point pen. 'He-ere we are.' Busily he began to write, his lips moving as he formed large childish letters on the paper.

Coffey looked at him. Here was a single man, a free man who next Monday would head up to Blind River; a man who could still dream youth's dreams, who could see himself as a magazine photographer travelling over the world, meeting beautiful girls, living life's adventures. It was an old dream of Coffey's; one he'd started to dream at the age of fifteen. And the men's magazines, the mail order courses, the talk of women as an inanimate pleasure to be enjoyed as you would enjoy a drink, the room jammed with evidences of boyish schemes, boyish pursuits – yes, it was familiar. A world of toys.

Yet Wilson was no longer a boy. The thin neck was clawed with age; there were grey streaks in the long untidy locks of hair; the hands were veiny, stippled with tell-tale brown moles. Was manhood what Wilson had missed?

'There we are,' Wilson said, folding the paper. 'Now you take this over to the bossman this aft. And write me out an I O U for five bucks, right?'

Coffey took the pen and wrote that he owed you, Warren K. Wilson, the sum of five dollars, signed J. F. Coffey. They exchanged slips of paper.

'See?' Wilson said. 'I knew we could make a deal if we talked things over. That's human relations for you. Now, here's my address up north. I'm trusting you to send me the dough, okay?'

'Fair enough.'

They shook hands on it; boys crossing their hearts. In the corridor, alone again, Coffey looked at the slip of paper.

Mr Mountain
Tiny Ones Depot
1904 St Donat Street

Dear Mr Mountain,
Here is a friend of mine, very reliable driver who has lots of experience in driving trucks and making deliveries and has part time night job which would suit you if you take him on 8 to 4 on my old shift.

Sincerly
W. K. Wilson

He put the piece of paper in his pocket. At least it was true that he could drive a truck. It was worth a try. With two jobs, he'd have enough money to support her and Paulie. And that was what mattered now. For after a morning's freedom, one thing was clear. It was too late to begin again, alone.

The small office at the rear of the *Tiny Ones* depot was decorated with a large lumber products calendar showing a young woman, her skirts entangled in a fly fisherman's cast. Her hands had gone up to shield the O of horror her pretty mouth made, instead of readjusting the resultant dishabille.

It seemed to Coffey as he stood beneath this calendar that the pretty girl's embarrassment perfectly mirrored his own.

Underneath the calendar sat Mr Stanley Mountain, his enormous weight severely testing a stout swivel chair. His most noticeable moving part was a stomach, large as a regulation basket ball, which bobbed regularly up and down, straining against his very clean white shirt and his yellow felt braces. His head of hair, white as detergent, bent in perusal of Wilson's note.

'Show me your driver's licence,' he said.

Coffey showed it.

'You a vet?'

'Yes,' Coffey said. It was so bloody hard to explain about the Irish Army.

'R.C.A.F. transport officer myself,' Mr Mountain said. 'And let me tell you I still run things by the book. Corp?'

A small man in white overalls put his head around the office doorway.

'Corp, take this man out to the yard, give him a truck. Test him.'

'Right now, sir?'

'Right now.'

So Coffey followed Corp out into the snow and was introduced to a small closed van which bore a picture of Winston Churchill, neatly nappied, and the legend: *Tiny Ones*. 'Drive her across the yard and park her between the two vans on the far side,' Corp said.

Coffey did this without difficulty, then waited as Corp joined him. 'Have a smoke, Paddy,' Corp said. 'Never mind about the rest of it. I just passed you.'

'Thanks very much.'

'I mean,' Corp said. 'I mean, I don't go for this service bull. Who does he think he is? The war's over, you know. I mean, you got to help other people,' he went on, becoming, Coffey thought, quite upset. 'I mean, you're out of work, Paddy, right? Probably got a wife and kids to support, right? Well then, good luck to you. Now here – give him this card. Finish your smoke. Then go on back.'

Coffey finished his cigarette as told, crossed the yard again and gave the card to Mr Mountain. Unconsciously, he assumed atten-shun! as he waited to hear Mr Mountain's verdict.

'Check,' said Mr Mountain. 'You're assigned, then, on a three-week trial. Terms of duty – Monday to Saturday. Hours of duty – oh-eight hundred hours to sixteen hundred hours. Truck to be checked and presented to your relief at sixteen ten. Morning check out inspection oh-seven fifty hours. Now, double on back to Corp and get your uniform.'

'Right sir,' Coffey said. 'Thank you, sir.' Involuntarily, he wagged Mr Mountain the old salute. Mr Mountain seemed pleased.

'Carry on, Coffey,' he said.

A battle dress jacket; a military cap with a badge which read: *Tiny Ones*; a machine for making change; a pair of sky-blue trousers and a pair of knee-length rubber boots. He signed for all, followed Corp into the locker-room and began to try them on. Off went his Tyrolean hat, his hacking jacket, his grey tweed trousers and brown suède boots. On the bench they lay, the last remains of Ginger Coffey. On went the uniform, anonymous and humiliating. He thought of the first time he had worn a uniform, as a private in the Regiment of Pearse; still a boy, still dreaming of wars, battles and decorations. And of the last time he took off his uniform on the day of his discharge. Of the relief he had felt then, knowing that it had all been a waste, that never again would he willingly become a number, a rank, a less than a man.

The uniform fitted him perfectly.

'Okay,' Corp said. 'You'll do. Take them off and stow them in your locker. Now you're a regular member of the shit brigade.'

Chapter Six

THE *Tiny Ones* depot was in the east end of the city. To return to the *Tribune* he must walk a long way. As he started off the sun moved west, unadmitted by the pale clouds which all day had curtained the frozen river and the city islanded within it. Thermometers outside banks and filling-stations began to fall. Four forty-five. Office workers, waiting release as the minute hand moved slowly towards the hour, looked at the darkness beyond their windows and saw edges of frosting begin to mist the panes. While below, approaching the financial district, saving the price of a bus, Coffey hurried on.

Five o'clock. In the financial district the street lights flared. Down came the office workers, spilling out into the streets, released, facing the freezing bus terminal waits, the long, slow-stopping journey home. Uptown they turned in their hundreds while down he went, down, still hurrying, no sandwiches in his pocket for the night's break, his night's work not yet begun.

Five-thirty. It grew colder. A policeman in fur hat and black greatcoat shuffled like a dancing bear under the harsh arena light of a traffic intersection. White mittpaw invited Coffey to cross. Crossing, Coffey scurried along the outer rim of light, raising his right hand to the policeman, giving the old salute.

Five-forty. On a corner, three blocks from the *Tribune* building, the red traffic light called: halt. Winded, Coffey waited, knowing he would be in time. In a newspaper kiosk an old woman squatting on her kerosene heater rose to serve a commuter, red-raw fingers fumbling in woollen mitts as she made change. The newspaper passing to the commuter's hurried clutch headlined a vaguely familiar word which made Coffey, crossing on amber, half-stop in the darkness, then walk close to the commuter trying to read what it said. On the opposite pavement the commuter, unfurling the newspaper, shook it out. Coffey read, and moved away, last lap, going through the *Tribune*'s revolving doors.

Cripple Mate Case:

I DID IT FOR LOVE

WIFE TELLS COURT

The elevator came and he rode up, thinking it should be Cripple Mate who told court he did it for love: Cripple Mate who tomorrow would climb into a fancy-dress uniform and go out to collect dirty nappies in proof of his love. Cripple Mate who, in one day on his onlie-oh, had more than doubled his earning power and who, no matter what she might have done with long drinks of water called Grosvenor, still loved her enough to want her back. Oh, he'd make her eat her words, so he would. She would never call him selfish again.

'Fourth floor, Editorial.'

Seven minutes to six. Coffey hurried into the *Tribune* cafeteria, rejecting supper in favour of a phone call. He called Grosvenor's flat, for Grosvenor would know where to find her. The number was busy. He waited, then dialled again. Still busy. At one minute to six it was still busy; still busy when the composing-room bell rang, forcing him once again to abandon the facts of his life for the facts of the world.

When the ten o'clock supper break came, he hurried to the cafeteria booth, still unfed, still trying. He spent the fifteen-minute break trying to reach Grosvenor in his flat, at the Press Club, and in three other places he remembered as Grosvenor's haunts. No luck. The bell rang. Back to work. And still, Oh God! he had not reached her, had not told her his news, had not been able to show what Cripple Mate could do.

At one a.m. the work over, he took the elevator down to the lobby, waited until Fox and the others had gone, then entered a pay phone booth under the *Tribune* clock. The lobby was quiet. Outside the phone booth an old night cleaner swabbed the Terrazzo floors with a wet mop as Coffey, for the umpteenth time that evening inserted his dime and dialled the number of Grosvenor's apartment. The number was busy. Hooray! Grosvenor was on the phone to someone – maybe to her? Giving her a lover's good night chat, sleep well, my lovely. Meantime, until the lovey-dovery chat was over, Cripple Mate must cool his heels.

Steady as she goes, Coffey warned himself. Wait a full five minutes so you won't be disappointed. And wait he did, smoking the last of his fags, watching the old cleaner slop the slimy, sursy mop over the Terrazzo fllooring, wetting the inlaid letters: *The Montreal Tribune.*

At one ten he watched the jerky minute hand complete its last revolution and again inserted his dime. Brrp-brrp-brr-brrp – Oh, rot your blabbering liver-lipped gob! By the holy, it was time someone put a stop to this. He replaced the receiver, dialled the operator and asked if FEnrose 2921 was out of order.

'Just one moment, sir, I'll check.'

Another wait. 'I'm afraid the receiver has been left off the stand, sir.'

And why would the phone be off the hook? So that a certain Gerry Grosvenor would not be disturbed. Well any man – *any man* – was justified in disturbing *that*, no matter how late it was. Out he ran into the icy streets, down one block, down another and there – little interior lights lit, drivers lumped over newspapers – a black snake of taxis lay in wait for night-birds near the entrance to an hotel. No time for economy now. In went Cripple Mate and gave the address, sitting forward, silently willing the driver to hurry as the cab moved off, its tyre chains rattling on the hard-packed snow, going up the mountain to Grosvenor's place.

Gerald Grosvenor lived in an apartment development opposite a large cemetery. Ten times as many people were located in the apartment development as in the graveyard which was very much larger in area. Therefore, slithering and twisting in the snowy drives among a huddle of enormous neo-Georgian buildings, Coffey's driver twice lost his way. It was five minutes to two when, his cab finally dismissed, Coffey found himself in the foyer of Grosvenor's building. To enter he must ring a bell beside Grosvenor's name plate. Grosvenor, alerted, must press a buzzer which electrically opened the foyer door. But if Coffey rang the bell, he would give Grosvenor a chance to slip Veronica out by the back way. And if Veronica were not there he would waken Grosvenor and would seem to Grosvenor a blithering fool. So he stood, irresolute. Maybe he should go away. Flute! He didn't *want* to find Vera there. And besides, she wasn't that sort of woman, she'd never leave Paulie alone in some boarding-house while she . . .? Or would she? What did he know about her after all?

Just then a late-returning tenant came up behind him and unlocked the foyer door. Coffey grabbed the door, met the tenant's suspicious stare with an apologetic smile and slipped in behind him, beginning the long climb to the fourth floor, remembering that curiosity killed the cat. And that if he were wrong he would look like an idjit.

But on he went in a curious mixture of wrath and shame. Went on, forcing himself into doing something his whole nature cried out against. Making a fuss, acting the looney, exposing himself to a stranger's scorn. On the fourth floor he paused, looking at the numbers. 81, 83, 85. He turned to the other side. 84. There were no overshoes or rubbers outside the door, though it was the custom for visitors to leave them in the corridor. Ah, she wasn't there at all: he was imagining things. Turn around now and go home. Ring Grosvenor in the morning. You'll find her tomorrow.

But just then a small man in a dressing-gown came out of Number 80 carrying an empty gin bottle and the wreckage of a box of potato chips. The man went to the incinerator slot at the end of the hall, passing Coffey with a suspicious stare, a stare which implied that Coffey might be up to no good; that Coffey had no business in the corridor; that he was loitering with some thievish intent.

And that stare, from a total stranger, made Coffey turn around and ring the bell of Number 84. Reassured, the small man turned and went back into his own apartment. Someone stirred inside Number 84. Someone was coming. Someone fiddled with a chain. Veronica's voice whispered: 'Who's that?'

Coffey had rung the bell out of funk, out of fear of a stranger. Now, he drew back as though he had been slapped, his lips tight under the curve of his moustache. Again her voice whispered: 'Who's that?'

But Grosvenor – for it was Grosvenor who stood there with her, it must be! – Grosvenor waited behind that door, probably holding his finger to his lips cautioning her to silence.

A loud buzzer noise sounded behind the door. Down four floors in the night silence of the hall the buzzer rang again, repeating the sound. They thought he was downstairs; that was it. Now they would open the door and Grosvenor would peep out, trying to see who was coming up.

The door did not open. Again, they pressed the buzzer, shaking in their shoes, the pair of them. Oh, he would bloody kill them!

But in that moment, waiting there, he remembered why he had rung the bell. He remembered that he would have gone away. Oh God, was it any wonder his wife was behind that door with another man? What was the matter with him that he wanted to avoid a scene? What was the matter?

But what's the matter with *her*, he thought. Why is it always me that's in the wrong? Oh, for God's sake, woman, what are you doing in there? Come home, for God's sake, you fool; how could you do this to me and Paulie? You were mine, you swore it, for richer or for poorer, for better or for worse, until death. Until death, do you hear?

And as though she heard, she opened the door.

'Ginger!' she said. 'Do you realize what time of night it is?'

Did he *what*? Well now, didn't that beat the band? In her dressing-gown and nightie, her feet bare, the brazen bloody nerve of her!

He pushed past her. 'Where's Grosvenor?' he asked. 'Hiding in the kitchen?'

'Gerry's not here. And shh! You'll wake Paulie.'

'Paulie?'

'Shh,' she said again. She followed him into Grosvenor's living-room, a bare, bachelor place with white walls, prints of Chinese horses and a long low bench of high-fidelity equipment. She motioned to a wicker and iron chair. 'Sit down. Shh. Gerry lent us his place. He's staying with a friend. The room I booked for us wasn't ready. Now, for goodness' sake, take that look off your face.'

'Where's Paulie?' he said. 'Where is she?'

'In there. Don't wake her.'

But he walked out of the living-room and opened the door she had indicated. He switched on the light. In a strange bed, clutching Bunkie, her nightdress-case doll, his daughter slept. He bent over her, saw her twitch, wake, and sit up.

'Daddy? What are you doing here?'

'I told you not to wake her,' Veronica said.

He stared at his daughter's face, still drowsy with sleep, at her fair reddish hair in tiny steel clips, at her breasts pulling tight against the buttoned pyjama top. Soon she too would be a woman. She too would leave for a stranger's bed.

'Are you satisfied?' Veronica said. 'Go back to sleep, Paulie.'

She switched out the light and shut Paulie's door. 'Do you realize it's three in the morning, and that I have to go to work at nine?'

He followed her back into the living-room. So *she* had to work, had she? Wait till she heard how *he* was working.

'Vera, there's something I want to tell you.'

'It's the middle of the night, Ginger. I want to go back to bed.'

'Vera, I have two jobs now. I'm earning a total of a hundred dollars a week. And Vera – are you listening to me?'

'What?' she said crossly.

'I said I have two jobs. I can well afford to support us now.'

She sighed, in swift exasperation.

'And I've left the apartment and I'm bunked in at the Y.'

'That's nice for you. Now, I really want to go to sleep, Ginger.'

'But wait – wait till I tell you. I'll give you both pay cheques next Friday. Every penny, mind you. You could make any conditions you like. I won't even ask you to sleep in the same room.'

She began to cry. He got up, went over, put out his hand to touch her shoulder. She moved away, leaving his hand hovering.

'Listen to me,' he said. 'I may have been selfish in the past and I may not have made the best fist of things. But listen – even though I'm not the best husband in the world, I know this much. Nobody loves you more than I do, Kitten. Nobody. No matter what you may think, or no matter what Grosvenor tells you, he couldn't love you the way I do.'

'You say you love me,' she said. 'Just because you miss me.

Well, you'd miss a servant if she'd been looking after you for fifteen years. That's not love.'

'Isn't it? Ah, for God's sake, woman, what do you know about it? Love isn't going to bed with the likes of Gerry Grosvenor, either.'

'Then what is it, Ginger? Tell me. You're the expert, it seems.'

'Well ... Well – dammit, Veronica, we're a family, you and me and Paulie. That's why we have to stick together, no matter what.'

He saw her bow her head. Her hand went up to her face; long fingers shielded her eyes, as though she prayed. Oh, Vera, he thought. How and under what mortal sky could you ever believe that you and Grosvenor will be as you and I have been? How could you have forgotten that life agreement we made fifteen years ago in Saint Pat's in Dalkey, me in a rented morning suit, a stiff collar choking me, praying to God Tom Clarke hadn't mislaid the ring, and you in white, your head bowed as now, kneeling before the altar – Love – oh, come on home now, and let's stop all this nonsense!

She removed the shield of her hand and he saw her eyes: bright, fixed in hate. 'So love is staying together for Paulie's sake?' she said. 'No thanks, Ginger.'

'Ah now, wait. I've changed, honest to God I have. Listen – do you know what this new job is? It's putting on a uniform and going about delivering babies' nappies and bringing back the messy ones. Now, if I was as selfish as you say, would I do the like of that? Would I, Vera?'

'I'm not going to listen to you. Oh, I knew you'd come back with some story. I knew it. It's not fair.'

'But it's no story. It's the truth.'

'All right,' she said. 'So it's true. Well, I'm sorry. And that's the trouble.'

'Vera, would you for the love of God give over talking in riddles?'

'I mean I'm sorry for you, Ginger. But that's all. You're not going to catch me again. You're too late with this, just as you've been too late with everything else.'

'Too late am I?' Coffey said. 'Maybe you're too late.

Grosvenor's five years younger than you. We'll see how long this lasts.'

'Yes, he is five years younger. You've used up the best years of my life, that's why.'

'What about my best years, Vera? Suffering J! What about my best years?'

'All right. Then why don't we try to save the years we have left? Why don't we get a divorce?'

'Divorce?' He felt his heart pull and thump in his chest. 'You're a Catholic,' he said. 'What's your mother going to say about the sin of divorce?'

'Don't you preach religion at me, Ginger Coffey, you that haven't darkened a church door since you came out here. Don't you talk about Catholics. What's wrong with you is that you never *were* a Catholic; you were too selfish to give God or anyone else the time of day. Oh, you may think I'm like you now, and I am. I never pray. But, once I did. Once I was very holy, do you remember? I cried, Ginger. I cried when Father Delaney said that unless we stopped practising birth control he'd refuse us the sacraments. Do you remember that? No, you never think of that any more, do you? But I do. You changed me, Ginger. What I am now has a lot to do with what you made me. So don't you talk sin to me, don't you dare! Sins – oh, let me tell you. Once your soul is dirty, then what difference in the shade of black?'

Trembling, she took one of Grosvenor's cigarettes out of a jar and, in a gesture familiar as one of his own, tapped it on the back of her hand before picking up a lighter off the table. The lighter was initialled G.G.

'Daddy?' a voice said at the door. Paulie, her pyjama trousers crumpled like accordion pleats around her calves, her sleepy eyes blinking in the bright light, came into the room.

'Paulie,' Veronica said. 'You go back to bed this instant, do you hear?'

'No.'

'Did you *hear* me, miss?' Veronica said.

'I'm not an infant, Mummy,' Paulie said. 'I've got a right to be here.'

'Go to bed!'

'No, I want to talk to Daddy.'

'Yes, Pet,' Coffey said. 'What is it?'

Paulie began to cry. 'I don't want to stay here. I don't want to stay with them.'

'With who?' Coffey said. 'With who, Pet?'

But Paulie, still weeping, turned to her mother, woman to woman, bitter, betrayed. 'You said it would be just the two of us. Just you and me. You said I was grown up now. I'm not going to be sent to bed every night like an *infant*, just because you want to let Gerry in the back door.'

'You little sneak,' Veronica said. 'That's enough. You'll do what you're told.'

'You're not in charge of me!' Paulie screamed. 'Daddy is. Daddy's in charge of me, not you. I want to go with Daddy.'

'Do you now?' Veronica said. 'Well, Daddy's living at the Y.M.C.A., aren't you, Daddy? No girls allowed, isn't that right, Daddy?'

Coffey did not look at her. He went to his daughter, taking her by the wrists. 'Oh, Pet,' he said. 'Do you really want to come with me?'

She was trembling. She did not seem to see him, to feel his hands. 'I can choose whoever I like,' she said, wildly. 'You're my father, not Gerry Grosvenor. I'm not going to be sent to bed just because she wants to see Gerry. It's not fair!'

'Of course it's not,' Coffey said. 'Now listen, Pet. If you want to come, I'll find us a place tomorrow. I promise you. I'll find us a place, don't you worry.'

'Will you, Ginger?' Veronica said.

'Yes, I will. Don't laugh. I will!'

But she was not laughing. She turned to Paulie. 'You say I broke my promise to you,' she said. 'But what about your father's promises? This promise he's making now, he'll break it. Ask him. Go on, ask him. How is he going to get a place for you tomorrow?'

'I don't have to listen to you,' Paulie said. 'Daddy's going to take me, aren't you, Daddy?'

He looked at the carpet, his thumb absently grooving the part in his moustache, hating that stupid foolish man who once again had shown him his own true image. Vera was right: his promises were worthless currency. How could he make Paulie know that this time he meant it? 'Listen, Pet,' he said. 'What your mother says is true in a way. But I have two jobs and as soon as they pay me, I'll have plenty of money, plenty! Now, listen – if you can wait until Friday, I swear to you on my word of honour that I'll find a place for us. A nice place. If you'll wait, Apple?'

'Of course, I'll wait,' Paulie said. But she did not look at him; proud of her rebellion, she stared at Veronica.

'Thank you, Pet,' he said. 'Now, would you go into your room for a while? I want to talk to your mother.'

Paulie went away: they heard her bedroom door shut. He looked at Veronica, thinking that, after all, this was a crush Vera had, it was – well, it was a sort of illness. It was up to him to try to make her see sense before it was too late. 'Listen to me,' he said. 'If I were you I'd put on my thinking cap to-night and wonder what's going to happen if you go through with this lunatic performance. Remember, if you change your mind, you can come back tomorrow. I promise you there'll be no questions asked and no recriminations. We'd just forget this ever happened.'

'Oh, go away,' she said. 'Go away.'

He picked up his little hat from between his feet, went unsteadily into the hall and knocked on Paulie's door. When Paulie answered, he took her arm and led her to the front door. As he passed a table with a telephone on it, he saw that the receiver jarred slightly on its cradle. That was why the phone had not answered. He replaced the receiver, then said in a whisper: 'All right, Apple. I'll come for you next week.'

'Wait,' Paulie said. 'Here's the address and phone number of the place we're going to. When you're ready to come and get me, phone and leave a message. And Daddy?'

'What, Pet?'

'Daddy, promise you won't let me down.'

He took her in his arms and crushed her against him. There, in the living-room, his wife sat alone, sick with some madness he could not understand. He held Paulie and she put her pale cheek up to be kissed. 'Word of honour, Pet,' he whispered. 'Word of honour.'

Chapter Seven

FIRST, park the truck, making sure that you are not beside a fire hydrant or in a no-parking area. Then check your book, Mrs What'shername, how many dozen last week, how many this week. Then find her parcel, hop down in the morning cold, ring the door bell, smile as she opens, and make change from your leather sporran. Thank you, Madam. Receiving in turn her apologetic smile as she hands over the long string sack containing her offspring's soilings. Then down the path, sky the sack into the back of the van and on to the next customer.

That first morning was a Saturday. So, although he was slow on the deliveries and late back at the *Tiny Ones* Depot, there was no panic. No proofreading that night. And the following day, Sunday, there was proofreading, but no *Tiny Ones*. Monday, now, that was another matter.

To begin with, by Monday morning he was stony broke. So when he arrived at the depot to pick up his truck, he put out a feeler to Corp. But Corp, the soul of friendliness until then, said: 'Why should I lend you five bucks, Paddy? After all, I don't know you from a hole in the wall. No dice.'

No dice. Coffey had twenty cents left in his pocket. He had not had any breakfast. And to cap it all, the first call on that morning's run, he ran into trouble. An apartment building it was; modern, with a plate glass door and a sign outside which said AMBASSADOR HOUSE. Four dozen, the order. He hopped down, hefting his brown paper parcel and went in through the glass door to check the apartment number on the board.

'Looking for something?'

A doorman in a green coat and peaked green cap tapped a white-gloved finger against Coffey's chest.

'Number twenty-four?' Coffey said. 'A Mrs Clapper?'

Anger came like a sickness on the commissionaire's wintry features. 'You blind or somethin', Tiny? Service entrance at the side. What's the matter with you?'

'I'm sorry, I didn't notice.'

'C'mon, c'mon, you're blockin' up the hall. Take your fuggin' diapers up the back stairs.'

Outside once more, Coffey tried Veronica's trick of counting ten. All that pushing and shoving: no need for that, was there? After all, people only saw things when they were on the look out for them. He remembered when Veronica was pregnant, he used to see dozens of pregnant women on the streets. But not since. Well, service entrances were like that. Unless you were on the look out . . .

Calming himself with these reflections, he found the service entrance, climbed four flights of stairs and rang the bell at the back door of Apartment 24. A uniformed maid opened to him. '*Tiny Ones*,' he said. 'Good morning.'

The maid took the package.

'That'll be two twenty, please,' he said.

'Just a moment,' she said. 'The mistress wants to see you.'

He stepped into the kitchen.

'Take your overshoes off,' the maid said. 'My floors!'

'That's all right, Anna,' a woman's voice said. A well-dressed woman, she was, too old to need *Tiny Ones* by the look of her. 'Does your firm rent cribs?' she asked. And Flute! She was from Dublin.

'No Madam.'

'Do they rent any other baby things, could you tell me?'

He felt his face grow hot. Not only was she Dublin, but Still-organ Road, Dublin, as stuck up as all get out. 'Well no, Madam. They don't.'

'Are you Irish?' she said.

'Yes.'

'I thought I caught a Dublin accent,' said she. 'Have you been over here long?'

'Ah – about six months.'

At that moment a younger woman (the nappy user's Mum, he guessed) came into the room. A blonde she was, in a tweed suit, all the latest style, who took one look at Coffey, her eyes getting bigger. 'Oh!' she said. 'Oh, I could have sworn – Excuse me staring like that. But you're the spitting image of someone I know.'

'But this man is from Dublin, Eileen,' the mother said. 'Isn't that a coincidence?'

'Oh? And what's your name?' the daughter asked Coffey, who wouldn't have had to ask hers. If floors could rise up and swallow a person – by the Holy, that wasn't just a figure of speech, for she was Colonel Kerrigan's daughter, the same girl he had danced with last winter at the Plunkett Old Boys' Dance in the Shelbourne Hotel. And had served under her old man in the army.

'My name is – Cu-Crosby,' he said.

'If I had a camera I'd take your picture and send a copy to this friend of mine,' she said. 'You're his double, right down to the moustache.'

'Whose double?' her mother asked.

'Veronica Shannon's husband, Mother. Ginger Coffey, do you remember him?'

'Oh, of course,' the mother said. 'Didn't he soldier with your Daddy once upon a time? And afterwards was in a distillery or something?'

'Yes, Mother.'

'But they went to Canada,' her mother said. 'I remember Mrs Vesey said something to me about looking Veronica up – '

As the mother talked, Eileen Kerrigan's eyes met Coffey's. Now, she knew. 'Anyway, we mustn't keep this gentleman here all day,' she said, cutting her mother short. 'Anna, would you get the bag?'

'Here you are,' the maid said and – Suffering J, let me out! – Coffey took it and backed out of the kitchen.

'Wait. Your money.'

He had to make change for a five-dollar bill, aware that Eileen Clapper, née Kerrigan, had informed her mother with a look. The maid shut the door on him. Now, the telling would begin – Oh yes, Mother, it could be and it is. I'm positive – Now the airmail letters would fly. Now it could be told in Gath and embroidered in the Wicklow Lounge, chuckled over in the offices at Kylemore, dissected in Veronica's mother's flat. And how glorious a comuppance it would seem to all the voices he had fled; how joyously they would savour each detail, the changing of his name, the absurd uniform with *Tiny Ones* on

111

the cap, the menial nature of his employment, the net result of all his hopes. They didn't even need to embellish it: though they would; like all Dublin stories it would lose nothing in the telling. Yes, the whole country could laugh at him now. He stood on the stairs and saw the whole country laugh.

Ha, ha! cried all the countrified young thicks he had gone to school with, who now, ordained and Roman-collared, regularly lectured the laity on politics and love. Ha, ha! cried the politicians, North and South, united as always in fostering that ignorance which alone made possible their separate powers. Hah! cried the archbishops, raising their purple skull-capped heads from the endless composition of pastoral letters on the dangers of foreign dances and summer frocks. Hah! cried the smug old businessmen, proud of being far behind the times. Ha, ha, ha! Emigrate, would you? *We told you so.*

Their laughter died. What did it matter? What did they matter, so long as he was not going home? And in that moment he knew that, sink or swim, Canada was home now, for better or for worse, for richer or for poorer, until death.

He went down the stairs, climbed into his truck and drove off, his tyre chains rattling in the freezing slush. What did anything matter now except his word to Paulie.

For lunch he had a ten-cent bag of peanuts and a glass of milk. After eating it, he felt like a starving man. Money he must have to last out until Friday. His proofreading pals? Ah, weren't they all boozers, counting their ha'pence from one pay day binge to the next? To last until Friday he would need more than the dollar loan they might afford. He would need at least ten dollars. Ten dollars required nerve. So, at the end of the day, he went to see Mr Mountain and nervously requested an advance on wages.

'Advance?' Mr Mountain's stomach heaved upwards in alarm. 'That's got to be done through channels, Coffey. I don't handle payroll, that's G.H.Q. stuff. Top man deals with that. And I might as well warn you that Mr Brott doesn't favour that procedure.'

'I'm afraid I'll have to chance that, Mr Mountain. I have to have the money.'

'Well, it's your funeral,' Mr Mountain said. 'It's strictly

against standing orders. However – ' he reached for one of the many forms he designed personally in the depot. 'Here's one of my unit identification check slips,' he said. 'It shows your rank, length of service and record in my outfit. If you want to try this, you'd better hurry. Head office closes at five.'

Hurry was right. The office was ten streets away and he had to Shanks mare it. So, chit in hand, with twenty minutes to get there, he set off through the darkening streets, wondering if he didn't win Mr Brott's clemency would he be able to pawn the lamp in his locker or sell some of his clothing second-hand? How did you go about pawning something here? Or selling clothes? But do not worry about that yet, he told himself. Cross that bridge when you come to it.

Shanks mare at five to five, pelting down an old street in the dock area past faded stores and warehouses stencilled with the names of unknown and unimportant enterprises: Pimlico Novelties; H. Lavalee Productions; Weiss & Schnee Imports; Wasserman Furs Ltd. And now, at one minute to five, he Shanks mared it into a building, rode up in an ancient latticed elevator, came out on the third floor and hurried down a corridor which smelled overpoweringly of Jeyes' Fluid, towards a frosted glass doorway stencilled:

TINY ONES INC.
Ring & Enter.

He rang and entered. Behind the counter which protected the office staff from the public, the desks were empty, the typewriters hooded, the file cabinets locked. He was late.

Still, someone must be here, he reasoned. The place was not shut. He rapped his knuckles on the counter, noticing a cubicle at the far end of the room in which a light still burned. He knocked again.

A small man appeared at the cubicle's doorway. 'Closed,' he said. 'Sorry.'

'But ...' Coffey began. But what? What the hell could he say?

The small man gave him a warning look, then shut the cubicle door. There was a name stencilled on the shut door, and reading it, Coffey felt his heart pull and jump. For wasn't this

113

the very man he was supposed to see? A. K. BROTT, PRES. Again, he knocked his knuckles on the counter. The door reopened. The small man came out, angry now.

'Mr Brott?'

'I said we're closed.'

'I – ah – I work at the depot, sir,' Coffey said. 'Could I see you a moment?'

'What about?'

'About – ah –'

'Come in, come in. I can't hear you,' the small man said, going back into his cubicle.

Coffey lifted the counter leaf and advanced among the empty desks. Inside the cubicle were several photographs in black frames, ex-voto scenes from the life of A. K. Brott. Brott with wife; Brott with children; Brott with first *Tiny Ones* van; Brott with first automatic washer; Brott with office staff; Brott with Chamber of Commerce outing. Coffey had plenty of time to study them as A. K. Brott, his shoulders hunched, whipped through the pages of a ledger. Brott with books.

At last, he raised his small grey head. Wary eyes studied Coffey. 'Well now. What's your trouble?'

'I've just started work for you as a driver, sir. I was wondering if I might have an advance on wages?'

Driver? Unbelievingly, A. K. Brott's small eyes travelled from the big fellow's florid moustache to his woolly-lined coat, his tweedy legs and suède boots. What sort of people was Mountain hiring these days? Looks like a burlesque comedian. And that red face: a rummy? 'No,' said A. K. Brott.

'But it's only ten dollars, sir.'

A. K. Brott's finger found a column, ran it down to a total. '*Only* ten dollars?' he said. 'Look at this. Off thirty per cent from last year. And that's not because the birth-rate is down. It's not down. It's up.'

He turned the pages, found another total, contorted his small grey features as though he had been seized with a sudden attack of indigestion. 'Look at this one,' he said. 'Worse. And *you* want ten dollars. You know what's going to happen here in *Tiny Ones*?'

'No, sir.'

'You're all going to be out of a job, that's what. Fifteen years I took to build up this business and look what's happened. Everywhere the same. Down twenty, thirty, even fifty per cent on some routes. All right, you're driving a route. Now, what is it? What's wrong?'

'What – ah – what do you mean?' Coffey asked.

'Disposable diapers, that's what I mean. Paper, that's what. I mean it's a goddam crime. There should be a law. There *is* a law, forest conservation, why don't they enforce it? And it gives the kids a rash, let me tell you, no matter what they say, paper skins a baby's ass raw. Ask any doctor, if you don't believe me. But it's new, and that's what people want, something new. Something easy. Now, you meet the customers on your route. Admit it. They're asking you for paper diapers, aren't they?'

'No, sir.'

'You're a liar.'

Coffey felt as though his face had been slapped. 'I'm not a liar,' he said.

'No? Well, come on then, wise guy. What *do* they want?'

What indeed? Coffey wondered. But if he was to get his advance, he must talk to this loony. Say something. What was it Eileen Kerrigan's mother had asked him for this morning?

'Well, as a matter of fact,' Coffey said. 'What most mothers want is to rent other things besides diapers.'

'What things?'

'Cribs and – and bassinettes and – and prams and so on.'

'Sit down,' Mr Brott said. 'What's your name?'

'Coffey, sir.'

'Well, go on. Let's hear it. If it's good, you won't be sorry, I promise you that.'

Coffey stared at Mr Brott, then exhaled in astonishment, his breath feathering up the ends of his large moustache. *Someone had asked his opinion.* Memories of former years, of the district manager of Coomb-Na-Baun Knitwear's unpleasant smile, of old Cleery in Kylemore Distilleries shaking his Neanderthal skull, ah, so many head men all unwilling to hear his ideas. Yet now, when he'd least expected it, here was a head man waiting. What could he say? He began to speak, making it up as he

115

went – 'Well, sir,' he said. 'A lot of families are small nowadays. I mean, they have one or two children, and buying prams and bassinettes and cribs is an expensive proposition for them. I remember in my own case, we only have one girl, and so we had to give all that stuff away when she was finished with it. Even the pram which was in tip-top condition. I just think if we could have rented those things, we'd have saved money.'

'Mnn ... hmm ...' Mr Brott said. 'Go on.'

'So – ah – if you rented those things, sir? Rent a crib, for instance –'

'Rent-A-Crib!' Mr Brott said. 'You think of that name yourself?'

'Ah – yes, sir.' What name was he talking about?

'Rent-A-Crib ... ' Mr Brott closed his eyes and sat for a long moment, as though trying to solve some problem in mental arithmetic. 'I don't say it's without merit,' he said. 'What's your name again?'

'Coffey, sir.'

'And you're a driver? You don't look like a driver.'

'I'm a New Canadian, sir. This is just a temporary job. I have a night job as well. But the trouble is, sir, I've just started in both jobs and haven't received any salary as yet. So that's why I came to see you about the advance, sir.'

'Advance?'

'Ten dollars, sir. If possible.'

Mr Brott shook his head.

'I mean, I could sign a receipt. I've earned more than ten dollars already. Couldn't you manage – ?'

Still headshaking, Brott took out his wallet and handed Coffey a ten-dollar bill. 'Advance nothing,' he said. 'You take it as a bonus. So you work at two jobs, eh? You know that reminds me of me when I was a young fellow. Ambitious, I was. How do you like Canada, Coffey?'

'I like it, sir. Very go-ahead country.'

'And you'll do well here, Coffey, you know that? You're a go-ahead fellow yourself. New Canadian, are you? Bet you never went to college, eh?'

'Yes, sir, I did, sir.'

'You *did*? Yet you're working as a delivery man. That's the spirit. Kids nowadays, they go to college, they think the world owes them a living. But it doesn't. I tell my Sammy that. I say to him, Sammy, you can have all the degrees in the world, they're no substitute for one good idea. What do you think, Coffey? Am I right?'

Coffey thought that A. K. Brott was not such a bad old geezer, after all.

'Yes, you're the kind we need over here,' Mr Brott said. 'Of course, this particular idea might not work. Might fail. Probably *would* fail. Lots of overhead on maintenance, that's one problem. Disinfecting the equipment, repainting, repairs, eh?'

'Yes, sir,' Coffey said. 'I suppose there would.'

'And then the pads, baby blankets, sheets, all that stuff? You figure on renting that too?'

'Well, why not, sir? You have a laundry. It would be just like diapers, wouldn't it?'

'That's right,' Mr Brott said. 'Cleaning tie-in. Yes, you're all right, Coffey, you know that? If you've got any more ideas, why you just come right up here and we'll talk it over. Okay? Nice meeting you.'

Pleased, confused, hungry for some supper, late because it was five-thirty now and he must rush, Coffey stood up, smiled at Mr Brott and wagged him the old salute. 'Good-bye, sir,' he said. 'And thank you, sir.'

'Don't mention it,' Mr Brott said. 'And you just keep that ten bucks, that's a bonus. Now, turn off the lights in the main office and shut the door when you go out.'

He switched off the lights, he shut the door. He hurried downstairs, hungry but content. Nice old geezer. It renewed your faith in Canada, meeting a man like that, a man who thought you were a go-ahead fellow. And he was a go-ahead fellow, dammit; he was no glorified secretary, no joeboy. He had been right to emigrate, no matter what. Tomorrow, he would find some place for Paulie and he to live and at the end of the week he would ask MacGregor for a raise. In a week or two he would be promoted. There was always a bright side: you just had to look for it, that was all. It was still uphill but, with a little victory now and then, you could keep on running. As long as you had hopes. And he still had hopes.

Chapter Eight

'MISS PAULINE COFFEY?' said the girl at the desk. 'Yes, if you'll just take a seat over there, sir. Won't be a moment.'

'Thank you,' Coffey said. He sat in the strange lobby and watched the girl – a nice little piece in a pony tail hairdo and a pink angora sweater – go upstairs in search of his daughter. He read a sign over the staircase: RESIDENTS ONLY: *No Gentlemen Allowed*. Which meant that Grosvenor was barred too. He was glad of that.

Still, it was strange to think that his wife and daughter were living upstairs in this place and that, he, their legal husband and father, could not go up. Not that Veronica would be up there at the moment. Oh no. Because, you see Veronica never came back from work until half past five. No, it was not unfair, or sneaky. Hadn't Veronica taken Paulie away in just that way? It was only tit for tat.

He had promised Paulie. He had kept his promise. Friday it was; here he was, a taxi at the door, a little flat rented, everything as planned. And now, as he watched the staircase, he saw the girl in the fuzzy pink sweater start down again, carrying two untidy bundles of possessions. Behind the pretty girl, his own Paulie, wearing sloppy white socks and saddle shoes, her winter overcoat a bit shrunken at the wrists and hems. He made a note to buy her a new coat. He went to her and kissed her pale cheek. 'Hello, Apple.'

'Be careful, Daddy, you'll make me spill this stuff.'

'I'll take it,' he said. 'I have a taxi outside.'

'Wait, Daddy.' She put her things down in the hall. 'We can't go yet.'

'Oh?'

'Mummy came home. She found out, I don't know how. She's upstairs pressing my good dress. She'll be down with it in a minute.'

'Oh?' he said.

'I'll put this stuff in the taxi, Daddy. You stay here. I think she wants to talk to you.'

'All right, Apple.' She was not going to take his Apple from him now: not after he had worked like a dog all week to get things ready. Just let her try.

He walked towards the stairs, ready to repel the enemy and as he did the enemy appeared on the landing above, carrying Paulie's party dress over her arm. He watched her come down, seeing not his wife but a stranger: a stranger who was more exciting to him than the woman who had been his wife. She had changed her hair style and her dark hair, now cut short, fitted her face like a helmet. She wore make-up and a dress he had never seen. He tried to imagine the familiar body beneath that dress; the full breasts with their large bruised nipples, the full thighs which swelled out of her slender waist, the familiar small mole beneath her ribcage. But it did not work: how could he imagine the body of this total stranger who now came towards him, smelling of an unfamiliar perfume? Was this what falling in love with Grosvenor had done to her; changed her from a wife to a beauty he would have envied any man's possessing? With shame, he realized that were she not his wife, he would preen and think of flirting with her; might even fall in love himself.

But when she spoke, she was Vera; no change. 'Hello, Ginger,' she said. 'Could we go into the lounge a moment? I want to speak to you.'

Yes. She was Vera and yet she was not. Again a stranger, as he followed her into the small lounge and shut the door so that they might be alone. But Vera once more as she handed him Paulie's dress, saying: 'I've just pressed this. Mind you don't crush it.'

He took the dress. He noticed that she was carrying her overcoat. She swung the overcoat out as a bullfighter tests a cape, whirling it on over her shoulders in a most un-Vera-ish manner. She pulled a new black beret out of the pocket and began fitting it on in front of the mirror over the fake fireplace. Was that what a crush could do to a person, make her exciting, a bit of a whore? What would she say if he were to kiss her this minute?

'What sort of place have you got, anyway?' she said, still adjusting her beret.

'It's a nice little place,' he said. 'Two bedrooms, a kitchenette and a living-room. Reasonable too. Seventy a month.'

'Does that include bedding?'

'Well, I – ah – I have the sheets and pillow cases from our old beds.'

'Yes, so you have.' Her beret now adjusted to her satisfaction, she began to powder her nose.

'Listen – ah – I – ah – I was just wondering? You – you wouldn't think of coming with us?'

'No,' she said, still powdering. 'If Paulie had been going to stay here, I'd have stayed. As it is, I'm moving.'

'Where?' The moment he'd said it, he knew it was a mistake.

'I've taken a cheap room,' she said. 'Not that it matters, as I don't suppose I'll be in it much.'

She looked in the mirror to see how he had taken that. 'Matter of fact, my things are outside now. Gerry's giving me a lift.'

Again, she looked at him through the mirror. 'Of course, I'd be willing to stay on here, if you'd leave Paulie with me?'

'Isn't that the height of you,' he said, bitterly. 'You trickster.'

'It's no trick, Ginger. I still feel responsible for Paulie. She's not a child any more and frankly, I don't think you'll be able to supervise her properly.'

'Who's talking,' he said. 'You have a bloody nerve talking of supervising a child.'

She turned from him, her face flushed, and went to the door. She opened the door. 'There's Paulie. I must say good-bye to her.'

He watched her through the opened doorway of the lounge as, impersonating his wife and Paulie's mother, she went up to Paulie, took her by the arms, and stood back looking the child over, as she had done a thousand times before sending Paulie off to a party.

'You'll have to let that hem down soon,' he heard her say. How could she say things like that, this brazen stranger who was going off with another man? 'Good-bye, darling,' he heard her say. 'I'll be over to see you in a day or two. And if there's anything you need or if there's any trouble, you know where to find me.'

Her hands reached out, took Paulie's shoulders and she put her lips forward to kiss the child's pale cheek. (Oh, if those stranger lips would only kiss him!) But he, standing in the doorway of the lounge, saw Paulie look at him as she drew back, suffering but not returning her mother's kiss. Poor bloody lamb, he thought. The pair of us wolves fighting over your body. Ah, Apple, Apple, I'll make all this up to you; from now on you'll be the only one that matters. Let her go; let that stranger go.

'Are you ready, Daddy?' Paulie called.

'Yes, Pet.' He went up to them. 'Good-bye, Vera.'

'Wait,' she said. 'I don't have your new address.'

He begged a sheet of paper from the girl at the desk and wrote the address down. Paulie went out to the waiting taxi. He handed the sheet to Veronica who folded it and slipped it in her purse. 'I'm leaving too, Miss Henson,' she said to the girl at the desk. 'You'll forward my mail, won't you?'

'Yes, Mrs Coffey.'

'Ready, Ginger?'

Silently he went ahead and held the door open for her. In silence they descended the steps to the street. There, its rear door open and Paulie inside, the taxi waited. Farther up the street, on the opposite side, Coffey saw Grosvenor's sporty little car. So she was not bluffing.

'Well?' she said. 'Sure you won't reconsider?'

He saw that she was afraid. Until now, this had been a threat. But now, she must cross the street and get into Grosvenor's car, cross the boundary into deed. She was afraid: she wanted to unpack and go upstairs, to go back with Paulie to the no-man's-land of the last week. And Coffey knew this: he who so rarely knew what her motives were, knew she was begging him to yield. And yet. Suffering J, wasn't she putting him in the wrong again, making it seem as if he were forcing her into infidelity by his stubbornness? He didn't want her to go, he didn't want her in Grosvenor's bed. But dammit, he was sick of this womanly blackmail.

'No,' he said. 'Go on, if you want to.'

'All right. Good-bye, Ginger.'

And yes, by the holy, she was doing it, walking away straight as a sword towards that bastard's car. Mad bloody woman, crossing the street in full view of her husband and daughter, to go off with another man. And why? Even now, she's sure that if only she goes through with it, I'll call her back, give her Paulie, admit she's won. Mad bloody woman.

She reached the car. Grosvenor opened the little red door and she settled in with a show of legs. A hot lust ran through Coffey as the little red door shut on that view of rucked up skirts. There was still time to call her back, time to bring that strange woman to his bed this very night, time to strip those stranger clothes off her and find beneath them a body which miraculously was his by law. Ah dear God! Wasn't it lust that made him want to stop her going off now? Wasn't it jealousy at Grosvenor's getting her? Wasn't it? For it was not pity, it was not love. No, it was not love.

He did not call. He stood watching, an oddly ridiculous figure in his bulky car coat and tiny hat. The engine of Grosvenor's car coughed to life.

'Daddy? Are you coming, Daddy?' Paulie called.

He looked at the taxi: there was one who loved him, one on whom he had no designs. He climbed into the taxi, shutting the door with a slam. He put his hand on Paulie's knee and tried to manage a Big Bear smile. It was starting to snow. Soft blobs of snow fell like moulting down on the cab windows as the little red sports car, its engine roaring, shot out and past them. Coffey and his daughter watched it go, their gaze following it as their taxi driver set his windshield wipers in motion. Chigchik, went the windshield wipers, wiping all out.

Chapter Nine

AND so, in his fortieth year, Ginger Coffey began playing house with a fourteen-year-old girl. It reminded him of his first days with Veronica. Getting used to each other took time. Keep her happy, that was it. Promise her little treats. And soon, when things improved, when he would have one good job instead of two poor ones, when he was not exhausted running from pillar to post, when he could sleep at night and not dream about that woman – soon, it would be plain sailing.

But, in the meantime, he was unsure. What did Paulie need in the way of clothes, for instance? If he gave her money to buy things, she was likely to go out and get something grown-up and unsuitable. He noticed she had taken to wearing nail polish. He mentioned it: she said all the other kids used it. What did he know? It was wrong, he felt, but he must not be cross. She was much alone in the flat, so it was only natural she'd want to ask her school friends in. But he was away day and night. What sort of children were these friends of hers? He worried that she was not studying enough: it was hard to scold her. He wanted to be friends.

And so, each day on his route, he tried to think of things that would interest her. He made plans. In a week or two when he'd be a reporter, they'd have much more time together. And then: 'Listen, Apple, how would you like it if we took up skiing? Wouldn't you like to ski, Pet? And maybe this summer we'll take a little cottage on a lake, just the two of us. We might rent a sail-boat. I've always wanted to sail a boat, ever since I was a little boy. What about you, Apple? Wouldn't you like to sail a boat?'

Ah, if she only were a boy. Or even younger. Remember when she was a tiny girl the fun we used to have playing games like snakes and ladders –

'I was thinking I might buy a draughts board, Apple? Give you a game on my night off, perhaps.'

But she was going to a skating party. Never mind, he would

go to a movie. Ages since he'd seen a film. Or perhaps he would just have an early night. Two jobs could be tiring, you know.

How tiring, he could not tell her. Each night when he shut the door of his bedroom and undressed, he stared at his solitary bed in an act of exorcism, telling himself he was sleepy, dead tired, couldn't wait to hit the hay. Exhausted, he would stretch out; exhausted he would attempt to sleep. But he did not sleep.

An elegant, familiar stranger followed a man into the foyer of an apartment house, followed him up four flights of stairs, waited as he unlocked the door of number eighty-four, smiling familiarly as she stepped across the threshold into a room with bare white walls, prints of Chinese horses and a long low bench of high-fidelity equipment. The man drew the blinds. Music was switched on and that elegant stranger began to remove her skirt, her blouse; walked in garter belt and black stockings to a bar, bending over the bottles, her new short hairdo no longer hiding the white nape of her neck. Sick, Coffey watched as the man went towards her. Sick, he saw the man begin to undress. . . .

Then, never mind, no, no count sheep, dead tired, think of Paulie, think of your promotion next week. J. F. Coffey, of the *Tribune,* think of your brother Tom in Africa, where is he at this minute? Think of little Michel and his robot toy, wonder how the little tyke's getting along. No one to play with. Think. . . .

But who would ever have thought this long drink of water would be such a Casanova? Look at him now, naked, laughing, bending his long knobbly backbone to press a button, releasing the couch bed which shoots out from the wall, standing up, turning to her with the face of that man in the Y.M.C.A. – Wilson, who talked of women as pigs. Oh God, don't watch now what Wilson is doing as he lays her down. Who is she, anyway? Some woman you don't know, someone you never knew, so go to sleep! Of course she's a stranger: Vera never did the like of that with you. You never saw the real Vera excited like that, a Bacchante kissing his hairy flanks. No, that's not Vera, that's some stranger with a beautiful body, a whore in black stockings, abasing herself with that man,

124

letting him pour wine over her breasts, laughing like a lunatic —

But she is not laughing. See? She is crying. Do you see that brown mole on her ribcage? Do you see that white nape, that long hair? Familiar, aren't they? Your Dark Rosaleen.

No chance to sleep, for now he must watch it all, must hear it all, must wait through the laughing, the music, the loud animal cries of fear and pleasure until, in the last hours of darkness, her voice starts to tell the man who she is, tell him how, for love, she crossed the street to get into his little red car, how in her husband's foolishness, the ticket money was spent, leaving her no choice. Telling on and on until the first winter light greyed the ceiling of his room, a false dawn which these two in that other room greeted with cries of drunken delight, becoming faceless, rolling and rolling there as he lay still, hearing them cry love, love, love until exhausted, they fell asleep in each other's arms. Then he too would sleep, a short sleep, murdered by the shrilling of his alarm clock. He would rise, put on the coffee, make the toast and waken his daughter. To sit haggard in the true dawn of his tiny kitchenette, the lights still lit in the winter darkness, a darkness presaging the night to come, the visions still in wait.

'Daddy, have you got a cold? You look pale.'

'No, Pet. Just tired.'

'Well, no wonder, working day and ni – '

'Won't be long, Pet. Matter of fact I'm doing very well down at the *Tribune*. I know they're pleased with my work there. I'm almost certain that old MacGregor's going to promote me to reporter any day now. Then I'll be able to drop the other job and spend more time at home. Tell you what. As soon as I get my promotion I'll take you out and stand you a bang-up dinner. Dress up in your best and – '

'Yes, but Daddy, you'd better hurry now. It's after seven.'

No faith. Her voice, like Vera's, cutting him off. Well, she'd see. On Friday. On Friday, his ship might come in.

On Friday he hurried to the *Tribune* office as soon as he had completed his delivery rounds. His pay cheque contained no notice of changed status. So . . . so as he had learned the *Tribune* style and had spent two weeks as a galley slave, wasn't it time MacGregor was reminded about that promotion? It was, it was indeed. He went to MacGregor's office. As usual, the door was open. Clarence, the fat man, stood on the right of MacGregor's desk, notebook at the ready. MacGregor himself was holding a telephone conversation with the *Tribune*'s publisher. 'Right, Mr Hound ... Yes, sir ... Right away, Mr Hound. Good-bye, sir.'

He replaced the receiver. His eye picked out Coffey in the doorway. 'Come in. State your business.'

'Well, sir. I've been in the proofroom two weeks, as of today.'

'Yes?'

'You see, sir, you said that I should learn the *Tribune* style. I think, sir, that I've got the hang of it now.'

'Well,' said MacGregor. 'Nice to know somebody's wurrking in this loafers' paradise. Good day to you, Coffey.'

'But – but I came to see you, sir, to see if perhaps there'd be an opening as a reporter.'

'We're still short staffed in the proofroom, aren't we, Clarence?'

'Yes, chief.'

'Very short staffed, eh, Clarence?'

'Yes, sir. Very short.'

Mr Macgregor looked at Coffey. 'We're short staffed,' he said.

'But, sir ... I've been counting on this promotion.'

'Tell him how many men want to become *Tribune* reporters, Clarence.'

'Dozens,' Clarence said. 'Literally dozens, Mr Mac.'

'So, we're not short of reporters at the moment, Coffey. You'll have to hang on.'

'But, I – ' Coffey felt his face hot. 'But, I have a family, sir. I mean, I can't support my family indefinitely on a proof-reader's wages.'

'What are you getting now?'

'Forty dollars a week, sir.'

'I'll gi' you forty-five. Now, go back to your wurrk.'

'Thank you, sir. I'd rather have the promotion, sir. I mean, forty-five dollars a week is still very little.'

'Did you ever hear such cheek?' Mr MacGregor asked Clarence. 'Did you ever, in your morrtal life?'

Clarence looked at Coffey with shock, reproach and disgust. But Coffey did not budge. There was a time and a tide. 'Well, sir. I . . .'

'Well, *what*?'

'I'd still like to know definitely when I may hope to be made a reporter, sir.'

'How the hell do I know?' MacGregor shouted. 'When I get a replacement for you, that's when. Maybe in a week or two.'

'In two weeks, sir? I mean, is that a promise? Because otherwise I don't see much point in my staying on.'

'All right, two weeks,' MacGregor said. 'You have my wurrd.'

'Thank you, sir.'

'Now, take your arse out of here. I have wurrk to do.'

'Yes, sir. And thank you, sir.'

Two more weeks. Still, it was better than a kick in the pants, wasn't it? A little victory. He hurried off to the *Tribune* cafeteria, had a quick sandwich, then phoned Paulie to tell her his good news.

'Listen, Pet. That promotion I was telling you about. We've only got a fortnight to go.'

'That's good,' she said, in an unbelieving voice. 'Daddy, Mummy was here today.'

'Was she?' He had been wondering when *that* would start.

'Yes, she took me out shopping,' Paulie said. 'She put down ten dollars on a new parka for me.'

He was hurt. 'But I could have bought you one, Pet. Why didn't you tell me you needed it?'

Paulie ignored this. 'Anyway, Mummy wants to come and visit me tomorrow. She wants to see you too.'

'I hope you told her we're getting along like a house on fire, Apple? Did you?'

'Yes, Daddy. Daddy – I have to hang up now. Kettle's boiling.'

He fumbled, replacing the receiver. All the good had gone out of his news with that mention of Veronica. Ah, hadn't he been the fool to think she would let them alone? Now she would start sneaking around to the flat behind his back, buying Paulie presents with Grosvenor's money, turning the child against him.

Tiny lights appeared before his eyes. He fumbled, feeling for the phone booth door. For a moment he blacked out, felt like falling. Oh, Dear Lord, if anything happened to him, what would become of Paulie? No insurance, nothing. His child would have to go and live with those two; would have to watch those things.

Steady as she goes, he warned himself. Steady now. If you go on like this they'll come for you in a little blue van and lock you up, so they will. Steady the Buffs. Put that woman out of your mind once and for all. You'll have to get rid of her.

But how? She was still his wife, the mother of his child. Divorce her. Get custody. Divorce her!

'Paddy?' a voice said. 'What's the matter?'

Uncomprehendingly, Coffey looked up, saw Fox buying cigarettes at the cafeteria counter.

'Are you sick?' Fox said. 'You look funny.'

'No,' he said. He joined Fox at the counter, knitting his hands in the steeple game. *Here's the church.* . . . He had been sick, that was it. Sick because he somehow believed he would get her back: sick because he had wanted her back. The cure was plain: divorce her.

'Come and have a beer,' Fox said. 'Pay night. It'll make you feel better.'

'No,' he said. 'I'll be better soon. Very soon.'

That night he went to bed in peace: he would sleep, he was sure. But the elegant stranger smiled. She sat in a restaurant, cigarette smoke stippling upwards in a thin spiral past her smiling face. Coffey, watching, saw her hold out a glass. That was not his ring on her finger. The ring with which he had wed her was a gold ring: it had belonged to his mother. This was a thin platinum circle, third finger, left hand, with these presents, kiss a new bride. Friends surrounded the newly-weds. An older woman leaned forward across the wedding feast and said: 'Didn't he soldier with my husband once? And was something in a distillery?' And the stranger who was once Veronica replied: 'No, he was just a Good Doggy.' Someone said: 'Uniform, would you believe it, with *Tiny Ones* on the cap? Diapers, it was. He delivers them to us every week. Of course, after that first week, I always made sure it was the maid who received him. Not to embarrass him, the creature.' The wedding guests shook their heads in sympathy and congratulated the bride on her fortunate escape. They thought her a nice woman: they had not seen her as he had, naked and frenzied with all those men in all those rooms. They had not seen her walk across the street in full view of her child and husband, showing her legs as she stepped into her lover's little red car. In their eyes she was a woman who had wasted her best years as wife to a glorified secretary; a woman who had saved herself before it was too late. She and her new husband would take tea with Madame Pandit. They would be invited to dinner by Louie, the Prime Minister of Canada. The Prime Minister would ask for the signed original of a G.G. cartoon. There would be a good little doggy in the border of that cartoon.

He lay in the darkness waiting for that first false light which would banish her and bring him sleep. He would divorce her and then he would rest in peace. Do you hear me, Vera? Don't laugh! I'm going to divorce you.

Yet, on Saturday, when the door bell rang and Paulie went to answer it, Coffey waited in the living-room of their little flat, his lips dry, his mouth betraying him in a hopeful smile. And when she came in, wearing a new and unfamiliar hat, he was gripped once more with a painful sense of loss. Look how strange we are to each other, all of us. Even Paulie, Paulie who takes her mother's coat to hang in the closet and now, formal hostess, asks if we would like some tea.

'Yes, that would be lovely,' Veronica said. And Paulie withdrew, the mistress of the house, while Veronica, a guest, waited to be entertained.

'Small, isn't it?' she said, looking around.

He did not answer.

'And how are you getting along, Ginger? I mean at your work?'

9 129

He said stiffly that he had received a raise; that in two weeks he would be a reporter. Everything was grand, thank you.

'But in the meantime these jobs must leave you very little time to spend with Paulie?'

'We manage,' he said. 'And it won't be for long. How are *you* getting on, Veronica?'

'Oh, I like my job very much. The woman who owns the shop speaks French but her English is poor. So we complement each other. As a matter of fact I made over sixty dollars with commissions last week. That's why I'm buying Paulie a new coat.'

'*I* could have bought it.'

'Ah, but you didn't, did you? And besides, I like doing things with my own money, Ginger. After all these years it's such a marvellous feeling to be solvent.'

He did not reply because, at that moment, Paulie came in with the tea tray. He noticed a box of assorted biscuits beside the teapot. Vera's favourites. In the time he and Paulie had been together, had she ever bought one of Daddy's favourite treats? No, she had not and watching the pair of them, listening to their womany voices, he felt alone, shut out, the heavy-fingered male. Listen to them, would you, chatting away like two old pals at a charity bazaar; Veronica going on about this bloody hat shop she worked in and Paulie regaling her with tales about the teachers at school, not seeming to know or care that her mother was a stranger who now had no mortal interest in Paulie and her school. Whereas he – all week he had hoped that Paulie would tell him about her little doings. He would have loved to hear her crack.

'More tea, Mummy? Daddy, would you get us some more hot water?'

He went into the kitchen and put the kettle back on the boil. The watched pot boiled all too fast for him. When he took the hot water back into the living-room, they were still at it, heads close, hens clucking. He sat across the room from them unnoticed, wishing she would go.

But no. After two more cups of tea, Veronica settled back comfortably on the sofa, showing her long, slim legs. He had always hated her carelessness in showing herself. Careless? It had been deliberate, probably. She blew a reed of smoke and said to Paulie: 'Look, darling, I wonder if you'd let your father and I have a little chat? Just for a few minutes?'

'All right,' Paulie said. 'I have to run down to the store for a moment. I'll see you when I come back.'

Paulie got her coat and went out, no secret look at him, nothing. And as soon as she had gone, the stranger sat up straight on the sofa, took her knee in her laced hands, letting her skirt fall away distractingly, and said: 'I've been thinking about Paulie. You and I must come to some arrangement about her.'

'What arrangement?' he said.

'Well, first of all, the expense; her school things and clothes and so on. And then there's this question of her being left alone so much. I could come in the evenings?'

'Could you?' he said sourly, watching that slim leg swing.

'Yes. I could be here at a quarter to six most evenings and I'd make supper and stay a while and –'

She talked. He watched her lips move; those lips which at night kissed a stranger's hairy flanks. Talking, making noises of motherhood, that mouth which each night he heard cry out in desire. He felt his own mouth open. To kiss those lips, to bite into that white neck, to take her now, tumble her back, tear the clothes from that stranger body which all week he had not been able to touch.

'So, what do you say, Ginger? Are you listening?'

. . .

'Ginger? What's the matter?'

The tea tray clattered, a cup fell sideways on its saucer. He lumbered across the room, his hands gripping her shoulders, his heavy body tumbling her backwards on the sofa. He tried to kiss her, his hands pulling up her skirt, quieting her hands as they tried to push him away. He felt her breasts come free within her dress as a shoulder strap snapped and heard his own breathing as he tried to control her kicking, struggling body.

A sudden pain made his eyes water. He let her go. She had caught both ends of his moustache and was pulling upwards by

131

the short hairs. She wrenched up cruelly, then pulled down, bringing him stumbling off the sofa on to his knees beside her. His hands caught her wrists, stopping the pain.

'Let go, Vera. Let go!'

She let him go. He stared at her, tears of hurt in his eyes, his lust lost at last in foolish pain.

'Are you out of your mind?' she said. 'You've torn my dress and my bra. My God, Ginger, what's the matter with you? How dare you?'

How dare he? Slowly, he got up off his knees. She had unbuttoned the front of her dress and now, one white shoulder out of it, was searching inside for the strap of her bra. Her hair had fallen over her eyes and there was a red mark on her neck as though she had been scratched. With an effort he looked at the carpet as, her dress fully open, she lifted one breast up, fitting on the ripped brassière. And all this time, scolding him. 'Getting me up here and leaping on me like a lunatic. What if Paulie had seen you? For goodness' sake control yourself.'

'I'm sorry,' he said.

'You should be. Look at that. You've torn the dress too. And I haven't even paid for it yet.'

'Grosvenor will pay for it,' he shouted. 'Let him pay for it.'

'That's enough, Ginger. I came here to see what I could do for Paulie. That doesn't give you any right to attack me.'

'No right? I'm your husband.'

'You *were*. You dirty rotten pig, trying to, just trying to – just your own dirty desires!'

She was crying: wouldn't you know? 'Ah, stop your whining,' he said. 'I'll bet that's nothing to what your fancy man does to you every night in the week.'

She stood up, buttoning her dress, distractedly trying to tidy her hair. 'I'm not going to stay here and listen to you. I want to help Paulie. I'm her mother, just remember that. I've got a right to help her.'

'You've got no right,' he said. 'Go on back to Mister Canadian Viewpoint. You deserted Paulie and you deserted me. I'm going to divorce you, do you hear? And when I do, I'm getting custody of Paulie.'

She sat still. Only her eyes moved in her face as she looked him up and down. Eyes bright with what he had once thought to be her bad temper, but which now he knew as her hate. 'Divorce?' she said. 'That's fine. I want one as much as you do. More.'

'Do you, Vera? Then you can help me pay for it.'

'Gerry will pay for it,' she said. 'I'll tell him to get in touch with you.'

'Why should Gerry pay for it?'

'Because he wants to marry me.'

He looked at his hands, joined them in the steeple game. Was that true? Would Grosvenor marry her? As they sat there in silence a key turned in the front door and Paulie came in with a bag of groceries and the afternoon paper. He stood up, protecting Paulie, afraid of losing her. 'You're just in time, Pet,' he said. 'Your mother's leaving.'

'So soon?' Paulie turned towards him and, suddenly, winked.

Veronica saw the wink. She stood up, walked to the hall closet and put on her overcoat. Then turned, trying to save her dignity, trying to smile and say the things a guest might say. 'Paulie, dear, you're turning into a very good housekeeper. Everything's so neat and tidy. Well, good-bye, Ginger. Good-bye, Paulie. And thanks for the tea.'

This time, she did not try to kiss Paulie. She opened the front door herself and looked at him, meaningfully, 'I'll have Gerry get in touch with you about that other thing on Monday. All right?'

'All right,' he said. The door shut. He looked around the living-room, smelling once again that unfamiliar scent, seeing the remains of her cake on a plate, her lipsticked butts in an ash-tray. He picked them up and carried them into the living-room and opened the door to dissipate the scented smell. He saw his face in the window-pane. That sad impostor considered him: he considered the lack of dignity in the actions of that graceless fool. Look at you. Had you no pride, no self-respect, jumping on her, letting her humiliate you?

He stood, staring at his image. Was that man really him?

'Daddy? What was that she said about Gerry Grosvenor getting in touch with you?'

The mirror man watched from the window-pane as he went to the sofa, sat down and absently bit into one of his wife's favourite sandwich creams. Tiny crumbs powdered his red moustache. 'Come here a minute, Pet,' he said. He waited until Paulie sat on the sofa beside him. 'Your mother and I are going to get a divorce.'

'But Catholics aren't allowed to get a divorce, Daddy.'

He sighed. 'Your mother and I aren't real Catholics any more. You know that.'

'Oh.'

'You see,' he said. 'Grosvenor wants to marry your mother. And she wants to marry him.'

In a gesture so rare that he had no courage to tell her he did not deserve it, Paulie slid off the sofa and sat at his feet, hugging his ankles. 'Never mind, Daddy,' she said. 'I'll look after you.'

Awkwardly, his hand stroked her head. 'You won't mind?'

'Of course I won't mind, Daddy.'

He touched her pale cheek. She loved him, yes she loved him. She was his, not Vera's; his own and only child. Wasn't that enough for any man, wasn't that a victory? He must prove worthy of that love. But as he decided this, he became afraid. How could he keep her love without a promise or two? Afraid, that foolish sad impostor spoke up. 'Oh, Pet,' the impostor said. 'We'll have a grand time, I promise you. You'll see, Pet, you'll see.'

'Yes, Daddy.' But why did she move her head away from his touch? Ah, dear God. She too was tired of promises.

Chapter Ten

ON Monday Veronica would have Grosvenor get in touch with him. He took that to mean that Grosvenor would telephone. But at four that afternoon as he returned his *Tiny Ones* truck to the depot, Grosvenor's little red midget car was parked outside Mr Mountain's office. His first thought was that Grosvenor must not see him in uniform. Skirting the little car, he drove his truck to the far end of the depot yard. He got out on the side away from the little car and began to double back towards the locker-room under cover of the line of parked vehicles.

About twenty yards from the locker-room, he ran out of cover. He was crouched behind a truck, trying to plan his next move, when a footstep from behind made him turn.

'Hello, Ginger. Thought I saw you.'

His face hot with rage and humiliation, Coffey went through the useless pretence of fixing his boot buckle. Then, unable to look Grosvenor in the face, he straightened up and turned towards the locker-room. 'I'm in a hurry,' he said. 'I have to change.'

'I'll come with you if I may?' Without waiting for permission, Grosvenor followed Coffey across the yard and into the locker-room where several other day-shift drivers were changing into street clothes. 'I came here because I wasn't sure how I could catch you,' Grosvenor said. 'You're a hard man to see, these days.'

Coffey, unable to think of a reply, stripped off his uniform and stood in his shirt, his legs oddly conspicuous in the heavy red underdrawers issued to drivers. 'I came to talk about the divorce,' Grosvenor said. 'Veronica says you're willing to go through with it. I think that's wise of you.'

The other drivers were listening. 'Would you mind shutting your gob about my private affairs until we get out of here?' Coffey said in an angry whisper.

'Oh – sorry.'

In awkward fury Coffey unbuttoned the underwear and stood naked before his enemy; remembered that naked was how he imagined Grosvenor each night. Hurriedly, he began to dress in his own clothes.

'Maybe when you're through, Ginger, we can go and have a drink some place?'

'You can drive me down to the *Tribune*,' Coffey said. 'But I'll not drink with you.'

'I'm sorry you feel that way, Ginger.'

Coffey did not answer. He finished dressing and set off across the yard to check out his day's receipts. When he had finished, Grosvenor was waiting in the little red car, its door open to receive him as passenger. He got in, his knees rising uncomfortably to meet his chest, thinking of her show of legs as she got into this car that awful day. It had not been deliberate. In this car, she could not help showing her legs. He had been wrong.

Wrong. Grosvenor started the car with a loud throttling roar. They shot through the *Tiny Ones* gate and into the street.

'The thing to settle is who's going to act as guilty party,' Grosvenor said. 'Now, of course, you'll think it should be her. But, if Veronica's the guilty party, the divorce will be far from a rubber stamp affair. You see, our Canadian divorce laws –'

'For crying out loud, will you stop lecturing?' Coffey said. 'Just tell me the quickest way.'

'The easiest way is to set up a false adultery scene,' Grosvenor said. 'I know a lawyer who can arrange it. They provide everything. A girl, a detective, the works. You check in to a hotel with the girl and half an hour later the detective shows up. Case is heard by the Senate divorce committee in Ottawa. It's a cinch.'

'And Vera gets custody of Paulie,' Coffey said. 'No thanks.'

'No, no,' Grosvenor said. 'Vera and I intend to get married and have children of our own, if possible. I know *I* don't want a fourteen-year-old daughter.'

Involuntarily, Coffey fingered the part in his moustache. Was that why she was marrying Grosvenor? To get the kids they'd never had?

'Another thing we talked about,' Grosvenor said, 'was the

136

expense of a divorce. Veronica thinks that because you're going to have the burden of supporting Paulie, it's only fair that we pay for the divorce thing. I agree. After all, you're pretty hard up at the moment. It wouldn't be fair to saddle you with an additional financial burden at this time.'

Coffey, his face hot, stared at the dashboard of the car. The ampere needle flicked, wig, wag, one side to the other. She went wig wag from him to Grosvenor, Grosvenor to him, telling each what she knew. Poor Ginger's too hard up to pay, you see. Now, Gerry, if you pop down and talk to him. Then tell me.

Last night he had not slept until dawn. Last night he had watched her in bed with Grosvenor as she laughed and made a story of poor Ginger's attempt to rape her. And Grosvenor had laughed too. Grosvenor, sitting here beside him, probably knew every secret thought or action he'd confided to Veronica in fifteen years of marriage. Bitch!

'All right,' Coffey said, in a hoarse voice. 'I want rid of her. You pay for the divorce and I'll be the target. When can we get it over with?'

'What about next Saturday night?' Grosvenor said. 'You don't work on Saturday nights, Vera says.'

Coffey nodded. 'Where?' he said. 'And how?'

'There's a hotel called the Clarence which isn't too particular. I'll try to set it up with the lawyer for Saturday night. You go there at ten. I'll have a girl waiting for you in the lobby. The detective will be along later.'

'Not much later,' Coffey said. 'I want to be home at midnight. I have my daughter to think of.'

'Of course. Shouldn't take more than an hour. I'll phone you and let you know the details, okay?'

Again, Coffey nodded. They drove the rest of the way in silence. When they arrived at the *Tribune*, Grosvenor reached over and put his hand on Coffey's knee. Coffey stared at that hand. It was very white, backed with very black hairs. He saw the hairy flanks she kissed in those nightly scenarios. Quickly, he moved his knee away.

'I just wanted to say thanks,' Grosvenor said, sounding hurt. For the first time since he had got into the car, Coffey looked

Grosvenor full in the face. It was an ordinary face. A year ago he had not even known it existed, yet now it was joined to his in a resemblance stronger than brotherhood, in an intimacy he and his true brother would never share.

What chemistry of desire made Grosvenor willing to face a surly husband to discuss the settlement of Veronica's divorce? What made him willing to pay for that divorce, to marry another man's woman, a woman older than he? Coffey did not know. He knew only that it was the same violent illness which, after fifteen years of marriage, had suddenly revived his own desire, making him prepared to commit any equal folly. He could not hate Grosvenor, for Grosvenor in turn would suffer the same feminine ritual of confidence and betrayal. He felt compassion for Grosvenor. He was cured of this sickness: Grosvenor had inherited it.

'Good-bye,' he said, and held out his hand.

Surprised, Grosvenor shook hands. 'Till Saturday then?' Grosvenor said.

'Saturday it is.'

His decision made, Coffey went to bed that night, confident that all his fevers had passed. He went to sleep and slept. He did not dream. In the morning Paulie heard him singing in the kitchen.

'Somebody's in good form,' she said, coming in, her hair in curlers, her toothbrush in her hand.

Coffey turned an egg on the pan, still singing. 'Why not?' he said. 'Less than two weeks to go, Pet. I wonder what sort of a journalist I'll make? I wonder now, will they send me off to far away places? That's a great thing about the journalistic profession, you never know where you'll end up. You see, you're very much your own boss in the journalistic field. Ah, it just shows you, doesn't it?'

'Shows you what?' Paulie said.

'That the old saying is true. The darkest hour is just before the dawn. You have to remember that. Hope, now that's what you need. While there's hope, there's life.'

'Somebody's in a very philosophical mood this morning.'

'And why not? Do you know another thing I was thinking

138

this morning, Pet? The old saying – man wasn't born to live alone. Do you know, that's a lot of malarkey. Man was, and the sooner he faces up to it, the better.'

'Does that mean you want to get rid of me?' Paulie asked.

'Never!' he kissed her on her brow, cold cream and all. 'By the way,' he said. 'That reminds me. I have to go out on Saturday night. I won't be back till nearly midnight.'

'But, that's perfect,' Paulie said. 'I was going to ask some of the kids over, anyway. Maybe you could go out early and leave us the place to ourselves?'

Well, he could go to a film, he supposed. Ah, he wasn't like some people: he knew that children hated grown-ups around when they were having a party. 'Good idea,' he said cheerfully. 'I'll do that. Go to a film, or something, and leave you a clear field.'

On Friday, when he returned from his *Tiny Ones* round, Mr Mountain handed him a message which had come in during the day. It was to call Mr Grosvenor before seven. So when Coffey arrived at the *Tribune*, he rang Grosvenor at home.

'Ginger? Good, I've been trying to get you. It's all set for tomorrow night. You're to go to the Clarence Hotel at nine forty-five. Go to the bar and there'll be a girl there wearing a green overcoat and a black fur hat. Her name is Melody Ward. Got that? Melody Ward. Have a drink with her, then take her upstairs. There'll be a visitor at ten-forty. Okay? And Ginger – you don't even have to pay the hotel bill. It's taken care of.'

'Fair enough,' Coffey said. He hung up, feeling like a man in a thriller. It wasn't sordid at all, it was an adventure. Melody Ward. He even found himself wondering would she be pretty? He did not think of Veronica. Because he was finished with all that, you see. He was cured.

Saturday evening, he returned from his delivery round in good spirits. He finished his supper at seven and, determined to be agreeable, put on his coat and hat and went out, leaving the flat free for the children when they came. He told Paulie he would be home about twelve.

It was a clear cold night, electric and anticipant. When Coffey alighted from a bus in the centre of the city, he was at once caught up in the hurry of a Saturday night spree. Neon lights promised, spelled pleasures, performed tricks. A neon Highlander danced a jig over a clothier's, a comic chicken popped its head in and out of the Q in a BAR–B–Q sign, a neon hockey player jiggled his stick over a tavern doorway. In movie house entrances, bathed in the fairground brightness of million-watt ceilings, diminished and humbled by enormous posters proclaiming current attractions, anticipant girls fidgeted, waiting for their dates; solitary boys consulted wrist watches and dragged on cigarettes, nervously checking their brilliantined pompadours in reflections from the glass-walled cashier's shrine. And as Coffey strolled slow, slower than the crowd, not sure what to do, he was swept up in a change of shows and eddied into one of these entrances. He stood undecided under the myriad lights, watching the anticipant girls smile and wave in sudden recognition ; the boys drop their cigarettes and hurry forward; the pairing, the claiming, the world go two by two.

Watching, he absently stroked the parting in his moustache: felt a sadness. All these thousands, hurrying to meet; yet he was alone. Saturday night and they came down in their thousands to laugh, to dance, to sit in the dark watching coloured screens, holding hands, sharing joys. While he waited to meet some unknown woman in a strange bar, to go upstairs with that stranger to an unknown room, perhaps to lie down on a bed with her, in make believe of an intimacy he now shared with no one. And when it was over, he would have no one: not even Paulie. For Paulie had put him out tonight so that she, with other youngsters, could laugh and dance, listening to shared music.

He had no one. He was three thousand miles from home, across half a frozen continent and the whole Atlantic ocean. Only one person in this city, only one person in the world, really knew him now: knew the man he once was, the man he now was. One person in the whole world who fifteen years ago in Saint Pat's in Dalkey had stood beside him in a white veil for richer or for poorer, in sickness and in health until death.

One person had known him: or known most of him. Would anyone ever know him again?

Well now, enough of that. Do something.

He went up to the cashier's little glass shrine; put a dollar in the opening. The cashier pressed a button and an aluminium machine spat a ticket at him. The cashier made change by manipulating another machine. A nickel dropped into its little metal change bowl. He picked it up. That was the way of this world. You saw someone in a glass cage, stepped up, exchanged things, but never touched. Oh, come on now! Enough of that, I said.

At the back of the theatre, penned two by two behind a velvet rope, a line of people waited. The usherette, a girl not much older than Paulie came up to him. 'Single, sir? We have seats in the first six rows.'

There was something about her: her accent was not Canadian. He smiled at her, drawn by that immigrant bond, and followed her from the lighted area into the darkness of the theatre. Poor kid. Her scapula bone stuck out at right angles against the maroon stuff of her uniform. New Canadians: thousands like her came here each year; thousands started all over again in humble circs. You heard such stories: lawyers forced to take work as checkers, doctors as lab assistants, professors driving trucks. And still they came, from every country in Europe, riding in old railroad colonist cars to the remote provinces of this cold, faraway land. Why did they do it? For their children's sake, it was said. Well, and wasn't he driving a truck now for his daughter's sake? Wasn't he one of them? Wasn't he too a man who would always be a stranger here, never at home in this land where he had not grown up. Yes: he too.

The girl's flashlight showed him an almost empty row, lowering its beam as she waited for him to enter his seat. He wanted to stop, take her by the arm, lead her back up the aisle into the light again. To say: 'I too am an immigrant,' to compare impressions, reminisce, to tell the things that immigrants tell. But the flashlight beam snapped off. He could no longer see her. He sat down, purblinded by the coloured images on the huge screen above. He looked around. Here were the solitaries. Some slept, some slumped in morose contemplation of the film giantess kicking yard-long legs, while some, like he, ignored her and peered about them in the shadows, hoping for a glance, a promise of company.

How long was it since he'd sat down here. Years, years. But he remembered: mitching away long school afternoons in the picture houses off O'Connell Street, huddled down in his seat for fear someone might see him and tell his parents. And later, as a university student, the lonely Saturday nights in cheap front seats, hoping that some American daydream would banish the private misery of having no girl, no place to go. Well, and was he going back to all that? For if he lost Veronica now, who would have him, a man nearly forty with a grown-up daughter on his hands? Wouldn't he end his days here among the solitaries?

Enough of that. He tried watching the film, but somehow the filmed America no longer seemed true. He could not believe in this America, this land that half the world dreams of in dark front seats in cities and villages half a world away. What had it in common with his true America? For Canada was America; the difference a geographer's line. What had these Hollywood revels to do with the facts of life in a cold New World?

At half past eight, unable to watch the film any longer, he went upstairs and sat in the lobby, waiting to go to the Clarence Hotel, waiting to meet a girl in a green coat and a black fur hat. He thought about her, Miss Melody Ward. How many of her customers really went to bed with her? Did she charge you extra for that? That made him smile. By the holy, it would be great gas to charge Grosvenor for that.

At nine-fifteen he left the theatre and began to walk towards Windsor Street. He thought of Veronica and wondered if she were thinking of him this minute as he started off to end it? And if she were thinking of him now, didn't she feel as he did, some sorrow that tonight, after all those years, it was ending? She must feel sorrow, he decided. Anybody would.

The Clarence was a small hotel opposite the Canadian Pacific Railway terminus. The neon sign over its side entrance read *Montmorency Room* and a display case showing photographs of glossy nonentities advertised *Continuous Entertainment*. He went in. The hotel lobby was on the right and consisted of a single desk-cum-cigar stand with three armchairs in a row facing the street window. At the desk was a night reception clerk and in the armchairs three old men stared out at the snow, watching traffic. On the left, in the Montmorency Room a pallid French-Canadian sang a cowboy lament to an audience of eight drinkers. Coffey entered, sat down at a table and ordered a rye. There was no girl in a green coat and a black fur hat. He was glad. Wasn't this whole thing daft? Why should he go through with it? He would not go through with it. Stranger or not, Veronica was his lawful wedded wife: his, not Grosvenor's. Why should Grosvenor have her? Why should he be the one who was left alone?

But the clock over the bar said nine thirty-seven and it was too late to ring Grosvenor and call this off. The girl would be here any minute, the detective was probably on his way already, the lawyer had arranged things –

And – and all his life, he had hated scenes, hated making a fuss. It was too late now, far too late to change things, because ... because at that moment a girl walked in. She wore a green overcoat and a black fur hat. She went up to the bar, spoke to the barman, then turned and looked around the room. She looked at him. And, by J, she was not the sort of girl who'd stand any nonsense. She was tall and pretty and tough. And, by J, she was coming right at him!

'You're Mr Coffey, right?' she said.

'Yes.' He stood up.

'The moustache,' she said. 'I was told to look out for it.'

Yes, he said, and would she please sit down. And what would she have to drink? A brandy? He called the waiter. He joined his hands under the table. *Here's the church* – How could he get out of it now? *And here's the steeple* – Because she wasn't the sort who would let him off lightly – *Open the gates* – good-looking too, in other circumstances he wouldn't half-mind –

The waiter brought a brandy and Coffey paid. The French-Canadian singer sang a song about Paree, Paree. The girl sipped her brandy, listening to the song. *And here's the minister coming upstairs* – Too late, wasn't it, of course it was! Besides, it wasn't his idea, it was Grosvenor's, all Grosvenor's fault –

And here's the minister ... Grosvenor's fault. He remembered sitting in the Ritz, his hands joined as now in the steeple game. And remembered what Veronica said in the Ritz: Gerry's fault? Not your fault, of course. Never your fault, is it, Ginger? –

He unclasped his hands and looked nervously at the girl. What sort of man would worry more about offending a strange whore than about losing his wife? Ah, dear God. The sort of man who had been ready to walk away from Grosvenor's apartment door one night for fear of a scene, who had only rung the bell that night because some total stranger gave him a suspicious look. The sort of sad impostor who now, seeing Miss Melody Ward applaud the singer, raised his hands and applauded too.

The singer bowed and went behind a curtain. The lights went on. 'Well,' said the girl, putting down her glass. 'I guess we'd better go up, huh?'

Who was he to talk about in sickness and in health until death? He, who half an hour ago had thought of taking this strange whore to bed, not of fifteen years of marriage. Who was he to condemn Veronica?

Miss Melody Ward stood up. She preceded him across the room and waited for him in the lobby. Through the reflection from the street window, the three armchair ancients watched him join her.

'Okay,' she said. 'Now sign us in as Mr and Mrs. Your right name, mind. But give an out-of-town address, like Toronto, huh? And act sort of loaded so's the clerk remembers you.'

He began, his large trembling dignity compromised by a sudden mulish stammer. 'Nu-no,' he said. 'No, I – can't.'

'Oh, come on,' she said. 'Don't worry.'

He avoided her eye, looked at the linoleum squares of the lobby floor.

'Oh, listen,' she said. 'This happens all the time. A lot of guys are nervous, so what? I mean, you don't have to do anything, see? I mean, we just go up and have a drink in the room and then I take a shower. I'm in the shower when the lawyer's man comes.'

The three old men sat silent in their chairs, their faces fixedly vacant in the manner of surreptitious listeners.

'So come on,' she said. 'I won't eat you.'

If only she knew: to come would be so easy. They were all waiting: the girl, the lawyer's man, the desk clerk, Veronica. All trying to shame him into compliance.

'No,' he said. 'I'm going home.'

'Well, for Christ's sake,' Miss Melody Ward began, her voice rising to a terrifying decibel count. 'What are you playing at, huh? I mean to say, I came all the way down here, I gave up another appointment –'

'You'll be paid,' he said. 'Good night.'

And turned away, his military manner failed completely in the desk clerk's curious stare, in the peering and whispering of the old men as he fled towards the sanctuary of the hotel door. Outside, he stood for a moment in the slush of the gutter and raised his face to the sky. Snow fell, wetting his cheeks. He felt his body tremble. Yes, it *was* a victory.

He went home. He had promised Paulie that he would stay out until her party was over, but in his victorious mood, he forgot all that. Somehow or other he must try to get Veronica back; that was all he thought of now. And so, at ten-fifteen, he paused outside the door of his flat, hearing from within that loud rockabilly nonsense that Paulie loved so well. He hesitated, but Suffering J, wasn't this *his* home as well as hers? Why shouldn't he take the bull by the horns twice in one night? He let himself in.

In the tiny living-room, furniture had been cleared against the walls and two boys danced cheek to cheek with two of Paulie's schoolmates. The girls he knew; like Paulie they were children playing at being women, their childish bodies tricked out in low-necked blouses and ballerina skirts; their faces unnaturally aged by lipstick and eye shadow.

The boys were older: they wore leather windbreakers, western style shirts, bootlace ties. Peculiar, brilliantined haircuts gave them the appearance of wet sea-birds. Where was Paulie?

He turned. In the narrow trough of kitchen, a third sea-bird faced him, eyes shut, spread hands distributed, one over Paulie's small rump, one on her back, pressing her breasts tight against him. Paulie's body moved in time to the music but her feet did not. Eyes shut, her pale face flowered upwards to the electric light bulb, she undulated in a fixed position, rubbing against the boy .

Coffey took three steps into the living-room and knocked the player arm off its thundering course. Eyes opened. The dancers stopped. The arm scratched in the silence, its needle frustrated: slipping, circling, slipping again.

'Daddy?' Paulie said, coming out of the kitchen. 'What time is it?'

But Coffey did not look at her. He pointed to the boy behind her. 'What's *your* name?' he said.

'Bruno,' the boy said. He had a slight inward cast to his eyes which gave him an aggrieved look. 'Why? You Paulie's Dad?'

'Do you go to school?' Coffey asked.

'Me?' the boy seemed puzzled by the question. He turned to Paulie. 'What'd *I* do?' he said.

'No, Daddy, Bruno doesn't go to school. He works.'

'I thought you said these were all school friends, Apple?'

One of the girls giggled. The boys exchanged glances and winks. 'Apple?' one of them said to Paulie. 'That what they call you at home?'

All laughed, except Paulie.

'Is there something funny about that?' Coffey said to the boy.

The boy, caught in Coffey's stare, was silent. The girls, saving him, said it was late, they really must go. The boys said they would drive them in their car. They ignored Coffey as did Paulie, who rushed around, helping them find their coats, talking pointedly about how sorry she was; it was early; it was a pity they couldn't stay.

'Night, kid,' said the boy who had been dancing with her.

'Be seeing you – *Apple*,' another boy said.

'Good night, Mister – ah – Coffey.'

'Good night.'

'Good night.' Paulie shut the door and went into the kitchen to clear away the litter of coke bottles and plates while her father started to restore the furniture to its former scheme.

'Why did you call me Apple in front of them?' an angry voice said from the kitchen.

'I'm sorry.'

'And why did you come home when you said you'd be late? You've ruined my party.'

He pulled the sofa back into place and paused, his lips shut tight under his moustache. After all he'd been through to-night! 'Come here a minute,' he called.

She came from the kitchen and stood in the doorway. Her face was pale. Her eyes were bright. Anger? She was his girl; she looked like him. But – he saw Veronica there. Not anger, no. Hate.

'Those boys,' he said. 'They weren't school friends. They're older boys, aren't they?'

'Yes.'

'Little thugs,' he said. 'If you ask me.'

'Nobody asked you, Daddy.'

Was it for this that he was working day and night? Was this all he had left now, this – this cheekiness?

He slapped his daughter's face. It was the first time in his life he had done such a thing.

Tears formed in Paulie's wide eyes. She stared at him as though she had lost her sight, then, with a wail of rage, began to weep. 'Leave me alone! You don't touch me. You – You – everybody'll be making fun of me. I'm not your Apple, do you hear? You and your Apple! I'm nearly fifteen.'

'Exactly,' he said. 'So what are you doing painted and powdered like an old woman? Go and wash that muck off this instant.'

'No, I won't!' she screamed.

He took her arm. 'Do what you're told, miss, or I'll put you over my knee and teach you some manners.'

'Don't you dare.' She wrenched free, ran into the kitchen and reappeared, an aluminium saucepan in her hand. 'Just you come near me.'

'Put that down, Paulie. Paulie, put that down.'

She threw it down. It clattered on the linoleum of the hall. She turned, ran into the bathroom and locked the door. Ah,

147

dear God. Contrite, he went to the door and knocked on it.
'Paulie? Now, listen Pet, listen to me –'

'I'm not your Pet. You're not going to bully me the way you
bullied Mummy. I'll run off with somebody too. I can run off
with Bruno. Just remember that.'

Run off with Bruno? He felt dizzy. He backed away from
the door and sat down on the first chair his hand touched.
In his mind, a child's voice spoke: Do you like big elephants
best of all, or do you like horses best of all? He remembered
her asking that. Or: Why do my dolly's eyes stay open when
she sleeps? Conversations which ended with him telling her
something she did not know. Now, she had told him something
he did not know.

Paulie came out of the bathroom. She crossed the living-
room. 'I'm going to bed,' she said. 'Will you put the lights
out?'

He heard her shut and bolt her bedroom door. She too
could run off with some male. Once, if Daddy liked big elephants best of all, then Paulie liked big elephants too. But
now. . . .

He covered his eyes, his fingers pressing against his eyeballs
until it hurt. Now, she was not his little Apple any more. Big
elephants were no longer relevant.

Chapter Eleven

BELLS, calling to the noon mass in the Basilica, tolled out across the city in a clear and freezing tone, waking him from an exhausted sleep into a world without end, amen. Slowly they focused, the facts of his life. Someone lost, someone stolen, someone strayed. But the morning habit of a lifetime, kicking now with its head cut off, must begin to balance the good with the bad. The habits of an habitual ratiocinator must be fixed in hope. And so, let's see. At least he had gained a little victory by running away last night. At least, last night, he had had his eyes opened to Paulie's true intentions. There was still time to stop her running wild. And so –

And so, when the bells stopped tolling and the worshippers went up the steps to pray, Ginger Coffey, with no God in whom he could place his trust, placed it as he must in men. By ratiocination, MacGregor had promised to promote him. And once MacGregor promoted him, as J. F. Coffey, journalist, he would have time to oversee and correct his daughter's upbringing. As J. F. Coffey, journalist, he would have a job he was proud of at last. No glorified secretary, no galley slave, no joeboy; but a Gentleman of The Press.

And so, he had been right to come to Canada, after all. He had picked a winner. In the winner's circle, by his habitual processes of ratiocination, he thought it natural that Veronica would salute his silks.

So, One – Two – Three, lift up your big carcass, you winner you. Up! And up he got, feeling a twinge in his left leg, going heavy and slow to the kitchen where Paulie was. He started right in.

'Hello, Pet. About last night. I mean – I'm sorry. Now, listen to me –'

The phone rang, postponing his armistice plans. He answered. It was Veronica. 'Ginger? I want to know if I can come and see Paulie this afternoon.'

'Of course you can,' he said.

'But if I come I don't want any repetition of the last time. I want you to be out.'

'Look,' he said. 'I have to have a chat with you.'

'Why?'

'Well – well, last night, I mean, last night I didn't go through with that business.'

'You didn't? Why.'

'Well, I'll explain it to you when I see you. And I want to talk to you about Paulie.'

'What about Paulie?'

'Little pitchers.'

'Oh, don't be ridiculous,' she said. 'Have you had a row with her? Let me speak to her.'

'No, wait dear, I want to explain –'

'Let me speak to Paulie!'

He sighed, put the phone down and beckoned to Paulie who was listening at the kitchen door. He went into the kitchen and listened himself, trying to make sense of what was being said. ... 'No, Mother ... No ... We had a row last night ... He hit me ... Yes, he did. Because, well, I'll tell you when I see you ... Yes, I'll come now.'

Paulie came back into the kitchen. 'Isn't your mother coming here?' Coffey said.

'No. I'm meeting her downtown for coffee. Now, if you'll excuse me, Daddy, I've got to get dressed.'

She went out. He looked at the stove. For the first time since they'd been together, she hadn't made his Sunday breakfast. He got up, spooned a dollop of instant coffee into a cup and sat down again, waiting for the water to boil. A few minutes later he heard Paulie go out. He sat alone, thinking of her meeting Vera in some restaurant, knowing that in their womany way, he would be blamed for all that happened last night.

Somewhere in the bowels of the apartment the furnace coughed and whirred into life. He drank his instant coffee. Upstairs, someone knocked on a radiator and the noise echoed down through the pipes to the basement. The whirring ceased. The furnace went off. Yes, it was hard to hope.

At ten minutes to two, the telephone rang. He expected it

would be Grosvenor, asking why last night's plans had gone agley. But it was Veronica.

'Ginger,' she said. 'Paulie's just left and she's on her way home. I want to see you at once, it's very important. After what she's told me, you and I have to come to some decision.'

'All right,' he said.

'Can you come up to my room?' she asked.

'When?'

'Now. Paulie has a key, hasn't she? You don't have to wait for her?'

'No.'

'All right then, hurry. Here's the address.'

In his dreams which were not dreams, he had sometimes seen her room. She did not spend much time in it, but it was large and elegant, furnished with spindly Swedish things and a large, unslept-in bed. It was close to Grosvenor's flat.

The reality was an Edwardian gingerbread house on the dividing line between the English and French sections of the city, a slum whose sagging porches and balconies were weighted with a winter's accumulation of crusted, filth-spattered snow. The hallway was bare and uncarpeted; the staircase supports were loose. Communal cooking devices were placed on the landings and large garbage pails stood sentinel at each turning of the stairs.

She lived on the third floor. She was waiting for him on the landing as he came up, his face slapped red by the cold, his car coat unbuttoned, his unhusbandly status plain by the polite way he took off his little green hat as he went to greet her. And she, still the stranger, wearing a navy blue dress and a white bead necklace, her stocking seams straight. He thought how a certain kind of drunkard hides signs of his failing in a meticulous attention to dress. A certain type of lady hides her nights of orgy. . . .

'Come on in,' said the lady, without preamble. 'I just got back myself a minute ago. Mind that step.'

Large? Modern? The room alarmed him. It was smaller than the cell he had briefly occupied at the Y.M.C.A. There was no closet, so her clothes were hung on hooks all around the walls. The bed was an unwieldy double, occupying two-thirds of the floor space. There was a small wash basin, its enamel browned with age. There was a small window, its panes covered with diamonded paper.

Of course she was never here: of course she just used it as a place to keep her things. Why then were there tins of food under the basin? Why was there milk on the window-sill, why those dishes stacked in a corner? He sat on the only chair; watched as she went to the mirror over the sink and unfastened her necklace. 'Filthy place, isn't it?' she said. 'They never clean it. I'm going to take my good dress off, if you don't mind. Oh, I'm in such a state about Paulie. I knew she was running around with boys. I just felt it.'

Desirable stranger pulled the dress over her head. Her white slip rose also, revealing her stocking tops and garter straps. It was the beginning of one of his nightly scenarios. He put his little green hat between his feet. The floor was not clean. How could she stay so clean here?

'I gather his name is Bruno,' she said. 'And that he's a mechanic.'

'He's a little thug.' Coffey said. 'And she's only a child.'

'Well, that's got to stop,' she said. 'No two ways about it, that's stopping right now.'

She went past him in her slip and reached behind the door for her dressing-gown. It, at least, was familiar. He had bought it for her as a Christmas present one hundred years ago in a shop in Grafton Street. She sat on the bed, reaching across the bed for her cigarettes while he stood, enormous and clumsy, in the tiny, ill-lit room, his hand trembling as he held out a match flame.

'Thank you.' She sucked in her cheeks, expelled smoke and leaned back on the pillows. She drew one knee up, lacing it with her joined hands. He looked at, then looked away from, her bare white thigh, her tan stocking top. Whorish beauty, cover yourself! But oh! Wasn't that gesture of drawing one knee up, holding it in her hands, wasn't that familiar from the years he had known her? Of course it was. Then, why had he never really looked at her in all those years? Why was it so distracting now? He did not hear a word she was saying. He shifted in his chair, shamed and troubled by his desire.

' – and supervision,' she said. 'No more leaving her alone every evening. So, what are we going to do about it?'

We. We is you and me. He looked again at the cans of food under the sink. Maybe his imaginings about her and Grosvenor had been only that? Maybe –

'Listen,' he said. 'If only you'd come back. I mean, even as a temporary arrangement until I get this new job. Listen, Vera – '

Listen? As he said the word, he saw her face. Of course she would not listen. As of old, she merely waited her turn to speak.

'For instance,' he said. 'Paulie's wearing lipstick and powder and her nails are orange. Now, I don't know about these things. She says the other girls in her class use them. How do I know?'

Veronica turned her face against the pillows. 'Oh God! It never changes, does it? Am I never to have any life of my own? The pair of you,' she said. 'You'd think you planned it. You can't look after Paulie and of course she refuses to come and live with me. And of course you won't go through with the divorce – oh, that would be too easy, that would be helping me, wouldn't it? And of course, Gerry can't wait for ever. Jesus Christ!'

She stubbed out her cigarette and sighed, a woman beyond all hope. 'All right,' she said. 'I'll go back until you get this other job. All right. Oh, it would have been too much to expect that I'd have some life of my own after all these years wet-nursing the pair of you.'

He avoided her angry eyes. He looked away and was caught in another stare, that of his own image in the mirror above the sink. The mirror man was flushed and guilty. Well now, fellow, and do you hear that? She's coming back for a while. Not because she wants to come, mind you, but because she has to stop you messing up Paulie's life. Do you follow me there, my *alter ego*? Do you want her?

He looked at her. Yes, he wanted her, no matter what the terms.

'And if I *do* come back,' she said. 'It's temporary. I'm keeping my job on. And I'm to be in charge of Paulie. Do you understand?'

He nodded, all right.

'And another thing,' she said. 'I'd like to have my own room.'

The mirror man watched his embarrassment. 'There's ah – there's only two bedrooms,' he said. 'There are twin beds in my room.'

She sighed in swift exasperation. 'Oh well,' she said. 'I suppose we may as well get started. Get my suitcases, will you? They're under the bed.'

The mirror man watched as he went down on his knees.

So, she came home. That night when he returned from his proofreading duties, he found her asleep in the twin bed next to his. Quickly he began to undress, remembering all the waking dreams of her absence, and in a few minutes, large, naked and vulnerable, he shyly approached her bed. He hesitated, then bent over and placed a bristly moustache kiss on the nape of her neck. Immediately – she could not have been asleep – she sat up and switched on the light. She stared at him. Naked, it was plain what ailed him.

'Go back to your own bed,' she said.

'Ah now, Vera –'

'Either you go back to your own bed or I'll dress and leave tonight.'

'Suffering J!' he said. But he went back to his own bed. He slept. He dreamed about her. And next morning awoke to a new torture. Covertly he watched as she got out of bed. She was wearing flannel pyjamas which were not exactly Gay Paree but which nevertheless brought him to sudden desire. He turned towards her, the ends of his moustache lifting in a hopeful smile. . . .

She stared him down. Without a word, she picked her clothes off the chair and went into the bathroom, leaving him alone, his desire dropping to a sadness. Unshaven and unfed (for she stayed in the bathroom) he fled to another day of diapers.

Still, wasn't it better to have her in the house, no matter how cold she was, than to torture himself with imaginings? Soon she'd thaw: the Keep Off The Grass signs would come down: Grosvenor would be forgotten. Soon they'd be friends again. Paulie would be friends with him too. Soon MacGregor would promote him. Soon everything would be all right. Soon. . . .

Yes, he put all his hopes in one basket, an ancient basket name of MacGregor. And that night, when he went to work at the *Tribune,* he attacked his galleys like a driven man. That night when MacGregor passed through on his usual sortie, Coffey looked up from the dirty steel desk, not in fear but in hope, proud of the great mass of corrected proofs on his spike, hoping MacGregor would see in him a man worthy of advancement.

But MacGregor did not single him out. MacGregor passed him by.

Ah well. Maybe tomorrow night?

Tomorrow was Tuesday. When he came back for his supper on Tuesday night, Veronica was not there. Neither was Paulie. Not that that made much difference as Paulie hadn't spoken two words to him since her mother's return. Still, it couldn't last much longer, could it?

He went to work. Again he drove himself to produce the greatest number of corrected galleys. Again he lived in hopes. And Hooray! At a quarter to ten, just before the supper break, a copy boy came into the composing-room and said Coffey was wanted at the city desk.

'Did you hear that?' Coffey said to Old Billy Davis. 'The *city desk.* Ah, now, MacGregor isn't such a bad old basket after all. He's given the order and the city editor's going to find a spot for me.'

Old Billy fingered his feathery goatee. 'Just so long it isn't trouble,' he said. 'Best you can hope for is keep out of trouble. Watch your step.'

Poor old sausage, what would *he* know? In joyful disparagement, J. F. Coffey, journalist, donned his jacket and hurried out into the great cavern of the city room, sure that now, his ship rounding the harbour bar –

False alarm. Leaning against a pillar a few steps from the city desk a visitor awaited Coffey. Waited, slightly disarranged as though the window-dresser had gone to lunch and left him unfinished.

'Hi,' he said. He turned towards the City Editor and said in a slurred, half-drunken voice. 'Okay if I borrow this guy?'

'Go ahead, Gerry boy,' the City Editor said.

Gerald Grosvenor waved his thanks, then detaching himself from the pillar, came towards Coffey. 'Come on in the cafeteria,' he said. 'I want to have a talk with you, Buster.'

He was drunk, that was plain. Uneasily Coffey accompanied him along the corridor to the cafeteria, praying that MacGregor would not spot them. Uneasily he waited as Grosvenor, after a noisy exchange of greetings with two reporters and the counterman, brought steaming mugs of coffee to the table. MacGregor had not yet paid his nightly visit; Coffey was supposed to be at his desk, not here. 'Look,' he said to Grosvenor. 'I'm busy and it's not my supper time yet. Now, what is it?'

'Want to talk to you,' Grosvenor said. 'Just left Veronica half an hour ago. You bastard. You're crucifying that girl.'

Uneasily Coffey looked around the cafeteria. The counterman was listening.

'Left her in tears,' Grosvenor said in a loud voice. 'At the end of her rope, see? Goddammit, I love that girl. And she loves me too. Yes, she does.'

To Coffey's intense embarrassment, Grosvenor began to weep. Worse, Grosvenor did not seem to care who saw him. 'What *are* you?' Grosvenor said tearfully. 'A dog in the manger, or something? I mean you're ruining Vera's life.'

'Will you shut up?' Coffey whispered urgently. 'Lower your voice and stop sniffling.'

'Forcing her to come back,' Grosvenor said. 'Using your daughter as bait. Don't you see what you're doing to both of them? It's criminal.'

'Shut up! Shut up, or I'll shut you up.'

'No, I won't shut up. You're a menace, Ging'r, that's what you are. You're one of those guys, you don't care about anybody except yourself. Veronica hates your guts, you know.'

'She does nothing of the sort,' Coffey said, unwisely.

'No? Only went back because you were messing up Paulie's life, didn't she? That's what she said tonight. I mean – ' and

156

Grosvenor reached across the table, his hairy black hand gripping Coffey's wrist. 'I mean, I'm not going to let you get away with this. I'm going to kill you, you sonofabitch.'

Quickly, Coffey disengaged his wrist. Until now Grosvenor had been merely a lay figure in his imaginings, a self-important dummy which Veronica had picked to affront him with. But now, look at him. Weeping, revengeful, not ashamed to make a fool of himself for love's sake. Is this why Veronica loves him? Because he cares more about her than himself, because, unlike me, he's prepared to weep in public? Suddenly – and for the first time – Coffey feared Grosvenor; feared the recklessness of Grosvenor's love.

'Now listen to me,' he said, staring at Grosvenor. 'Listen now. Veronica's my wife and I intend to hold on to her. Get that straight. I'm a newcomer in a new country and I've had my troubles finding a spot, as who wouldn't? But things have changed. I'm on the right track now. I'm getting a better job soon and we're going to be all right, all of us. So bugger off, Grosvenor. I'm warning you, if I catch you sloping around Vera any more it's you that will be killed!'

'You don't scare me,' Grosvenor said drunkenly. 'You big Irish ape. You and Veronica are finished, do you hear? She loves *me*. She's coming back to *me*. Know what I'm going to do? I'm going to beat the piss out of you, Buster.'

With that, Grosvenor stood up, wiped his wet eyes with the back of his hand and moved out from the table, spilling coffee from the untouched mugs. He stood in the aisle, raising his arms in the exaggerated stance of an old-style barearm boxer. Drunkenly he began to circle Coffey, who hesitated, embarrassed by the rapidly forming audience of reporters and copy boys, uneasily aware that MacGregor might walk in at any moment, yet itching to lay Grosvenor in his tracks.

'Come on,' Grosvenor jeered. 'Fight! I'm going to kill you, you sonofabitch. Somebody should have done it long ago.'

His face ruddy with anger, Coffey ducked the long loping clout which Grosvenor aimed at him. Then he moved in. He knocked Grosvenor's right arm aside and stiffened Grosvenor with a vicious punch in the mouth. Grosvenor stumbled, hit a chair and sat down in it, his hands going to his mouth. After a moment a trickle of blood ran down his wrists. He took his cupped hands away and stared into the bloody spittle in his palms. There were bits of teeth there. The spectators looked at Coffey with new respect and one of the older reporters came forward, blocking his path. 'Hold on,' he said. 'Guy's hurt.'

Coffey did not need the restraint. His anger bled to shame at the sight of Grosvenor, pathetic and beaten, the underdog beloved by the crowd. Whereas he, the man with right on his side, stood convicted as a bully. He dropped his arms and at that moment, as though announcing the end of the contest, the composing-room bell rang in the corridor. Supper break. Now, it did not matter if MacGregor walked in. A victor, wanting the crowd to think him a good sport, he went over to Grosvenor and tried to help him up. 'Come on,' he said. 'You're in no condition to fight. Better cut off home.'

Grosvenor pushed him away. He stood up, watched by all the cafeteria customers and, staggering slightly, put his hand to his mouth as though he were about to vomit. He rushed into the corridor, Coffey following.

'Do you want to go to the Men's Room?' Coffey called after him. 'It's the other way.'

'Go to hell,' Grosvenor mumbled. He lurched along the corridor, one hand over his mouth, the other fending the corridor wall away. At the end of the corridor a service elevator waited, its gate open, its operator squat on his little stool. Grosvenor lurched aside, then turned, looking curiously like a performer on a tiny, bright-lit stage. He pointed an accusing finger at Coffey. 'You won't get her,' he shouted. 'She's coming to me. Irish Ape, you'll fail! She's mine, do you hear me? Mine!'

That crying voice, that bloodied mouth, that accusing finger, the sight of Grosvenor in the bright-lit elevator cage: all filled Coffey with an unreasoning dread. It was as though Grosvenor had formally pronounced a curse on him. And at that moment, MacGregor appeared, Jehovah at the far end of the corridor, attended by Clarence, his fat ministering angel. In sudden panic Coffey ran forward, tried to close the elevator gate. 'Take him down,' he whispered to the operator. 'Hurry, hurry –'

Startled, the elevator operator closed the gate. The elevator cage fell shuddering into the black shaft. Coffey turned and walked back up the corridor towards MacGregor, a man approaching the altar of his hope. Surely in this minute his luck must change? Surely in this very minute MacGregor would dispel the curse of Grosvenor's hate?

Clarence, riffling through his notebook, said: 'Eleven hundred lines, sir.'

'That's it,' MacGregor said. 'Shoe Week Convention. Tell the city desk to send a man to cover it. Good advertising tie-in.'

'Yes, Chief,' Clarence said.

Coffey was level with them now. He turned towards MacGregor, his face like a child's in its longing.

'A few wee features on the local page,' MacGregor said. 'To keep the advertisers happy.'

'Right, Chief.'

They passed him by. They had not seen him. He did not exist. *Irish ape, you'll fail!*

That night when he got home, Veronica was sitting up in bed reading a book. 'What did you do to Gerry?' she said.

'He started it. He came in drunk and acting like a blithering idiot.'

'So you broke two front teeth for him?'

'That was an accident, dear. Besides, he asked for it.'

'An accident?' she said. 'Well, let me tell you, you're wasting your time.'

'What do you mean?'

'I mean, hitting Gerry, what good's that going to do you? Gerry's more of a man than you'll ever be. Gerry loves me. That's why he was so upset tonight when I told him I'd have to stay here. That's why he got drunk.'

Coffey began to undress.

'And another thing,' she said. 'I've no intention of staying here one minute longer than I have to. Today, I spoke to the mothers of those girls Paulie goes around with and we're all going to make sure that gang of hoodlums are chased out. We're going to arrange more evenings at home for Paulie and the others. I can come over here two or three evenings a week and supervise. I don't have to live here all the time, just for that.'

'Ah now, wait, Kitten – why, at the end of this week, I'll have that new job and maybe then we could – '

'New job,' she said. 'Oh for God's sake!'

'No, I'm getting it, dear. Honestly.'

'Want to bet?' she reached up and put the light off. 'Good night,' she said. 'I have to work tomorrow.'

Slowly, he finished undressing. He put on his pyjamas. If she left now ... He went over to her bed, sat on the edge, and put out his hand. It hovered over her, then settled on her shoulder. 'Vera?' he said.

'What?'

'Vera, I know Grosvenor loves you. But I do too.'

'Ha, ha!'

'Don't laugh, Vera. I do love you. Honestly I do.'

'Listen to me,' she said. 'You don't know what love is. Just remember this, Ginger. Love is unselfish, it's doing things for other people and not asking them to do things for you. If you really loved me, you'd let me go. You'd give me a divorce. You'd think of my happiness and not your own. Gerry does. Now, go back to your own bed. Good night.'

He stood up. Heavily he recrossed the room. He got into his bed and lay down on his side, looking at the darkness where she was. *Unselfish*. So that was what she wanted. Some proof of devotion greater than self. Was that the thing that would win her back? Was it? He rolled over and stared at the invisible ceiling. Love is unselfish. Was that what she had found lacking in his love for her? Was that why Grosvenor, weeping but prepared to wait, had won her instead? If only he could think this out. If only his brain could puzzle out what she had said and find the answer, that absolute answer he felt he had almost grasped.

It was tiring to think. He was not used to thinking in abstractions. But still – was selflessness what he lacked? Was *that* true love? Would the greatest proof of his love for her be his willingness to sacrifice himself, the way Jesus had sacrificed himself, for mankind? Jesus considered that the highest form of love, didn't he? Well, there you are, then.

'Vera?' he said.

'Go to sleep.'

160

'Listen, Vera,' he said. 'I've made up my mind. If I don't get that reporter's job at the end of this week, I'll bow out. If I don't get it, you can go back to Grosvenor and you can take Paulie. And I'll give you your divorce into the bargain. Now, isn't that unselfish of me? Isn't it?'

He waited for her answer. There was no answer. 'I mean it,' he said. He did mean it.

Chapter Twelve

NEXT morning he awoke on the cross of his new obsession. He woke and went to work, a man who had decided to gamble his all on one event. He started fresh on that Wednesday morning, convinced that if he got the job, all his worries would end. Veronica would stay, Grosvenor would disappear, Paulie would be his Apple again, his future would be assured.

And if he did not get the job? If he did not get the job he would go down like a man. Lonely and proud, he would cast himself adrift from all who knew him, his boats burned for ever. He would prove to her that he was a man of his word, the most unselfish lover in all the world, a man who could do a far, far better thing than Grosvenor ever would.

Not that he thought he'd have to, mind you. No, he was going to get the job, for sure. J. F. Coffey, journalist, Coffey of the *Tribune*, why that was only a matter of days and hours now. And so, that Wednesday morning, fixed on the cross of his obsession, he began to measure off those hours. As he drove through the city delivering diapers, his mind moved from hopes to *faits accomplis*. By mid-afternoon he had convinced himself by his habitual processes of ratiocination that he had no time to lose. For, since he was getting this new job on Friday next, he should be starting his preparations now, shouldn't he? Right, then. He had no time to lose.

At four-thirty that afternoon, his delivery route completed, he walked into the *Tiny Ones* depot and gave notice.

'What?' Mr Mountain rose up in alarm, his great stomach overlapping the military array of folders on the desk. 'What's the matter, Coffey, we not treating you right?'

'It's not that, sir. It's just that this other job is more in my line. The job with you was more or less a stopgap.'

'Well, eff me,' Mr Mountain said. 'Reporter, eh? What paper?'

'The *Tribune,* sir.'

'The *Tribune,* eh?' Distractedly, Mr Mountain ran four

plump fingers through the soft thickness of his detergent-coloured hair. 'This puts me on a spot,' he said. 'What am I going to tell the boss?'

'What do you mean?'

'Well, this is strictly classified info, Coffey, but the fact is you're up for promotion.'

'Oh.'

'Mr Brott himself is interested. Told me to keep you happy. Said he was finding an office spot for you soon. It's going to reflect on my department, you walking out like this.'

Now that was nice to hear, wasn't it? Damn right it was. He wished to goodness Veronica were in the room. They want to keep me on and promote me. Well, Vera, what do you think of that?

'Look, I'm not unhappy with the job or with the way I've been treated,' Coffey told Mr Mountain. 'I'll be glad to explain that to Mr Brott, if you like.'

'Tell you what,' Mr Mountain said. 'I think this is a case for top brass. Tell you what – ' he paused, staring with great solemnity at Coffey. 'I'm going to the boss himself!'

He picked up the phone, a man assuming command. 'Wait outside,' he said.

So Coffey stepped outside. In a moment or two, Mr Mountain dashed to the door, beckoning him. 'Wants to speak to you *himself*,' he whispered. 'Mr Brott.'

He handed Coffey the telephone. At the other end of the line a crackly, testy voice said: 'That you, Coffey? A. K. Brott here!'

'Yes, sir.'

'What's this about quitting? Now, you listen to me. You come right over here. I want to talk to you.'

'But I have to start my night job, sir, I wouldn't be able to manage – '

'What time you start?'

'Six, sir.'

'Give me Stan.'

Coffey gave him Mr Mountain. 'Yessir,' Mr Mountain said briskly. 'Right sir, Roger, sir. Thank you, sir.' He put the phone down. He picked up his hat, stared at Coffey with some distaste. 'Get in my car,' he said. 'I've got to deliver you.'

So they got in Mr Mountain's car and drove up to the *Tiny Ones* head office. There was no conversation *en route*: Mr Mountain clearly believed this disruption in the chain of command to be above and beyond the call of duty. Coffey felt embarrassed. It was not Mr Mountain's job to chauffeur him. Especially when it was all a waste of time.

Among the display of ex-voto scenes in A. K. Brott's office several advertising roughs were pasted on a board. They bore a vaguely familiar slogan:

RENT-A-CRIB SERVICE

Why Buy? We Supply

Tiny Ones Inc.

'That's right,' Mr Brott said, pointing to the board. 'I checked into that idea, had a survey done and now I'm ready to go. That's what I want to talk to you about. What's this about you quitting?'

'I'm going to become a journalist, sir.'

'Reporter?'

'Yes, sir.'

'Never saw a reporter in this province you couldn't buy off for twenty bucks in a plain envelope. So, forget that. You're a smart fella, Coffey, and I'm going to make you a good offer. A once-in-a-lifetime offer – take it or leave it.'

Coffey fiddled with his little green hat. Nice to know that old Brott thought well of him, but to tell the truth, if he never saw a nappy again, it would be far too soon. Still, it was a good omen, wasn't it? The tide was turning, his luck had changed and surely, surely, in less than forty-eight hours, Mac-Gregor would come through and J. F. Coffey, journalist, Coffey of the *Tribune* –

'Matter of fact, I should have acted sooner,' Mr Brott said. 'Just goes to show, in things like this you've got to pee or get off the pot. So, okay. Here's what I'm going to do. I'll make you my personal assistant at ninety bucks a week.'

Personal assistant to the managing director of Kylemore

Distilleries. Personal bumboy to old Cleery in the advertising, glorified secretary at Coomb-Na-Baun. Coffey stared at A. K. Brott's small grey face.

'No,' he said in a strangled whisper.

'No? Look, what's the matter with you? Personal assistant, do you realize the chance I'm giving you.'

'Do I?' Coffey echoed. 'Fetch me this and fetch me that. Run down for cigarettes. Book me a table. I'm no glorified secretary, I'll have you know. I'm going to be a reporter by the end of this week.'

'You're crazy.'

'Ah no,' Coffey said. 'What do you think I came to this country for? Sure, didn't I leave a job as personal assistant in a far bigger company than this – this laundry will ever be. No thank you.'

'Well, that's your mistake.' Mr Brott said, shaking his little grey head. 'Rent-A-Crib, now there you were using your head, Coffey. When a guy gives me a worthwhile idea, I like to pay for it. As my assistant you could have had yourself a nice steady job. Reporter? You're nuts. Come on now?'

'No,' Coffey said. 'I want to be a reporter.'

'Well, it's your funeral,' A. K. Brott said. 'Sorry you feel this way. Stan?'

Mr Mountain appeared in the doorway. 'Yessir?'

'Stan, drive Coffey down to his newspaper. And get a replacement for him. He's quit us. Take him off the payroll.'

'Rodger Dodger,' said Mr Mountain.

Personal assistant! It just showed you, unless you had the guts to believe in yourself, what you started off as you would wind up as, even over here. Thanks be to God he would never go back to that, thanks be to God he had the strength to refuse once and for all. Glorified secretary, indeed! Running errands now and for ever more, amen. Ah, shove your bloody personal assistant once and for bloody all! Shove it!

'What's the matter with you, you look mad?' Fox said.

'Nothing,' Coffey said. 'I was just thinking about something. I turned down a job today.'

But Fox did not seem to hear. He fed two new galleys in Coffey's direction. 'Let's get rolling,' he said. 'Old Billy Davis has reported sick tonight. We're a man short.'

'What's the matter with Old Bill?' Benny asked.

'A cold, he says.'

Blast Old Billy, Coffey thought. What's he getting sick for when I need him here? But a cold was nothing. No need to panic, was there? Right, then. He picked up a fresh galley.

Next morning, Coffey broke the breakfast silence with an announcement. 'This is my last day on the delivery job,' he said.

'What happened?' Veronica wanted to know. 'Did they lay you off?'

Now, wasn't that typical? 'They did not lay me off,' he said. 'I resigned. Matter of fact they offered to promote me and take me into the office. That's how well they think of me, if you want to know.'

'And you *resigned*?'

'Too right, I did. I told you, I'm going on the editorial staff of the *Tribune* as of next week. Friday will be my last night in the proofroom.'

'Honestly, Daddy?' Paulie said. It was the first direct word she had spoken to him in days.

'Yes, Pet. Word of honour.'

'Oh, that's super,' Paulie said, looking pleased. 'Then you and I can go skiing. Remember, you promised?'

'Don't count your chickens.' Veronica said to Paulie. 'And hurry now, you'll be late for school.'

Don't count your chickens. Wasn't that the height of her, putting the child against him every chance she got? But he would not let her annoy him. He went off to his last day of *Tiny Ones* deliveries and spent it happily, settling up his accounts with the housewives on his route. Naturally, he told all his customers the good news. And the ladies were impressed. A reporter, now that was a glamorous job, one woman said. And another said he was a credit to his family. Yes, they congratulated him, wished him the best of luck and one or two of them even offered him a tip. Which was well meant, not mortifying at all; there was no harm in it. He took the money so as not to hurt their feelings and bought candies for all the little boys on his route.

At four sharp, he turned over his uniform, his accounts and his truck to Mr Mountain. At four thirty, after saying good-bye to Corp and the other lads, he walked out of the depot, a free man. By six he was at the *Tribune*, ready for a good night's work, his hopes high, his obsession well stoked. And at five past six – hooray! Fox came in with a brand new proofreader.

A new man. Coffey studied him. He was elderly, the new man. He wore long combinations under his rolled-up short sleeves and he read the first galley as carefully as if it was his own insurance policy. Ah, good man yourself, New Man. You'll do a night to learn the ropes and Ginger Coffey will give you all the hand you want. And lend a hand he did, hitching his steel chair close to the new man's, keeping a brotherly eye on the new man's performance.

MacGregor came at ten, did not look at Coffey, examined the new man's work with his customary displeasure, said that Old Billy Davis was still sick, and passed on out of the composing room. Later, Fox told them that Old Billy had flu.

'Flu,' Coffey said. 'Sure, that's nothing.'

'Old Billy's seventy-two, you know,' Fox said.

Coffey put that worry out of his mind. Next morning when he woke, he believed his only remaining trial was how to wait out the day. For it was Friday. Mafeking Relieved. Irish Guards Pull Out. He lay late, listening to the indistinct mumble of his womenfolk in the kitchen, half-wishing that he had a day of diaper deliveries to occupy him until the news came through this afternoon.

At half-past eight, just before she left for work, Veronica put her head in the bedroom door. 'Isn't today the day you expect to be promoted?' she said.

'Didn't I tell you it was?'

'You did, Ginger. You also made a promise to me the other night in bed. Do you still feel that way?'

'You never even answered me the other night,' he said, reproachfully.

'What was the use answering you, when you'll renege on it for certain.'

'Did I say I'd renege on it?' he asked her.

'Well – are you going to?'

'I am not,' he said. 'As I told you the other night, if I don't get that job today you can have your divorce and Paulie and all the rest of it. I'll show you who's selfish!'

'Do you mean that, Ginger? Honestly and truly?'

'I do,' he said. 'But I *am* getting the job, don't forget. It's promised.'

'All right. I was only asking. I wanted to see if you were serious.'

She went out. He lay for a while, thinking of their exchange. Wasn't that women for you, never letting on they heard a word and then, two days later, coming out with the whole thing. So she thought he'd renege, did she? Well, he'd show her. Not that he'd have to, of course. Of course not.

He lay abed, listening as Paulie left for school in her usual, late-flying rush. Then he got up, shaved and dressed with the care of a man preparing for some court function. His only worry, as he saw it, was how to wait until four. At four, the night staff were entitled to go and pick up their pay cheques. And as all staff changes were reported on pay day to Mr Hennen in the pay office, Mr Hennen would know. But Flute! It was a long, long morning.

At a quarter to four, having already waited fifteen minutes in the corridor, Coffey went into the *Tribune* business office and idled by the cashier's wicket, trying to catch Mr Hennen's eye. Mr Hennen, an old bird in his cage, busied himself with his ledgers, aware of Coffey, but determined to make him wait each agonizing second until the hour. The office clock's second hand circled, the minute hand jerked up one black notch, the hour hand moved imperceptibly closer. At the precise moment that all three reached the hour, Coffey stepped up to the wicket. Mr Hennen laid down his pen, fussed with his black sleeve protectors and looked in Coffey's direction. 'Name?' he shouted.

'J. F. Coffey.'

Mr Hennen riffled through a sheaf of pay cheques and

slipped one through the wicket. 'Don't spend it all at once,' he said.

'By the way – I – ah – I wonder if you'd have a note about a staff change?' Coffey said. 'A transfer for me?'

Mr Hennen cocked his old parrot head to one side. 'Transfer?' He opened another ledger and took out four little yellow slips. He riffled through them. 'These here are all the new staff changes. Your name's not in.'

'Perhaps it hasn't come down yet?'

'All changes came in at noon. So it won't be for next week, fella.'

'But Mr MacGregor promised me . . .?'

'Did he now?' Mr Hennen said, and winked.

Coffey turned from that wicked parrot eye, afraid. What did that wink mean? Surely –

'Hey, wait a minute,' Mr Henney said. 'One of your fellas is sick. Phoned up, wants someone to take his cheque over to him. Let's see. Davis is the name. Want to take it to him?'

Old Billy. *There* was the reason he had not been promoted. That was what Mr Hennen knew and had not said. Coffey went back to the wicket, heartsick with anger against old doddering Bill. Why did he have to get sick this week, of all weeks? It was not fair. Bloody Old Bill! 'All right,' he said. 'I'll take it to him.'

Mr Hennen passed over an addressed envelope and Coffey went out into the streets again. Bill's place was a room over a small clothing store, in a street three blocks from the *Tribune* offices. The landlord, an aged French-Canadian who spoke no English, looked at *W. Davis* on the pay envelope, then nodded and led Coffey up the back stairs to a door at the end of a dark corridor. Coffey knocked. 'Come in,' an old voice called.

The room reminded Coffey of Veronica's, but there was a difference. Old Billy had lived here a long time. There was a small electric hotplate, an old icebox with a tray of ice in it, a green card table on which a large orange cat licked its paws. The walls were shelved with many books in fruit crate containers. There were several snapshots on the walls, and an ingenious device of extension cords and three-way plugs so that Old Billy could turn on and off the lights from any chair or corner. On the bed lay the master of the room, his frail body invisible beneath a heap of quilts, his plumy goatee jutting upwards in the direction of the water-stained ceiling. 'It's Paddy, isn't it?' he said. 'Did you bring my cheque, Paddy?'

Coffey removed a fold-up chair from the stack beside the card table. The cat made a hissing noise of dislike. The chair had not been opened for many a year; dust lay thick in its crevices; its hinged joints were stiff. He put it at the head of the bed and sat down. He handed over the envelope.

Frail old fingers fumbled with the flap. 'Full cheque,' Old Billy said. 'Didn't dock me sick pay, I see. Good. And how are you, lad? What's new?'

Coffey did not answer. He looked at the old man's arm, protruding from a worn pyjama sleeve. On the skeletal wrist was a faded tattoo. A harp, a shamrock and a faint script: *Erin Go Bragh*. Above this tattoo was another, a heart pierced by an arrow and entwined with a motto: *Bill loves Min*.

'Are you Irish, Billy?' Coffey said. 'That harp?'

'Course I'm Irish,' Old Billy said. 'William O'Brien Davis. Fine Irish name.'

'But you were born over here?'

'No, sir. I'm an immigrant, same as you. Donegal man, born and bred. Came out here when I was twenty years old, looking for the streets that were paved with gold.' Billy's mouth opened in a chuckle, showing his hard old gums. 'Yes,' he said. 'I've been all over, Atlantic to Pacific and back again. Been north of the Circle too and down south as far as the Gulf of Mexico. Yes, I've been all over the States, seen them all, all forty-eight. Never found any gold streets though. No sir.'

But Coffey did not join in the old man's laugh. He stared at that skeletal forearm. *Bill loves Min*. Where and in what long ago had Bill loved Min? Where was Min now? How many years had Old Bill lain here in this room, watched over only by the inhuman, unblinking eyes of his orange cat?

'Yes, all I got to show now is forty dollars a month on the old age pension,' Bill said. 'A man can't live on that nowadays. Even me and I don't hardly eat but a bowl of Campbell's soup once a day. And beer. Beer's what keeps me going. That's why this proofreading job was such a blessing. Lots of beer.'

'But you still have the proofreading job,' Coffey said. 'We've been expecting you back tonight.'

'Not tonight,' Old Billy said. He touched his chest. 'Got something in here, the doctor says. I've got to rest.'

'But you'll be back,' Coffey said. 'In a day or two – '

'It was the *Tribune* doctor who saw me,' Old Bill said. 'They have my number. Hear they hired a new man already.'

'The new man's not a replacement for you,' Coffey said. 'He's my replacement. They're making me a reporter next week. Now listen, Bill. Tonight, I'm going to see MacGregor. I'll tell him you'll be back in a day or two. You'll be up and about in no time.'

The old man's eyes had closed. He appeared to be sleeping.

'Bill, listen?' Coffey said. 'Bill, are you asleep?'

'Plenty of time to sleep,' the old voice said. 'Not much else to do but sleep when you're living on the old age. Be all right, though. I've got all my things here. Bowl of soup, that's good enough. And a beer. The odd beer . . .'

His toothless mouth remained open on that sentence. His hand, holding the pay cheque, slid over the quilt and bumped against Coffey's knee. The envelope fell on the floor. Carefully, Coffey picked it up and put it on the card table. Carefully, he leaned over the old face. Yes, Bill was asleep.

'I'll be back, Bill,' Coffey said in a whisper. He lifted up the skeletal arm, covered it with the quilt. Yes, J. F. Coffey, journalist, would come back, oh yes, Billy, I promise you, I'll come back every week, I won't forget you. I'll bring beer. Every time, a case of beer.

But would he? Another promise. Would he Judas Old Billy along with the rest of them? For Old Billy might not come back to work. Old Billy might never be back. Coffey tiptoed to the door, opened it with infinite precaution, and went out into the dark corridor.

Irish. *An immigrant, same as you.* A young wanderer, once, travelling through this land of ice and snow, looking for the bluebird. *Erin Go Bragh*. But was it really Erin Forever? What trace of Erin was left on William O'Brien Davis save that harp and shamrock, that motto, faded as the old reminder that *Bill Loves Min*. Would Ginger Coffey also end his days in some

171

room, old and used, his voice nasal and reedy, all accent gone? 'Yes, I'm Irish. James Francis Coffey. Fine Irish name.'

No, no, that wasn't going to happen to him. Not to J. F. Coffey, journalist. Never mind Old Billy, he was going to get that reporting job. Tonight he was. It was all arranged. He wasn't going to wait for MacGregor to speak to him, he must speak to MacGregor himself, remind him – yes, MacGregor was a busy man, it might have slipped his mind. And a promise is a promise. So, all right then. See MacGregor.

Because it was pay night, Fox and the others had spent their usual two hours in the tavern before coming to work. This meant that only Coffey and the New Man were not under the weather. So Coffey read the major number of galleys before the first edition. He and the New Man worked at the same desk, sober men and true. Ah! New Man! Good man yourself. You front-line relief!

At ten, when supper bell sounded, MacGregor had not put in an appearance. Coffey could wait no longer. He went to the office. But MacGregor was in conference with the telegraph editor which meant that Coffey had to wait in the corridor until ten past ten. At last, when the telegraph editor went out, in went Coffey.

'What do you want?' MacGregor said.

'It's the two weeks, sir. It's up, as of tonight.'

'What two weeks?'

You see! It *had* slipped MacGregor's mind, so it was a lucky thing Coffey had decided to take the bull by the horns, wasn't it? Glad that he had come, he spoke up. 'You remember, sir, about making me a reporter? You promised two weeks ago.'

'Aye,' MacGregor said. 'Well, we're still short-staffed in the proofroom, as you know. Man sick.'

'Yes, sir. But I went to see Old Billy Davis today and he's feeling much better. He'll be back to work in a day or two at the latest. Now I wondered, in view of that, perhaps you'd make the change now and start me off as a reporter next week?'

'No.'

172

'But I've been expecting it,' Coffey said, feeling his face grow hot. 'I've been counting on it, sir. I hardly think it's fair.'

'Fair? What? What the hell are you talking about? Now go on – take your arse out of here before I kick it out.'

'No!' Coffey said, in a sudden shocked rage. 'You made me a promise. I've been working like a bloody slave for the past three weeks in hopes of this. I gave up another job because of it. I promised my wife and daughter. You don't know how much this means to me, sir. It's very important.'

'Clarence?' MacGregor shouted. The fat man rushed in, notebook at the ready. 'Now, Coffey,' MacGregor said. 'Tell it to us again.'

'You promised me,' Coffey said, feeling his tongue thick and confused. 'You promised that you'd promote me as soon as you had a replacement in the proofroom. Well, that new proof-reader's been here three days now. He's a good man too.'

'What new reader?'

'Rhodes, sir,' Clarence said. 'Replacement for old Davis.'

'But Billy's coming back,' Coffey began. 'He needs the job, you're not going to throw him –'

'Doctor said bronchial trouble, sir,' Clarence told his chief.

'Aye.' MacGregor nodded his head. 'Bronchial trouble. He won't be back.'

'But you promised me,' Coffey turned to Clarence. 'You were here. You heard him.'

'I don't recall any promise,' Clarence said.

'Aye,' MacGregor said. 'Go on back to your desk, Coffey.'

'No, it's not fair! Dammit, is that the way you keep your word?' Coffey shouted.

'Perhaps I'd better phone the lobby, sir,' Clarence said. 'And ask them to send Ritchie up.'

Ritchie? Ritchie was the doorman. A blackness sealed Coffey's eyes. For a moment he stood, dizzy, their voices fading in his ears. Doorman? To throw him out?

' – had quite enough of this,' MacGregor's voice said. 'Now go on back to your wurrk or you'll not be paid.'

'That's it, fella,' Clarence said. A hand took Coffey's arm. 'Come on, now.'

'No . . .' Coffey said. 'Dammit, no!'

173

'Listen to me, you.' The blackness cleared from in front of Coffey's eyes and he saw MacGregor leaning across the desk. A large blue vein pumped in MacGregor's pale bony skull. 'If you think I have any notion of making you a reporter after the way you carried on tonight, you're sadly mistaken. Now, get back to that proofdesk and thank your stars I don't kick your arse right out of this building. Is that clear?'

Clear? He shook himself free of Clarence's arm. He turned back into the corridor. The composing-room bell shrilled, calling the readers back to work. Dazed, he walked towards the sound of the bell.

The new proofreader, Mr Rhodes, was surprised at the difference in the Irishman's behaviour when the Irishman came back from his supper break. Until now he had thought of the Irishman as the hardest-working, most respectable man on the shift, the only one you would not be ashamed to introduce to your friends. Obliging, sober, well-spoken, not cursing and half-drunk like the rest of these bums.

Mr Rhodes was on pension from the railroad and had only taken this job to help his wife make payments on a little place they were buying up north. He had been unpleasantly surprised by the class of man he found himself working with and, in fact, would have resigned the second night, had it not been for the Irishman's helping hand and courtesy. But now, when the big fellow came back and sat down at the desk beside Rhodes, he began to show signs that he might be every bit as unstable as the others. For one thing, he hardly did a tap of work for the rest of the shift. He sat there, his face like a wooden idol, muttering filthy language under his breath. Had he too been drinking, Rhodes wondered? Indeed, it would be no surprise, for in all Rhodes's years in the railroad's accounting department, he had never met such a low class of man as Fox or Harry or that young lad with the eczema. So at the end of the night's work, when he heard the big fellow say that he would go out for drinks with the rest of them, well, thought Rhodes, I was mistaken, he's a bum like the others. No money was worth it, to be forced to spend your retirement years in the company of men like these. No. Next Friday, Rhodes decided, I'll give my notice.

'Come on, Paddy,' Harry said. 'We'll have a jug at Rose's place.'

They stood on the steps of the *Tribune* building. Down the street, brightlit in the night silence, a sign winked on and off. FIVE MINUTE LUNCH. 'Rose?' Coffey said.

'Rose of the Rosy teats,' Fox shouted. 'Come on, lads.'

The Five Minute Lunch was open all night. There, under the rumble of transcontinental trains leaving on track, arriving on track, gathered a nightly cross-section of city owls. Bus drivers on the late trick, their change machines extracted and placed carefully beside their coffee and eggs; coloured sleeping-car porters from the railroad terminus across the street, magpie collections of abandoned newspapers and magazines stuffed in the handles of their overnight bags; consumptive-looking French-Canadian waiters stealing a break from the boredom of fifth-rate night clubs; middle-aged whores, muffled in babushkas, snow boots and sensible woolly scarves, condemned by the winter to come in often out of the cold; night postal clerks; ticket collectors; cleaning men. And behind the long mica and chrome serving counter, under framed, hand-lettered cards – WESTERN SANDWICH KNACKWURST & BEANS SPAGHETTI & MEATBALLS – the queen of this night hive moved, never off her paining feet, never hurried, never done. Rose Alma Briggs.

'Rosy, dear,' Fox said, rapping his cane on the counter.

Rose sent two eggs, sunnyside up, flipping on to a plate. She turned, acknowledged the greeting with a nod. She was powdered and clean; she wore a white nylon coat, white rubber shoes and white lisle stockings. Under the transparent coat, a white slip. And biting tight into the soft pink flesh of her fat soft shoulders, white straps like tiny tent ropes converged to a double support of the mammary mountains trembling in bondage underneath.

'Evening, Mr Fox. What'll it be?'

'Ever practical,' Fox said. 'We will have the usual. Three times. This is our co-worker, Mr Coffey.'

'Pleased to meet you,' Rose said. She opened a glass jar, removed three pickled eggs, put three slices of rye bread on three plates, then, turning again, looked at Coffey. 'What's the matter with him?' she asked Fox.

'He needs cheering, that's all,' Fox said. 'Go, lovely Rose, bring us that which cheers and doth inebriate.'

'Now watch yourself,' Rose said. 'The Provincials was in here last night. They'll be back.'

'We'll wu-watch it,' Harry assured her. 'Give us tu-two cu-cokes to colour it.'

From beneath the counter, Rose took a large paper bag, added two coke bottles to its contents, and handed the bag to Harry. Fox led the way into a small back room near the toilet. The bag was opened and a large bottle was placed on the table. The label read: *Vin Canadien Type-Sherry.* Fox uncorked it and drank several swallows. 'Now, Harry,' he said. 'Pour the cokes in. And if any policeman pays a call we are enjoying the pause that refreshes. Right?'

'Right,' Harry said. The cokes were added and full glassfuls distributed. 'Du-drink up,' Harry said.

Coffey picked up his drink. It tasted sweetish but not strong. He drank it down and poured another. Yes, what matter if he got drunk? Drink and these companions would be his future life. Down, down, down, all his boats burned. He had failed. Now he must do a far, far better thing. . . .

'Count your blessings,' Fox told him. 'Think of old Billy. You have your health and strength.'

He drank a third glass, not listening. Alone he would be, an ancient mariner who had looked for the bluebird. He would grow a feathery goatee, his voice would change, nasal and reedy. Old Ginger Coffey, fifty years a reader, a man in humble circs. He stared through the open doorway at the customers in the outer room. Humble circs, all of them. How many of them had dreamed, as he had once, of adventures, of circs not humble in the least? And what had happened to those dreams of theirs? Ah dear God, what did you do when you could no longer dream? How did you reconcile yourself to those humble circs? 'Suffering J,' he said. 'So this is what it's like.'

'What *what's* like?' Fox said, pouring.

'The bottom. The dustbin. The end of the road.'

'Bottom?' Fox shouted. 'Why, you don't know what bottom is, Paddy. Now, take me. Three years ago you could find me up the street outside Windsor Station, panhandling dimes at two in the morning. Without an overcoat, mind you, and the weather at zero. That's bottom, Paddy. Bottom is a dime. A dime and a dime and a dime until you can buy your peace of mind in the large jug of Bright's Hermitage Port. Bottom is when your clothes are too far gone for anyone not to notice, and there's no chance of a job because they do notice. Bottom is that, Paddy. Not this. Why, this is regular employment.'

'Bottom's when you lose your wife,' Coffey said thickly. 'That's bottom. Bottom's when bloody liars make promises and bloody wife-stealers run off with your wife. Bottom's this bloody country, snow and ice, bloody hell on earth – '

'Yu-you leave Cu-Canada out of this,' Harry said menacingly. 'Gu-goddamn immigrants. Go on back where you came from.'

'No, we have room for all sorts,' Fox said. 'We're the third largest country in the world, remember. We need our quota of malcontents.'

'I'm sorry,' Coffey said thickly. 'Didn't mean to insult you fellows. Thinking about my wife. Not Canada. Leave Canada out of this.'

'He doesn't want to talk about Canada,' Fox said. 'Leave Canada out. There you have the Canadian dilemma in a sentence. Nobody wants to talk about Canada, not even us Canadians. You're right, Paddy. Canada is a bore.'

'No, I didn't mean that,' Coffey said. 'I'm just – listen, I've just lost my wife. And my little girl. Lost them.'

But Fox was not listening. 'Poor old Canada,' he wailed. 'Not even a flag to call its own. Land of Eskimo and Mountie, land of beaver and moose – '

Coffey poured another glass and tried to stand up. Suffering J, what was in this wine, what's the matter? His legs felt like melting wax. How could he go home tonight to tell her that he would keep his word? How could he make his lonely exit in dignity, and him half drunk? Ah dear God –

'Sit down,' Fox shouted.

He turned towards the shouting voice, confused. 'Must go,' he said.

'Sit down!' Fox's cane caught him a smart blow behind his woozy knees and Coffey sat down. 'I'm speaking to you, you bogman, you!' Fox shouted.

In trembling pain Coffey leaned across the table, inches from his tormentor's stubbled face. Cruel cripple doomsayer! He bunched his fist, raising it to strike that yelling mouth –

'Now don't hit me. Don't!' Fox shouted.

Dully, Coffey lowered his fist. At once Fox picked up the wine jug, swinging it in a menacing sweep. 'Don't you dare walk out on me,' he yelled. 'I can't stand people walking out on me!'

White shoes, soundless on their rubber soles, moved up behind Fox. Rose Alma Briggs deftly caught the swinging jug. 'That's enough of that,' she said.

'Oh, Rose of all the world,' Fox shouted. 'Go, lovely Rose.'

Rose moved behind him, reached under his armpits, set him tottering on his feet. 'Out,' she said. 'That's an order. And this is the last time you use my place as a wine drop, any of you. Come on Harry. Help him.'

For an instant Fox's glazed eyes grew bright with rage. He gripped his cane, raising it like a club; held it suspended over the table for a moment, then lowered it. 'No,' he said. 'No violence. No police. No doctors. Give me liberty or give me death, right, Rose? Yes, Rose. Yes, all. Good night, all.'

Harry took his arm. Together they threaded their way among the tables of the outer room. The street door opened with a huff of wind, then banged shut as the drunkards met the winter snow, circling like lost birds on the pavement. Rose Alma turned to Coffey. 'Poor man,' she said. 'He was in the asylum, you know. Dee-tees.' She bent and began to stack the dishes on the table. 'You don't want to get mixed up with the likes of them. They're winos.'

Coffey felt for a chair and sat down. His legs were trembling, the sweat on his brow was cold, his head felt swollen and heavy. 'Not mixed up,' he said drunkenly. 'This job – just a stopgap, you see. I'm a New Canadian, you see.'

Rose looked at him. 'You married?'

'Yes.'

'Well, why don't you go home to your wife then? It's late.'

He put his hands up; felt his face fall into them. He rested his face in his hands. 'My wife's leaving me,' he said.

'No wonder,' Rose said. 'If you carry on like this.'

'I didn't carry on. She did.'

'Maybe she had a reason, did you ever think of that? Now, go on home.'

He raised his face from his hands. Two Rose Almas stacked dishes, side by side. 'A reason?' he said.

'Carrying on like this,' said the double images of Rose. 'You men. Do you know what women have to put up with? Now, go on home.'

'Home?' he said. 'I have no home,' he told them.

'Where do you sleep then?'

'In my own bed. Not allowed in hers, you see.'

'Come on now.' The two Roses came close to him. 'This way.'

They raised him up. He tried to focus on the outer room. There were twins of all the customers. He rubbed his eyes, trying to make them come together, but they, like Rose, remained bi-focal. 'Come with me,' Rose said. 'Watch out for those girls over there. You don't want to get in trouble, now do you?'

'What girls?' he said. 'Where girls?'

Rose took his arm, led him across the room, past the whores' table. 'Have a girl,' he said. 'My own little girl. Going to lose her now.'

'No, you won't,' Rose said. 'Now come on. Bus stop's right across the street. You got a ticket?'

He nodded, not hearing, hearing only words.

'You'll feel better tomorrow,' her voice said. 'Things will look better then.'

'No.' He stopped, turned to her, his face pale and confused. Behind that large trembly dignity, behind that military façade of moustache and middle age, Rose Alma saw his true face. Like a boy, she thought. Lost.

'Never better now,' he mumbled. 'Got to give them up ... promised ... word of honour ... word – of – honour. My

179

Paulie too. Growing up. Trouble with boys. I – made mess that too.'

'Never mind,' Rose Alma said. 'They need you. Go home.'

She opened the café door and suddenly he faced the street. A gust of wind struck a near-by rooftop, whirling a powdery gust down to blind him, covering his moustache and eyebrows with a fine white granulation. Aged white in one moment, old Coffey crossed the street, stumbling over a snowbank, headed for two street lamps each labelled with a tin sign: BUS. BUS. He was going home, wake Veronica, renounce her and then, lonely, his barque cast adrift, he would leave again, going into the Arctic night, condemned for ever to this land of ice and snow, this hell on earth, alone for ever in his Y.M.C.A. room....

He tried to focus down the street, looking for a bus. No bus. Instead, a huge trailer truck came uphill, red warning lights aflicker, a groaning giant condemned to move at night. It drew near and bi-focally, two tiny drivers looked down on Coffey from their high riding cabs.

The driver looked out, saw the man standing under the lamp, tiny green hat snowmatted, his moustache and eyebrows white, peering up, a lost drunk nightface. The great truck rode on.

A night wind crossed the frozen river, whirled along the empty ice-locked docks, rushed into the street. Coffey bent his head to the wind and, cold, confused, began to feel a natural urge which would not wait. The street was quiet. Only in the Five Minute Lunch was there light. Still trying to focus, he peered at the buildings on his side, looking for a lane. There was no lane. But there was a large darkened doorway, some office building entrance, and there, unable to wait any longer, he stepped into the shadows.

A police prowl car turned the corner from the railroad goods depot behind the station, its tyres noiseless in the thick night snow. In the front seat, two uniformed constables looked over at Rose's place then swept their searchlight beam along the front of the hotel opposite. The constable who was not driving rolled down the window and stopped the searchlight glare on what he saw. In the main doorway, legs apart, head bent in humble concentration, a man.

180

'*Tu vois ça?*' the constable said to his colleague.

'*Calvaire!*' the driver said, revving his engine.

Coffey, fumbling to adjust his dress, heard the engine sound. Still blinded by the harsh eye which had picked him out, he did not see the constable but felt a hand touch his elbow.

'*Viens ici, toi,*' the constable said.

'I – what?'

The constable did not reply, but led him towards the waiting prowl car. The other constable sat quiet at the wheel.

'What do you think you're doing?' the first constable asked.

Coffey told him. 'Just waiting for the bus, waiting a long time, you see, so I had a call of nature. I mean, there was nobody –'

'You hadmit the oohfense?' the second constable said in a strong French-Canadian accent.

'Well now, look here –'

'Where do you work?'

'The *Tribune*.'

Constable One looked at Constable Two. This was a matter for caution. Police and Press relations. 'What do you do there, sir?' said Constable One.

'Proofreader. Galley slave.'

'*S'qu'il dit?*' the second constable asked the first.

'*Zéro,*' said the first.

'He's been drinkin' the wine,' the second constable said, sniffing Coffey.

'Well, I was with some friends – look here, officer – ah now, for the love of God, man, be fair. I'm not drunk –'

'Get in the car.'

'Ah now, we don't have to do that, we can settle this, can't we.'

The first constable seized Coffey's left wrist and jerked it up against his back, bending Coffey double. In that way he was led towards the car. 'Get in!'

So he got in and the first policeman got in the back beside him. The car started its engine, the police radio crackled and the driver made a report to radio control as they drove through the deserted streets. The report was in French, so Coffey did not understand it.

At the police station they made him wait. He sat on a bench, staring at a room full of two-headed policemen. Veronica must not know. Paulie must not know. Must get out of this. Just a fine or a warning, probably. Now see here, Sergeant ... Reason with them. Ach now listen, to me Sergeant, married man, little girl and wife, one over the eight, no harm meant, hmm?

But still ... there were so many tabloid weeklies in this cursed city. Suppose it were reported in one of them. All full of rape they were, and other sexual misdemeanours....

He exhaled, feathering up the ends of his large moustache. IMMIGRANT CHARGED WITH DISORDERLY CONDUCT. A nice thing for Paulie to see. Nice thing indeed. Flute! You're not going to let that happen, are you? Not likely. He'd give a false name, that's what he would do. False name, that was the ticket. With any luck he'd get a fine and be home by morning. Right, then!

The double images had diminished to single ones by the time he was called up to the sergeant's desk. 'Name and address?' said the sergeant.

'Gerald MacGregor,' Coffey said, and gave the address of Madame Beaulieu's duplex.

The desk sergeant started a long conversation in French with the radio car officers. They reached an agreement. 'Okay,' the sergeant said to them. He turned to Coffey. 'We're not booking you on a vag,' he said. 'We're going to book you for indecent exposure. That's the charge.'

'Wait a minute, sergeant,' Coffey said. 'Couldn't we settle this here – it was all an accident. A mistake.'

'Now, put all what's in your pockets in this bag,' the sergeant interrupted.

'Ah now, sergeant –'

'And take your tie off.'

'Ah, sergeant, ah now, listen, I'm an immigrant here, I didn't know it was any crime –'

'And give me your belt.'

'Sergeant, did you hear me? Listen – I'm a married man with a little girl. Ah God, you've no right to enter a thing like that in the record.'

'*Prends lui,*' the sergeant said to the jailer. '*Numéro Six.*'

The jailer took him in the back and led him down a flight of stairs. A detective was coming up. They stopped to let him pass. The detective, a fat young man with a crew cut and a moustache almost as large as Coffey's, stopped and said: '*Le gars, s'qu'il a fait, lui?*'

The jailer laughed. '*A fait pisser juste dans la grande porte du Royal Family Hotel.*'

'Oh-hoh!' the detective said, grinning at Coffey. 'What's de matter? You don' like the English, eh? Or the Royal Family? Or maybe you just don' like the hotel?'

'What – what do you mean?' Coffey said. 'What does he mean?' he asked the jailer.

'Move your ass,' the jailer said. He pushed Coffey towards the last flight of steps, led him along a corridor and unlocked the door of a cell. There were two men sleeping inside. Coffey, undignified, holding up his trousers with both hands, made one last appeal to justice. 'Listen to me,' he said. 'Please, will you let me speak to the sergeant again?'

'Don't piss on de other boys in here,' the jailer said, shoving him in. 'Dey won't like it.'

The cell door shut. The lock turned. The jailer went back upstairs. Sick, Coffey let his trousers sag as he groped for and found a bench. He sat down, hearing the harsh cough of his cellmate. The cell was clean but stank of beer or wine or something. Or, was it he who ...? He did not know. One floor above him he heard the policemen walking about, talking, laughing at an occasional sally or bit of horseplay. Up there, just one flight of stairs, men were free. While down here – Oh God! Childish memories of being shut in a closet, of calling out to playmates who had run away, of beating on the door, unanswered: these swam in on him now, making it impossible to say chin up, steady as she goes, or any of the rest of it. Ever since he could remember he had read of prison sentences in secret dread. *Jail.* Yes, they could send him to jail. Oh God, he prayed....

Oh Who? What did God care, if there were a God? Or was it God who had pulled the rug out, once and for all, who had now decided to show him once and for all that he had been a lunatic to have hopes, that his ship would never come in, that he had lost his wife and child for ever?

Steady. Steady as she goes, he told himself. Don't panic. Steady on there.

But it was no good. Upstairs, the policemen broke out in another round of laughter. He put his face in his hands, his lower teeth biting into the hair on his upper lip. Ah no, no, there was no sense blaming a God he could not believe in, there was no sense blaming anyone. Vera was right. *He was to blame.* If he had been content with his lot at home, he would never have come out to this cursed country. If he had never come out here, he would not have lost Veronica to Grosvenor; Paulie would not be running around with young hoodlums older than she. If he had not come out here, he would not be a proofreader with no hope of advancement, he would not be in jail tonight. Why hadn't he gone straight home? Whose fault was it he was drunk? His fault.

Yes, his fault. What a bloody fool he had been giving that wrong name and address. They had put his belongings in a bag, but if they looked in his wallet they would crucify him. He should call out now, go upstairs, apologize, get a lawyer, tell them his real name.

He went quickly to the cell door and peered out of the small judas window at the corridor. The window was thick-glassed, with a wire-netting grille. He could see no more. He stepped back, trying to peer sideways down the corridor and, as he did, he saw his own face, angled in the reflection from the glass pane. He stared at that sad impostor, at that hateful, stupid man. Yes, look at you, would you? You that promised you would drop out of sight. You that would do a far, far better thing, look at you! What sort of man would call out now, what sort of man would disgrace Veronica and Paulie because he was afraid of being locked up?

He stepped back into the darkness of the cell again. He could not bear to look at that hateful, stupid man. He was not that man. He was Ginger Coffey who had given a false name to protect the innocent and now must take his punishment.

He sat down, his trousers loose around his hips. It was dark. He was afraid.

But oh! he knew something now, something he had not known before. A man's life was nobody's fault but his own. Not God's, not Vera's, not even Canada's. His own fault. *Mea culpa.*

Chapter Thirteen

SHORTLY after dawn someone in a near-by cell began to beat on the door and call out in French. This woke everyone up. The jailer came downstairs, unlocked the cell and led the prisoner out. One of Coffey's cellmates wiped his nose on his sleeve and said: 'They never learn.'

'What d'you mean?'

'They'll take him up in the back room now and tire him a bit.'

'Oh?' Coffey went to the cell door and listened. He could hear no sound upstairs. He heard his third cellmate say: 'You bother them, they tire you, that's right. Just keep quiet is the best.'

Several minutes later the jailer brought back the man who had been shouting. The man held both hands over his stomach and his face was pale. After he had been locked in again, he could be heard retching. Coffey's cellmates exchanged nods. One said: 'In Bordeaux they beat the shit out of you whether you bother them or not. Minute you get in, they fix you.'

'Where's Bordeaux?' Coffey asked.

'Provincial jail. What are you up for, Jack?'

'Ah – I was taking a leak in the open last night and the police found me.'

'A vag, eh?'

'A vag?' The word was familiar. 'No, it wasn't that they called it. Indecent exposure, it was.'

His cellmates exchanged glances. One of them coughed. 'Well,' he said. 'I'd rather it was you, not me.'

At eight o'clock a bell rang. A jailer came down to the cells, called a roll from a typewritten list and ordered the prisoners to line up at their cell doors. Several other policemen appeared. The prisoners were marched upstairs and Coffey, with three other men, was put in a waiting-room. There was a policeman in the room. One of the prisoners begged a light.

186

'NO TALKING!' shouted the policeman.

At eight thirty-one, Coffey and three others were taken to the back door of the police station. A van was backed into the alley, its engine running. A policeman helped them up, a second policeman handed the driver a list and the doors of the Black Maria were locked. There were already two prisoners in the van and it stopped at three police stations in the next half-hour. By the time it reached a court-house somewhere in the harbour area, the van was crowded with men and reeked of alcohol and sweat. They were disembarked in a yard and, as they waited to be marched away, Coffey saw a newspaper kiosk in the street outside, its walls plastered with tabloid headlines. One of them read:

CADI SENTENCES 'FOUL EXPOSER'
MERCY PLEA REJECTED

Suffering J! Better they sentence him to jail than Paulie ever read the like of that. This was his fault. Everything was his fault. He must pay for it himself.

'Right,' said a warder. 'MARCH!'

One of the prisoners, an old man, said: 'Is there a toilet inside? I need to go to the toilet.'

The warder turned and bellowed as though struck. 'NO TALKING IN THE CORRIDORS.'

They were marched downstairs and locked up.

Above the judge there was a large crucifix. The Christ figure seemed to recline, head to one side, as though trying to catch the half-audible mumble of the clerk of the court. '– criminal code – statute – section – said Gerald MacGregor – night of – premises – indecently expose himself – as witness –'

A lawyer, arriving late, entered the courtroom and hurried up the aisle, shaking hands with his colleagues. The reporters on the Press bench were reading a newspaper called *Le Devoir*: they did not appear to have paid attention to the charge. The judge, a florid man who might have been mistaken for a bookmaker, was having trouble with his Parker pen. He signalled a court functionary who went through the door leading to the judge's chambers. A detective-sergeant came in and stood beneath the judge, waiting. The clerk of the court finished his mumble and sat down. The judge unscrewed his Parker pen, and noticed the waiting detective-sergeant. The sergeant stepped forward and whispered. The judge looked at Coffey.

'Swear the accused,' he said.

Coffey was sworn in. The judge said: 'Now – is your name Gerald MacGregor?'

Coffey looked desperately at the crucifix over the judge's bench. The Christ figure lent an ear: waiting.

'I warn you,' the judge said, 'No one by the name of MacGregor lives at the address you have given. Do you still say that is your name?'

In terror, Coffey looked at the detective-sergeant. Vera and Paulie? – must protect – 'Yes, your honour,' he said.

'All right.' The judge nodded to the sergeant. 'Bring your witness in.'

The sergeant signalled to a court attendant and the court attendant went outside. In her best blue coat, her eyes downcast, Veronica was escorted to the bench. She was sworn in. Her eyes met Coffey's, then flittered towards the Press bench. The reporters were taking notes now. She gave her name and address.

'Is this man your husband?'

'Yes.'

'What is his given name?'

'James Francis Coffey.'

'You may stand down. Clerk, read the charge again in the name of James Francis Coffey.'

She went to a front seat and sat down. She looked up at him and her fingers fluttered in a tiny, surreptitious greeting. She was afraid.

'Now, Coffey,' the judge said. 'Why did you give a false name?'

'I – ah – didn't want my wife and daughter mixed up in this, you see.'

'I do not see,' the judge said. 'You have heard the charge. Have you any idea of the gravity of this charge?'

'Well, no, your honour. You see – I mean, I wanted to avoid

– I mean, it wasn't their fault. I didn't want them to be worried.'

'This charge,' the judge said, 'carries a maximum penalty of seven years in prison.'

Coffey looked at Veronica. She seemed about to keel over. *Seven years.*

'Well, Coffey? What do you have to say for yourself?'

'I – I'm an immigrant here, your honour, and I've not done very well getting settled. My wife . . .' He stopped and looked at Veronica, who lowered her head, not answering his look. 'My wife and I had agreed to separate unless I did better. I'd promised her that unless I got a certain promotion, I'd let her go back to – I mean, leave me. And I promised she could take my daughter as well. So last night, I didn't get the promotion and so . . .'

He could not go on. He stood, looking down at her, looking at the white nape of her neck beneath the hairline of her new short haircut. The judge said: 'What's all this got to do with perjuring yourself?'

'Well, I'd lost them anyway, your honour. I didn't want them to suffer any more for what I'd done. So I thought of a false name . . .'

The judge looked at the sergeant. 'Is the prisoner represented by counsel?'

'*A pas demandé,*' the sergeant said.

'This case is being tried in English,' the judge said, testily.

'Sorry, sir. He didn't ask for a lawyer.'

The judge sighed. He put both halves of his Parker pen together, screwed them tight, then laid the pen down.

'How do you plead?' he said to Coffey. 'Guilty or not guilty?'

'Not guilty, your honour.'

'Very well. Call the first witness.'

Constable Armand Bissonette, Radio Mobile Unit, Station Number 10, took the stand. Following the witness's testimony, he was cross examined by Judge Amédée Monceau.

His Honour: 'Was there anyone else in the street at the time?'

Witness: 'Not so far as we could see, sir.'

His Honour: 'Then no one witnessed the act except the police?'

Witness: 'Maybe there were people inside the hotel lobby who saw it.'

His Honour: 'Did you actually see any people?'

Witness: 'No, sir.'

His Honour: 'And the doorway was dark?'

Witness: 'Yes, but there were lights in the lobby, inside the door.'

His Honour: 'Were those lights visible from the doorway?'

Witness: 'Yes, if he had looked in, he would have seen that it was a hotel lobby. But he was on the wine, sir. He could hardly see straight.'

His Honour: 'He was intoxicated?'

Witness: 'He's a wino, sir. I smelled the wine off him.'

His Honour (to accused): 'What did you have to drink?'

Accused: 'Your Honour, I had some glasses of wine. It was a sort of mixture of sherry and Coca-Cola. I didn't intend to get drunk.'

His Honour: 'You're Irish, by the sound of you. Is that an Irish recipe?'

(LAUGHTER)

His Honour: 'If that didn't make you drunk, it should have made you ill. Were you ill?'

Accused: 'Yes, Your Honour. I felt a bit dizzy. And I had been waiting a long time for the bus.'

His Honour: 'How long?'

Accused: 'More than twenty minutes, sir. Maybe half an hour.'

His Honour: 'Half an hour? Well, I can see you're not a native of this city. Half an hour is not a long time here.'

(LAUGHTER)

Coffey looked at them: the judge grinning at his witticism, the lawyers looking up to laugh with the bench, the spectators lolling back in their seats like people enjoying a joke in church. Seven years in prison and yet they laughed. But why not? What was he to all these people except a funny man with a

190

brogue, not a person; an occasion of laughter. His whole life, back to those days when he ran past the iron railings of Stephen's Green, late for school, back through the university years, the army years, the years at Kylemore and Coomb-Na-Baun, through courtship, marriage, fatherhood, his parents' death, his hopes, his humiliations – it was just a joke. All he was this morning, facing prison and ruin, was an excuse for courtroom sallies. So what did it matter, his life in this world, when this was what the world was like? Unsurely but surely he came to that. His hopes, his ambitions, his dreams: what were they but shams? Only one face in that courtroom suffered with him, knew him as more than a joke, was one with him on this awful morning. One face, which fifteen years ago in Saint Pat's in Dalkey had turned from the priest to look at him and say 'I do'.

The judge rapped on his desk. The laughter stopped.

His Honour, Judge Amédée Monceau addressed the prosecution. His Honour stated that under the circumstances, the lateness of the hour, the absence of proven intoxication, the lack of witnesses to the action, the fact that there was no known previous criminal record, there was some question in His Honour's mind as to why the police had preferred the more serious charge. A charge of vagrancy might, His Honour suggested, have been more appropriate in this instance.

Detective-Sergeant Taillefer: 'Your Honour, this act was committed in the front lobby of one of the biggest hotels in the city.'

His Honour: 'Yes, but you have not proved that there were any witnesses.'

Detective-Sergeant Taillefer: 'Well, the police took such speedy action, sir, that nobody was disturbed.'

His Honour: 'Sergeant, if the police department is ever in need of a public relations officer, I'll be very happy to recommend you. But if there are to be any further compliments to the police department this morning, will you please allow them to come from me?'

(LAUGHTER)

Down there in the courtroom the spectators looked up, enjoying the discomfiture of the police sergeant. No one looked at him, the central figure in this drama. No one, not even she. For she sat, her head bent; humiliated. Was she humiliated because this laughter was a criticism of her, a mockery of her taste in marrying a man who had indecently exposed himself to the world's ridicule, whose sufferings merited the world's attention only as a subject for farce? Likely that was it, he thought. For didn't she want shot of him too, wasn't she here only because the police had found his true address and ordered her presence in this court? Oh, Vera, Vera, look at me would you . . .?

But she did not look at him. She did not care for him any more than the rest of them. Nobody cared for him.

His Honour: 'Accused, stand up. Have you anything to say in your defence?'

Accused: 'I didn't know it was a hotel, Your Honour. I thought it was an office building. It was an accident.'

His Honour: 'I see. And in your country is it common practice to relieve oneself in office doorways? Are you asking me to believe the Irish are uncivilized?'

Accused: 'No, Your Honour.'

His Honour: 'I see. Well, let me inform you, Coffey, your actions last night constitute a serious crime in this province. Now, as I understand it, there were certain extenuating circumstances. It was late at night and you were at the mercy of the Montreal Transportation Commission –'

(LAUGHTER)

His Honour: 'And certainly, having imbibed the concoction which you described to this court there is every reason that your system should seek to expel it as soon as possible in one way or another.'

(LAUGHTER)

His Honour: 'However, the fact remains that your action in a public – a very public – place might have caused considerable shock and outrage to innocent bystanders. In the event of your action being committed deliberately to shock and outrage such bystanders, the charge laid against you by the police would seem justified. And, as I have already told you, the maximum sentence for that offence is seven years in prison.'

Veronica raised her head. There were tears in her eyes and her face was terribly pale. She stared at him as though only she and he were in the room. He looked at her: his legs no longer trembled. He saw it in her eyes: it was not shame of him, it was fear for him. He looked up at the judge, no longer afraid.

His Honour: 'Now, Coffey, in the absence of defending counsel, this court considers you to have thrown yourself upon its mercy. And despite the charge laid against you by these officers, I am inclined to believe that in view of the mitigating circumstances there was no criminal intent on your part. So I am giving you the benefit of the doubt. I hereby sentence you to six months in prison –'

His eyes left the judge's face: went to her below him. Something had happened. A court usher and a spectator were bending over her. Fainted? The court usher was helping her from her seat. Watching, Coffey barely heard the judge's next phrase.

'– however, in this case, sentence will be suspended, in view of the fact that you have no previous conviction and are an immigrant with a wife and child to support. I am dealing with you leniently, Coffey, because I am sorry for your family. To be alone in a new country, with their breadwinner in jail, seems to me a fate which your wife and child do not deserve. But let me warn you that if for any reason you again find yourself before this court, you will, I assure you, have every cause to regret it.'

They had taken her outside. He was all alone now. He stared at the judge.

His Honour: 'In conclusion, let me remind the police officers concerned that in cases of this kind all available evidence should be weighed before a charge is preferred. It is because of carelessness in determining the charges against defendants

193

that this court has been obliged, time after time, to render verdicts against the prosecution. That is all, gentlemen.'

A warder tapped him on the shoulder. He was led back to the detention room.

'My wife – ?'

One of the warders stepped on Coffey's toes. It hurt. 'Sorry,' the warder said. 'What's that you said?'

'My wife, is she –'

The detective-sergeant, smiling, stepped on Coffey's toes. 'Twenty years on the Force,' he said. 'And I never saw a judge give a guy a break like you got. Luck of the Irish, it must be, eh, Irishman?'

The sergeant poked him in the ribs. It was not a friendly poke. The warder made him sign for his belongings. Then, they let him go.

The corridor outside was crowded with people. Witnesses, waiting their turn in court, lawyers in corner conference with clients and colleagues, policemen walking up and down with the proprietary air of museum guides. He ran past them all, ranging this way and that, finally emerging into a large hall where two court ushers sat on a stone bench near the main door. He went to them.

'Excuse me,' he said, newly afraid, for they were policemen. He expected them to shout 'NO TALKING'. But instead they were the police he had always known.

'Yes, sir?'

'Did you see a woman? I mean a woman fainted in the court there, did she go out this way?'

'In a blue coat, right?' the usher said. 'Yes, we put her in a taxi a minute ago.'

'I'm her husband,' he said. 'Do you know the address she went to?'

They thought this over. One said: 'A number on Notre Dame Street, I think.'

He thanked them and turned towards the doorway. He felt weak, as though he had risen from a month in bed. Notre Dame Street was Grosvenor's office. Ah, God, it was plain as the nose on your face. She had fainted: she had not even

194

waited to hear the whole thing. She had not waited for him but had gone off to her lover. Ginger's in jail. Gerry we're free.

Yes, he had been wrong to hope. He was right the first time. She did not care about him. Nobody cared.

Through the main doorway, under the Latinate scrolls to justice and truth, he moved, his step that of an old, old man. He was a wanderer who had sought the bluebird, who had seen all, who knew now that this was what the world was like. He stood at the top of the wide fall of steps which went down to the streets of the city, that city of which he had hoped so much, which had laughed at his hopes, which had turned him out. He looked up at the sky. Grey clouds ballooned down like the dirty underside of a great circus tent. Yet, oh! Never since he had lain in a field as a small boy had the heavens seemed so soaring, so illimitable. And in that moment his heart filled with an unpredictable joy. He was free. The night that had passed, the cells below stairs, the shouting warders, the terrifying laughter of the spectators in court; it had happened and yet it had not. It was a nightmare washed into nothingness by the simple and glorious fact of freedom. The city, its roofs and cornices crusted with snow, its rushing inhabitants muffled in furs, seemed a busy, magical place, a joy to be abroad in. For one liberating moment he became a child again; lost himself as a child can, letting himself go into the morning, a drop of water joining an ocean, mystically becoming one.

He forgot Ginger Coffey and Ginger's life. No longer was he a man running uphill against hope, his shins kicked, his luck running out. He was no one: he was eyes staring at the sky. He was the sky.

A passer-by bumped against him; went down the wide steps. The moment detached itself, leaving him weak and wondering. That was happiness. Would it ever come again? Wishing would not bring it back, nor ambitions, nor sacrifice, nor love. Why was it that true joy, this momentary release, could come even in his hour of loss and failure? It could not be wished for: it came unawares. It came more often in childhood, but it might come again and again, even at the end of a life.

Slowly, he descended the court-house steps. Yes, a momentary happiness might come to him again. But was that all he could hope for now – a few mystical moments spaced out over a lifetime? Yes, it might be all.

Wish, if I could wish, what would I wish for now?

But he thought of her. He thought of his promise to go away. He must not wish. He must go. Yes, he must go.

Chapter Fourteen

He let himself in, cautiously. There was always the chance that Veronica might have come back. But when he opened the hall closet, her coat was not there. As Paulie was at school there was no further need for him to be quiet. He went into the bedroom and began to pack a suitcase. He took shirts from the dresser drawer, avoiding the man in the mirror. He no longer felt any interest in that man. He no longer felt any interest in Ginger Coffey. He felt like someone else.

Suddenly, down the hall, the shower went on. Saturday! Of course. Paulie was at home. He wanted to hide. He did not want questions; did not want to be forced to explain why he must go. Hurriedly, he tried to finish the clumsy job of stuffing his clothes into the suitcase. But the suitcase slid off the bed with a thump. The shower stopped. He heard Paulie's footsteps in the corridor.

'Mummy, is that you? . . . Mummy? . . . Who's that?' Her voice changed from inquiry to doubt, to fear, and of course it was not fair to frighten her by letting her think he was a thief or something. He opened the door and there was Paulie in her bathrobe, her face and neck still dewed with shower steam. 'Oh, it's you, Daddy,' she said. 'Where were you?'

'In here.'

'No, I mean where *were* you? We were nearly demented. And then, this morning, when that policeman came in the car for Mummy, I was sure you were in a hospital or even killed. Now what *happened*?'

'I was in jail,' he said.

'Oh, you're joking!' But as she said it, she ran to him and hugged him. 'I was worried, Daddy.'

'Were you, Pet?' He was surprised. He took her face in his hands and raised it up. Yes, she took after him: there was something of him in her reddish hair, her worried eyes. She was his child and she had worried for him. If he asked her to come away with him now, she might come. . . .

But where? And why? His hand stroked the back of her head. She loved him: it was more than he had a right to expect. Let her be.

'My hair's just set,' she said. 'Please don't mess it, Daddy.'

He released her. He must finish his packing, without her knowing. 'What about getting me some coffee?' he said.

'Okay, Daddy. But what *is* all this about jail?'

'It's a long story, Apple. I'll tell you some other time.'

'Tell me now.'

'Some other time,' he said.

She went to the kitchen. He shut the bedroom door and picked the bag off the floor, repacking it. She had worried for him: she loved him. That moved him more than he thought he could be moved again. Still, he had made a promise. He must go. He shut the suitcase and, so that she would not see it, he went to the hall closet and hid it. After the coffee, he would slip away. . . .

But the hall door opened as he closed the closet. Veronica. Slowly, he turned to face her. It was like those long ago days when, having failed the examination, you must face the anger, the reproach.

'Is it you?' she said.

'Yes.'

'But you're supposed to be in jail?'

'It was a suspended sentence.'

'Oh.'

He looked at her. She looked at him. Caught, like strangers who eye each other on a train, they pretended the glance was accidental. 'Well . . .' he said. He opened the closet and took out his car coat.

'Are you going out?'

He put on his coat and reached in again for his little green hat. 'I'm going away. They're not going to make me a reporter, now or ever. So you can get the divorce. I'll be in touch with you.'

He stood for a moment, facing the closet; feeling watched; not wanting to meet the eyes that watched him.

'What about Paulie? Does Paulie know?'

'No,' he said.

'Well, don't you think you should tell her?'

'You tell her.' He turned, little green hat in one hand, suitcase in the other. 'Would you open the door for me, Vera?'

Their eyes met. One person in the whole world who had known him; one person who knew him as more than a joke. A person who, fifteen years ago in Saint Pat's in Dalkey had knelt beside him at the altar and promised. . . .

'Before you go,' she said. 'There's one thing I want to explain. I didn't run away this morning.'

He put down his suitcase. He would have to open the door himself. She wasn't going to help him.

'Listen, Ginger. When I heard the judge say "six months", I keeled over. Then, when they took me out, I thought the best thing to do would be to go to Gerry's office and try to get a lawyer so that you could appeal.'

He opened the door and picked up his suitcase.

'You don't believe me, is that it?'

'It doesn't matter,' he said. It did not matter.

'Gerry refused to help you,' she said. 'That's why I came back here.'

'Look, Vera, I have to go now.'

'But, just a *second*, will you?' Her voice was urgent and strained. 'I want to tell you what Gerry said to me. He said it was the best thing that could have happened. He said it would make the divorce easier. That's all he cared about.'

'Well, it doesn't matter, does it?' he said. 'It's former history.'

She bent her head, and suddenly rubbed at her eyes with her knuckles, leaving a smudge of mascara on the bridge of her nose. 'Dammit,' she said. 'I'm sorry. Don't you see, I'm sorry?'

Sorry? What was she sorry about? What did sorry cure? She'd told him that once. Now, he knew what she meant. He stood, suitcase in hand, at the open doorway. He must go.

'Wait,' she said. 'There's something else too. Only I can't tell it, with you standing there like some door-to-door salesman. Come into our room a minute. I don't want Paulie to hear.'

Unwillingly, he put down his suitcase and followed her back

to the bedroom. What use was there in all this? Why must she make it so hard?

She shut the bedroom door. 'Now, listen,' she said. 'I never slept with Gerry. On my word of honour. I wouldn't do it until you and I were legally separated.'

He nodded. Get it over with.

'You should have seen Gerry just now,' she said. 'He behaved like a total stranger. How could anyone love a person who'd let someone go to jail and be glad of it? He doesn't love me, either, he just wants me. Whereas you – you stood up in the courtroom this morning and gave a false name for my sake and for Paulie's –'

She stopped. She seemed to be waiting for him to tell her something.

'All right then,' she said. 'If that's the way of it, won't you even kiss me good-bye?'

Kiss this stranger? Unwillingly, he put his arms around her. She was shaking. He looked down at the nape of her neck, bared by her new hairdo. It was unfamiliar, yet familiar. Ah God! Had he been wrong in that, as well? For, now that he held her, she was no stranger at all, but Veronica, the woman he had slept with how many thousand nights. Veronica: older and heavier than the girl he had married, her breasts a little too big, her eyes edged with small white lines, her hand, now touching his cheek, roughened by years over sinks and washtubs. Veronica. No stranger: not desirable.

'Ginger,' she said. 'You still love me, don't you? You said you did.'

Love her? This body familiar as his own. Desire her? This woman growing old.

'Even if you don't love me,' she said. 'There's Paulie. That child wept half the night, worrying about you. You can't walk out on her now.'

Didn't you walk out on Paulie, he thought. But what was the use in blaming her. Blame was his. 'Look,' he said. 'You'd better off, you and Paulie . . .'

He did not go on. Someone else was saying all this. Not Ginger Coffey. Someone who had stopped looking for the good in the bad; who had stopped running uphill in hopes; someone who knew the truth. He did not love her: he could no longer love. He did not want to watch her cry. She was getting old: she was just another illusion he no longer had. He began to button his overcoat.

'No, we wouldn't,' she was saying. 'Because it wasn't only your fault, it was mine. When I saw Gerry just now – I mean, saw the real Gerry – I knew it was my fault. What I mean is, I'd like to start again. Listen, we *could* start again if you wanted to? You could get that job as Mr Brott's personal assistant, if you went and asked for it.'

He looked down at her. Yes, that was true. He might get that job. He could become, now and for ever more, amen, the glorified secretary she always thought he was. What did it matter? What was so terrible about that? Didn't most men try and fail, weren't most men losers? Didn't damn nearly everyone have to face up some day to the fact that their ship would never come in?

He had tried. He had not won. He would die in humble circs.

'I'm sure he'd give you the job,' she said. 'Honestly, Ginger, I'm sure of it.'

He smiled. Wasn't that familiar, somehow?

'Don't laugh,' she said. 'You'll see!'

'I'm not laughing,' he told her.

'Why, listen,' she said. 'In a year or two we'll have forgotten this ever happened.'

He did not feel like someone else now. She did.

'And if you do stay,' she said, 'I'd never ask you to go home again. You were right. Home is here, we're far better off here. Why, in a month or two, with my job and your job, we'd be sitting pretty. You were right. This was only a crush I had. Why, I'll bet you –'

'A brand new frock, Vera?'

She stopped. She looked at him, her eyes blinding with tears. 'Oh, Ginger,' she said. 'I sound like you.'

'I know you do.' He went to her, put his arm around her and opened the bedroom door.

'Your coffee's ready,' Paulie called from the kitchen. 'And do you want an egg, Daddy?'

Beside him, Vera waited his answer.

'I'll have two eggs,' he said.

'Good. I'll put them on,' Paulie said.

'No, *I'll* do it,' Vera said. Quickly, she went out of the room and down the hall.

He pushed the bedroom door, let it drift shut. He unbuttoned his overcoat. In the dresser mirror, the man began to cry. Detached, he watched the tears run down that sad impostor's face, gather on the edges of that large moustache. Why was that man boo-hooing? Because he no longer lusted for his wife? Because he wasn't able to leave her? Ah, you idjit. Don't you know that love isn't just going to bed? Love isn't an act, it's a whole life. It's staying with her now because she needs you ; it's knowing you and she will still care about each other when sex and daydreams, fights and futures – when all that's on the shelf and done with. Love – why, I'll tell you what love is – it's you at seventy-five and her at seventy-one, each of you listening for the other's step in the next room, each afraid that a sudden silence, a sudden cry, could mean a lifetime's talk is over.

He had tried: he had not won. But oh! what did it matter? He would die in humble circs: it did not matter. There would be no victory for Ginger Coffey, no victory big or little, for there, on the court-house steps, he had learned the truth. Life was the victory, wasn't it? Going on was the victory. For better or for worse, for richer or for poorer, in sickness and in health until –

He heard her step outside. He went to join her.

MORE ABOUT PENGUINS
AND PELICANS

Penguinews, which appears every month, contains details of all the new books issued by Penguins as they are published. From time to time it is supplemented by *Penguins in Print*, which is our complete list of almost 5,000 titles.

A specimen copy of *Penguinews* will be sent to you free on request. Please write to Dept EP, Penguin Books Ltd, Harmondsworth, Middlesex, for your copy.

In the U.S.A.: For a complete list of books available from Penguins in the United States write to Dept CS, Penguin Books, 625 Madison Avenue, New York, New York 10022.

In Canada: For a complete list of books available from Penguins in Canada write to Penguin Books Canada Ltd, 2801 John Street, Markham, Ontario L3R 1B4.

THE REVOLUTION SCRIPT

Brian Moore

'Workers of Quebec, start today to take back what belongs to you; take for yourselves what is yours ... your factories, your machines, your hotels, your universities, your unions. Don't wait for an organizational miracle.'

The manifesto of the Front de Libération du Québec, composed by the members of the Liberational Cell and broadcast on the national TV network in prime time. They had kidnapped James Cross, Britain's Senior Trade Commissioner, and they threatened to execute him if their demands were not met.

But there would be no release of political prisoners, no plane to Algeria, no $500,000 in gold, because the Chenier Cell went one better and Premier Trudeau invoked the War Measures Act – the most repressive laws ever invoked in a democracy in peacetime. Mr Cross lived to tell his story but Labour Minister Pierre Laporte did not.

Brian Moore, now a Canadian citizen, tells the FLQ kidnapping story with a skilled blend of detachment and intimacy that provides a valuable insight into the manners and motivation of the urban guerrilla.

CATHOLICS

Brian Moore

A confrontation between the old and the new doctrines of Catholicism takes place on a tiny remote island off the coast of Ireland, where the secure cocoon of an island brotherhood is torn apart by a visitor from Rome.

'The island community is beautifully portrayed and a larger, metaphysical world evoked in the confrontation between faithless Kinsella and doubting Tomas. And all done with such quiet, observant patience, in a prose honed down to absolute clarity and precision' – Janice Elliott in the *Daily Telegraph*

'Attention is gripped . . . every word has to be read. There is a flavour of George Bernard Shaw about, with the difference that here the protagonists are not mocked' – Julian Symons in the *Sunday Times*

'In purely literary terms a beautiful little book, a masterpiece of reverberant concision' – J. W. Lambert in the *Sunday Times* (Choice of the Year)

'Mr Moore is surely one of the most versatile and compelling novelists writing today' – Elizabeth Berridge in the *Daily Telegraph*

FERGUS

Brian Moore

'Brian Moore is a novelist of enormous talent' – Claire Tomalin in the *Observer*

Fergus Fadden is an Irish-born writer, a man fashioned in the traditional mould of priests and Guinness, poetry and prayers. But like many before him, he has been lured to the high altar of the new world: the celluloid scene of films and fantasies. Here, in California, figures from his past come as hallucinations, to haunt his conscience and force him into a drastic self-appraisal.

'With the wry, beguiling brilliance one has come to expect of him, Mr Moore brings absolute conviction to this terrible and comic haunting – so nearly fatal. As for the living, he conveys entertainingly as usual the tissue of domestic life and adds, for bonus, some sharp encapsulated visions of the West Coast movie scene' – Janice Elliott in the *Sunday Telegraph*

THE GREAT VICTORIAN COLLECTION

Brian Moore

When Anthony Maloney woke up one day in Carmel, U.S.A., he glanced out of his hotel window and noted, with surprise, that his dream of the night before had come true. A vast open-air market stretched in front of him, filled with the most exquisite and priceless collection of Victorian objects.

'A book which I can recommend without reservation' – Robert Nye in the *Guardian*

'Mr Moore's book seems to me to be a survey of his own literary career and a shrewd allegory about the situation of the artist in contemporary society' – Philip French in *The Times Literary Supplement*

'Decidedly a major novel' – Myrna Blumberg in *The Times*

'Delicate and witty ... perfectly proportioned and written with total ease' – Francis King in the *Sunday Telegraph*